Burning Secrets

Titles by the same author

A Good Liar

Forgiven

Fallout

Cruel Tide

Fatal Reckoning

Burning Secrets

Ruth Sutton

First published in United Kingdom
by **Hoad Press** in 2018
2 Lowther Street, Waberthwaite, Millom, Cumbria LA19 5YN
www.ruthsutton.co.uk

ISBN 978-0-9929314-3-8

A CIP catalogue record for this book is available from the British Library.

Editorial: Lynn Curtis
Typesetting and Page Layout: Chris Moore
Cover design: Kevin Ancient
Typeset in Adobe Garamond Pro 11.5/14.5pt

Printed and bound in UK by TJ Books Limited, Padstow, Cornwall.

Acknowledgements

The Foot and Mouth outbreak of 2001 had disastrous and tragic consequences for many parts of the UK. For almost six months, Cumbria was like a war zone. Farming suffered badly, as did many other businesses dependent upon tourism. Out of respect for my Cumbrian community, I wanted to present an accurate account of the outbreak and its effects. I am therefore extremely grateful to those who took time to give me first-hand accounts of their experiences during the crisis: Adam Day (auctioneer and stock valuer), Peter Frost-Pennington (veterinary surgeon), David Thompson (Cumbria Police), Robin Watson (Cumbria Police, CSI), Terry O'Connell (Cumbria Police, retired).

Once the research was complete, I began working with a new editor, Lynn Curtis, whose advice on the outline and fine-tuning of the story has been invaluable. Thanks are also due to Chris Moore for typesetting and page layout, Kevin Ancient for another beautiful cover, and Karen Atkinson for proofreading.

Author's Note

Almost all the place names in this novel are real, with the single exception of Brinfell Farm, which does not exist, and the names of individual streets and houses are also invented. All the characters are fictional, but some of the stories they tell are derived from my interviews and conversations with those who lived through this difficult time in Cumbria's recent history.

Ruth Sutton, Waberthwaite, 2018

Chapter 1

Cockermouth, 2001

On a cool Friday afternoon early in March, Helen Heslop stood on the pavement outside Cockermouth School, waiting. The street was quiet, everyone else had gone home. She was twelve, old enough to catch a bus on her own, but no buses went close to her home at Brinfell Farm, and it was too far to walk. When she'd seen Granny Jo in Carlisle last weekend, they'd talked about going back home to the farm for the weekend. Someone would come and pick her up, unless Dad stopped them.

Helen didn't want to go back to the house in Pond Street where she was staying, in case Uncle Harry was there. She certainly didn't want to be alone with him. Harry was her dad's cousin. He and Auntie Chris had taken her in when Foot and Mouth Disease broke out and Dad didn't want her coming and going every day in case she brought the disease back to his precious cows. Uncle Harry was really creepy. He walked round the house in just his tracksuit bottoms, showing the thick black hair on his chest. He'd said she was a big girl for her age, and tried to touch her. Helen hadn't told anyone about that, not her best friend Emma or even Granny Jo.

There were other things Helen didn't like about the Pond Street house. There was never any food in the cupboards or the fridge, for instance. They ate takeaways most of the time, off their laps in front of the telly, not properly round a table like Helen's mum always insisted on back at the farm. Auntie Chris was out a lot, and the washing piled up on the kitchen floor. Helen's two cousins, David and Ryan, obviously didn't want her staying there because now the boys had to share a bedroom while she occupied Ryan's. She hated the footballs on the bed cover and the stinky trainers in the wardrobe, and she wanted to take his stupid posters off the wall, but she dared not, in case Ryan got David to push her around. Helen had really wanted to stay with Emma, whose parents had offered to help by giving her a room during the Foot and Mouth crisis, but Dad had said she couldn't live with 'strangers'. Sometimes Dad put his foot down about really stupid things.

Helen checked her watch. Five to four. If no one turned up soon she would go and meet her cousins at the Market Café where they often went after school. At least she wouldn't get stuck with creepy Harry.

Then she saw someone she knew, standing by a blue van parked across the street. His name was Alex and she liked him. He was about the same age as Uncle Harry and her dad, but he was funny and friendly, not like either of them. He'd come into the café a few times and sat with her and David and Ryan, just chatting. Helen had thought he must be lonely. And now he was here and she was pleased to see him. She waved. Alex waved back, and she crossed the road to speak to him.

'I'm waiting for someone to take me home,' Helen said. 'Mum hasn't mentioned it, but I think it's meant to be a surprise.'

Alex took a last draw on the roll-up he was smoking, then flicked the dimp away into the hedge. He smiled. 'Well, guess what?' he said. 'Your mum asked me to pick you up for her.'

Helen was surprised. 'You know my mum? You never said.'

'Oh, yes, Rose and I go back a long way. She texted me.' He took a small black mobile from the pocket of his jacket and held it up. The screen looked to be blank.

'But she doesn't have a phone like that,' said Helen, puzzled.

'Yes, she does,' said Alex. 'And she asked me to take you home.'

Helen hesitated, but only for a moment, then she clapped her hands. 'I knew Mum would sort it out! Shall I go and get my things?'

Alex shook his head and smiled. 'She said you won't need anything. I've even got a drink and some cake for us both in the van.'

'It won't take long to get there, will it?' Helen asked as he politely opened the passenger door for her.

'No time at all,' he said. 'In you get.'

'What's that funny smell?' she asked, as she fastened her seat belt and they drove away.

Carlisle was even busier than normal on a Friday afternoon. Ever since the FMD outbreak had started the city had been crowded with strangers: vets, haulage contractors, slaughtermen – all of them needed in greater numbers than ever before. The rest of the county had emptied: footpaths closed, farms barricaded, no animals visible, no visitors, sporting and leisure activities suspended. But Carlisle was booming. DC Maureen Pritchard cursed the traffic on the road from Workington. By the time she'd found a place to park she was in a foul mood.

Her father's hairdressing salon in the centre of town was packed and noisy. Maureen went through to the tiny staff room, dropped her bag on the floor, flopped down on one of the old chairs and kicked off her shoes. There was a full-length mirror on the opposite wall and she glanced in it automatically. Her reddish-brown hair still looked good, thanks to Dad, but the face underneath had seen better days. There was more weight under the dark trouser suit and white shirt than there used to be too, but she was reasonably comfortable with that. No point in fighting biology, and she was pushing fifty. Maureen had spent her early adulthood working in this salon, leaving over twenty years before to join the police, but right now it felt more welcoming than the CID room.

Cyril Cornthwaite had watched his daughter come in and recognised the signs. He put his head round the door: even in the middle of winter his tanned face betrayed an addiction to the sun bed in a backroom of the salon. 'Bad week?'

'Shitty,' she confirmed.

Cyril looked critically at himself in the mirror and tweaked the collar of his blue shirt to a more fashionable angle. 'I'm just finishing off Mrs Evans and then I've got a break. Make us a coffee. Back in a bit.'

Maureen hung up her coat and made the coffee, trying to deal with a sudden urge to tell Detective Inspector Stanley bloody Bell where he could stick the job.

'What's up?' said Cyril when he returned. 'You look like death warmed up.'

'I'm pissed off,' said Maureen. 'You remember last year… no, the year before… when I went to the DI and said it was time they gave me a sergeant's job? And they told me the only way I'd get to be sergeant was to go back to uniform.'

Cyril nodded. 'Bloody daft,' he said. 'They must know how good you are.'

'So this time around I didn't even bother applying when the sergeant's job came up again.' She shook her head. 'Well, the new sergeant started Monday, and guess what?'

'Don't tell me, a woman?'

'Right, ten years younger than me by the look of her, voice like cut glass, just come out of the army and doesn't know one end of the county from the other. Detective Sergeant Anna Penrose. I thought Bell was going to have a stroke.'

Cyril shook his head. 'Doesn't make sense.'

'Bob Carruthers reckons it's to do with some Home Office big shots who came up before Christmas, asking questions about why we don't have enough women in the senior ranks. He thinks they took the first one that came along, to make the statistics look a bit better.'

'What's the point in that? Doesn't do women in the police any good if they put someone in who can't do the job.'

'Exactly,' said Maureen. 'You can see that, why can't *they*?'

'And Dinger's unhappy, is he?'

'You know what he's like. Thinks it's the beginning of the end. Bet there's been some moaning at the Lodge.'

Cyril sipped his coffee without further comment. He was proud of his daughter, but she could put her foot in it sometimes. 'So what's she like, this Penrose woman?'

Maureen shrugged. 'Too early to tell. She's been a sergeant with the Military Police apparently, but this is different, chalk and cheese. She looks the part, I'll give her that. Very fit, good-looking in a gym bunny kind of way, well up on spreadsheets and all that. She and Bell talk about overtime figures and clear-up rates, all the stuff he gets from the bosses. Probably knows the PACE Act back to front.'

'That's all the procedural stuff, isn't it?'

'Came in 1983, after I started. With that and all the new forensics, policing's not the same any more.'

'No more slamming people against the wall and stuffing evidence in your pocket,' said Cyril. 'Ah, the good old days.'

She pulled a face. 'It wasn't as bad as that.' Then she smiled reluctantly. 'Well, sometimes it was, but don't tell anyone.'

Cyril looked at the big clock on the wall. 'Got to go,' he said. 'You can help us out for a bit if you want.'

'Can't tonight. Meeting Paddy in The Crown. He always went there on a Friday with our Jack, so now Jack's away he's meeting me instead.'

'The lad OK, is he?' Cyril asked.

'You know Jack, hard to tell the reality from the razzle-dazzle sometimes. Paddy still can't get used to a son of his working in the theatre.'

'Paddy's a good man, solid.' said Cyril. 'This new sergeant got anyone?'

'Bob said summat about a fiancé who got killed in the army. Maybe that's why she looks so tense.'

'You'll cope with this, you always do,' said Cyril, giving her a quick hug.

She held him close for a moment. 'Thanks, Dad.'

Maureen put on her coat, picked up her bag and went out into the dark damp evening to meet her husband and forget about work for a while.

Anna Penrose sat in the empty kitchen of her cottage and looked around. It was a daft decision to rent an unfurnished place, but she'd lived in army houses with army-issue furniture for too long. She had a couple of chairs, a table, a sofa, a bed and the basic kitchen stuff, and that was it. When she'd moved in a week before, the boiler had refused to work, and it had taken her all week to sort it out. Her father had offered to help, but it suited Anna to have him in Dorset, so far away that he couldn't be round doing jobs all the time. She could put him off without sounding as if she was trying to avoid him, even if she was.

She'd found someone local to fix the boiler and now at least the little house was warm, but there was a draught coming from somewhere and the wind outside was whining in the trees that surrounded the house and the yard where she'd parked the car. It would have made more sense to live nearer Workington and the station but it was the mountains, not the sea, that had drawn her to Cumbria. This place on the Whinlatter forest road was only twenty minutes from Keswick, and she could get to the Workington office in half an hour, downhill all the way in the opposite direction. This was the place that Mark would have chosen. Together they had walked most of the fells on this western side of the Lake District.

She poured herself a whisky and listened to the wind. The landlord of the pub in the village had told her that the power often went off when it was wild like this, but it hadn't happened yet. The weekend stretched ahead. She'd go into Cockermouth on Saturday and do some shopping, have a proper look around. Seemed like the kind of town where you could get decent coffee, and there was even a good bookshop.

It had been difficult since she'd started the new job, much harder than expected. She and Bell had talked about some useful things, but she could tell he didn't want her around. And that Pritchard woman… what was up with her? They'd hardly spoken all week. It must be hard to take orders from someone who's so much younger. She had done her best to show that she was decisive and business-like: it had worked before, but in this place things didn't feel the same.

Everything here was unspoken, indirect. She didn't know where she stood and people didn't explain things properly. Everyone knew she was a stranger and might need help to find her way around, but when she'd asked that weaselly DC Carruthers where the police station was in Whitehaven, he'd started off with, 'Well, you know the big garage where Loop Road starts…' What an idiot! If she knew that, she wouldn't need directions, would she? She should have told him how unhelpful he was being, but they'd all just have stared at her, and the Pritchard woman would have rolled her eyes. Again.

Pritchard was going to be a problem. She'd been on the job for twenty years, twice as long as Anna, and worked with the Drug Squad all over the county before she came to Workington. She knew everybody and everywhere in Cumbria. Sickening. Anna had noticed that on Friday afternoon the office emptied pretty fast. Granted there was nothing to deal with that couldn't wait, but it didn't say much for their commitment. And another thing: Pritchard and Bell were both overweight. Maybe she should suggest a fitness check.

The Foot and Mouth emergency was getting worse by all accounts, and now the army had been called in. Not before time apparently, but things might tighten up a bit with a military presence. God knows, there was room for improvement. She'd seen cattle carcasses lying beside a farm gate on her way home, and the smell of the pyres outside Carlisle spread far and wide on the wind. The place was like a war zone already and Anna knew all too well that any war brings out the worst in people as well as the best.

Nothing in the fridge, and she was hungry. She'd only had one whisky, so it was OK to drive. She put on her expensive cagoule, climbed back into the car and drove down to the pub in search of food and someone to talk to.

The spring days were lengthening. Drifts of snowdrops hid under hedges on the lane leading up to Brinfell Farm. Soon the stand of larches beyond the empty fields would burst into soft green, and on the higher fells tight whorls of bracken would push up into the light. Rose Heslop was still in the lambing shed when she realised it was nearly time for her to ring her daughter Helen in Cockermouth. Things were calming down after the hectic rush of lambing a few weeks earlier. Just a few orphans to feed now; she sat patiently on a straw bale as two of them pulled at the teats of the bottles she held in her gloved hands, their tails wriggling with pleasure.

When bellies were full and bottles empty, Rose walked back to the farmhouse. The end of the day was grey and damp. Low cloud sat on top of the fells, blocking the sun and covering everything with a fine drizzle. She took off her boots in the porch, peeled off the long purple gloves she wore for working with the sheep, opened the door of the Aga and threw the crumpled latex into the flames. The bright red Aga was Rose's pride and joy, the only improvement to the old kitchen that Eric had been willing to pay for. He'd always worried about money but these days he was much worse and Rose was hungry for things to change.

Helen had been living with Eric's cousin Harry Strong and his family for two weeks, since she'd insisted that she wanted to stay in school and Eric had insisted that she couldn't come and go from the farm every day because of the risk of contamination. He'd gone on and on about how easily the disease could spread, on shoes, car tyres, clothes.

Rose believed her daughter would be best off not missing school. It was only her second term at the comprehensive and there were friendships to make, and new subjects to get to grips with. Time out now could set Helen back just as her classmates were finding their feet. Rose had her reservations about the Strongs, though. Fortunately, Eric didn't know that she and Harry's wife Christine had a bit of history, and Rose wasn't going to tell him.

When the arguments had started about going to school, Rose's elder son Aidan had jumped at the chance to stay on the farm. He was close to sixteen and would be leaving education for good in a few months. He was as tall as his father now, and filling out, not a child any more.

Brian was only six and liked being at home with his mum and the animals. When the outbreak started he'd been frightened that they would send him away. Rose wondered how much Brian really understood about what was going on. It was hard to tell because he didn't talk much at the best of times, which this definitely wasn't. He still played with his toy farm, but she noticed that he was lying the animals down on their sides rather than standing them upright on their plastic legs. Brian missed his sister, and wanted Rose to sleep in his bed at night. Eric didn't seem to care. He was obsessed with the cows, checking them constantly. And he was drinking too, passing out in the big chair in the kitchen almost every night. No wonder he complained about backache. He and Rose hadn't had sex for months: that was another thing that couldn't be talked about.

There was a time when she and Eric had been happy. Eric had been at Sellafield when they first got together, clean work, with good money and regular hours. But the contractors he worked for sent him away for weeks at a time, and he and Rose seemed to lose touch with each other. She'd started going out with girlfriends, drinking too much and getting up to things she couldn't tell Eric about. That was the problem with Christine Strong: she knew far too much about those days, and Rose didn't trust her.

Just before Helen was born, Eric's dad got too ill to manage the farm and the relatives expected Eric to take it on – something about keeping it in the family, and being your own boss. Looking back, Rose couldn't fathom why he'd gone along with it without thinking about what it would mean for her and the children. He'd just assumed that Rose would support him, and he didn't want his dad to think that he couldn't control his wife. They'd moved to the farm in the spring, and during that first summer Eric seemed to revel in the freedom farming gave him, but soon Rose could see the novelty draining away. When she tackled him about it he claimed he'd been pissed off with Sellafield, that it was too 'oppressive,' and he was glad of the chance to get away, but that was just to avoid admitting the move had been a big mistake.

Rose made herself a drink and thought about the mess they were in. If only they'd talked about it properly at the time they wouldn't be stuck here on this windy hillside, cash poor, working all hours and all weathers. But Eric never did talk much, not to Rose anyway. For a while this had made her sad: now it made her angry, and she could see Aidan going the same way.

The only joy the farm gave Rose was her sheep, just a few dozen Swaledales, but they were hers. Eric told her that it was just a hobby, that she was too soppy about them, spent too much on feed when they should be outside, but in the end he let her get on with it. When she'd wanted to get a part-time job in town, for the company and some proper money, he'd objected until she cried and begged. Working at the auction mart had made her life tolerable, but it had been forced to close a few weeks before, and now she was suffocating, although the pills were helping. Just one fragment of Rose's freedom remained. Upstairs in a private drawer was a small black mobile phone that only she and one other person knew about. It was their secret.

In the quiet farmhouse kitchen, Rose picked up the landline phone and dialled the familiar number to talk to Helen. It rang for a long time. Then a boy's voice said, 'Hello?'

Another voice in the background instructed, 'Ask who it is, dummy.'

'Who is it?' said a high-pitched voice she recognised as Ryan's.

'It's Auntie Rose, Helen's mum,' she said. 'Is she there?'

'She's not in. Dunno where she is.'

'What about your mum? Is she in?'

There was a lot of whispering. Rose strained to hear what the two boys were saying. She'd never liked them much. David, the older one, looked like a bully and Ryan seemed very childish for ten. It was David who finally spoke to her.

'Our mam's here, but,' he hesitated, 'she's not well… she's asleep.'

Rose raised her voice. 'David, listen to me: if Helen's not there I need to speak to your mum. Or is your dad in?'

'No, he's out getting pizzas for tea.'

'Well, wake your mum up. Tell her it's Rose and I need to speak to her. It's important.'

A few moments later the voice that said 'Hello?' was slurred.

'Christine, it's Rose here. Where's Helen?'

There was a pause. 'Helen? She must be upstairs.' Rose heard the sound of clattering on the stairs. Chris has been drinking, she thought. Typical.

'She's not here,' the woman announced. 'Could be at Emma's. Wait a minute.'

Rose heard her say, 'What? Who told you that?' before she spoke once more on the phone. 'Rose, David says that Emma told him Helen was coming home this weekend. She thought her gran had arranged it.'

In the farmhouse kitchen, Rose stood quite still. 'But she's not here.'

Chris hesitated, then said slowly, 'She's not here either.'

'Oh, Christ,' said Rose. 'Where is she?'

'Search me,' said Chris.

'We trusted you!' Rose shouted into the phone. 'You said you'd look after her like your own.'

'Now look here,' Chris spluttered. 'Don't you…'

Rose slammed down the phone and ran to the back door in her slippers. The yard outside was wet and muddy but she didn't care. When she reached the door of the cowshed she stood and shouted until Aidan appeared. He stared at her just like his dad did sometimes, as if she were a child. Rose caught hold of him. 'Where's your sister?'

'No idea,' said the boy. 'What you asking me for?'

Eric walked down the shed towards them. 'What's the racket?' he said. 'You'll scare the beasts, hollering like that.'

'Helen,' Rose was gasping now. 'She's… I don't know where she is.'

Aidan looked at his father. Eric took Rose by the hand and led her back across the farmyard to the house. Inside he sat her down at the table and stroked her hair back from her face. 'Calm down, Rosie,' he said. 'Helen's in Cockermouth, isn't she, at Harry's?'

Rose stared at him. 'No, she's not. They say they don't know where she is.' She stopped and swallowed, breathing hard. 'She's not there, Eric. They thought she'd come home, that my mum had arranged it.' She reached up and seized the edge of his stained jacket. 'Helen was with her last weekend, in Carlisle, but not now. Where is she, Eric? Where's Helen?'

'Stay here, love,' he said, squeezing her hand. 'I'll fetch your pills.'

A little later, when the pills began to take effect and Rose was calmer, Eric rang his mother-in-law.

Chapter 2

Maureen Pritchard was in the bar of The Crown waiting for Paddy to struggle through the crowd with their drinks when her mobile buzzed in her pocket. She pushed her way to the door for the quiet she needed to answer it.

'Dad? What? You'll have to speak up... Yes, I know Jo Haile... Helen Heslop?... Is that Jo's grand-daughter? Was that the young girl she brought to the salon with her last weekend when I was there? About twelve, thirteen, pretty little thing... When did they see her last?... In school? That was hours ago. So she's not in the house in Cockermouth... What about where her family lives, on the farm?' She listened again, frowning. 'OK, give me the details.'

She scribbled down facts and various phone numbers. 'Leave it with me, Dad. Call Jo back and tell her she did the right thing, and to let the parents know we're on to it. Yes, I'll call you later. 'Bye.'

Maureen dialled her new sergeant's mobile number.

'Sounds like a missing child, ma'am. Not been seen since the end of school, in Cockermouth. Twelve-year-old girl, Helen Heslop, staying with a family in town while the FMD outbreak is on. Parents' place is,' she checked her notes, 'Brinfell Farm, outside Lorton. That's near your house, isn't it?'

'Yes, I know,' said Anna. She didn't know, but she was learning to fake it. 'Could you attend the Cockermouth house and I'll go to the farm?… No sightings? None at all?… That's more than three hours. Doesn't sound good. What have we checked so far?'

Maureen went through the details. 'Mother rang the Cockermouth house as usual around six, and was told Helen wasn't there. She panicked and her husband rang the grandmother, Mrs Jo Haile in Carlisle, who knows my dad, who called me. You know how that works.'

Anna's irritation was obvious from her voice. 'Sounds like typical Cumbria. All around the houses. Why didn't the parents call us if they were that worried?'

There it was again in Penrose's voice. Was she condescending… patronising? Whatever, it got on Maureen's nerves.

'Comes to the same thing, ma'am,' she said. 'What about DI Bell?'

DI Stanley Bell was normally referred to as 'Dinger' but Maureen wasn't sure how Penrose would react to that. Dinger himself didn't seem to care about that nickname: the one he'd never liked, and rarely heard since his elevation, was 'Short Arse'. The fact that both the women who reported to him were taller than he was annoyed him on a daily basis.

'Leave that to me,' Anna said. 'We might need him on this one. Let me know how you get on. See you back at the station to cross-check, about eight.'

Maureen's second phone call was to the home of Mr and Mrs Harry Strong, in Pond Street, Cockermouth. Before the doorbell rang there half an hour later, Chris Strong had time to tidy up, gulp down enough coffee to clear her head, and send David out to find his dad and bring him back. When she opened the door, the plump woman standing on the doorstep pulled an ID card from the inside pocket of her coat.

'Mrs Strong?' she said. 'DC Maureen Pritchard. We've had a report that a child, Helen Heslop, who's been living with you, has gone missing. I need to talk to anyone who has information about this.'

'My husband's not here…'

'So I'll talk to you,' said Maureen, 'and not on the doorstep. This is a serious matter.'

Chris stepped back, stumbling as she did so. Maureen looked at her closely, noticing the unsteadiness and the smell of wine under the coffee. Years in the Drug Squad had left their legacy, and there was something familiar about this woman. It would come to her.

'In here?' Maureen asked, going into the front room. 'I'll need to talk to your sons, Mrs Strong, so can you get them, please? And your husband.'

'He's out. I've sent the older lad to fetch him,' Chris said. 'Ryan!' she called up the stairs, 'get in here!'

The boy sidled into the sitting room. He was still wearing his school clothes, which looked and smelled as if they needed a wash. Maureen sat down on the sofa and patted the seat next to her. 'Ryan, is it?' He nodded, a wary expression on his face. 'My name's Maureen. How old are you, pet?'

'Ten,' said Ryan, 'just.'

Maureen smiled. 'And which school do you go to?'

'St Paul's,' he whispered. 'Miss Woodhead's class.'

'So, do you know why I'm here?'

'Helen.'

'That's right. She's gone missing, and we need to find her.'

Ryan looked at his mother. 'Don't know,' he said in a babyish voice. 'Don't know where she is.'

Chris kneeled down on the floor in front of her son. 'It's all right, pet, you're not in trouble. Just tell the lady what she wants to know, OK?'

'When did you last see Helen?' Maureen asked.

'This morning, before we went to school.'

'Not since then?'

Ryan shook his head.

They all heard the back door open and a man's voice raised in anger, saying, 'Where are they?'

Maureen raised her hand to stop Chris answering and stood up to face the door, holding up her ID card. The man who came in was dressed in black, tall and fleshy, with dark eyes that flickered up and down the woman in front of him like a heavyweight boxer weighing up an opponent.

'Mr Strong? DC Maureen Pritchard, Workington CID. We need to talk to you about Helen Heslop.'

'What about her?'

'She's not been seen for some time and we need to find her.'

'She's at home, back on the farm. The lad told me. Not that lad,' he pointed at Ryan, who was sucking his thumb. 'The other one. David... get in 'ere.' A teenager put his head round the door. The small front room was crowded and he hovered awkwardly in the doorway.

Maureen stepped towards him. 'Come in, David,' she said. 'Join the party.' She extended her hand to Harry, who shook it reluctantly. 'I need to talk to both the boys. They may have been the last people to see Helen today.'

'I don't like the police in my house,' said Harry, trying to stare her down.

Maureen looked briefly away, and then back at him. 'Well, that's fine, Mr Strong. We can talk here or we can take all of you back to my office, in Workington police station, and talk to you there.'

'Harry, for God's sake,' said his wife. She turned to Maureen. 'He had some trouble, you know, when he were a lad. He doesn't mean it. If you want to talk to our boys, it'll be here, OK? Not down the nick.'

She pulled Ryan towards her and the child wriggled uncomfortably at the unusual show of affection. Harry swore under his breath. 'Get on with it then,' he said, leaving the room. Maureen followed him to the door. 'I need you to stay in the house for now, Mr Strong, or I can take you down the station to make a statement separately. This child's been missing for too long already.' She turned back to the others. 'Is there anything you can tell me, David? When did you last see Helen?'

'Lunchtime. At school. Her mate Emma told me Helen said she was going to the farm this weekend. Said her gran in Carlisle had fixed it up as a surprise.'

'Emma?'

'Emma Talbot. Lives at the Redhouse B&B in town.'

'OK, what about since then?'

'Didn't see her after school.'

Maureen scribbled in her notebook. 'Did you and Ryan come straight home?'

'He comes up to meet me at the gate,' said David, gesturing towards his brother. 'Then we walk home together. Helen wasn't at the gate but she has her own key now, doesn't have to wait for us. When we got back she wasn't here. We thought she'd gone to the farm.'

Maureen looked at them both. 'Do you always come straight home from school?'

Ryan immediately looked at his brother, who answered, 'Sometimes we go to the café, downtown.' Maureen noticed that

David didn't look directly at her and pulled at a bitten fingernail when he'd finished speaking.

'Which café?' she asked.

'The Market. We have a drink and wait till Mam gets home.'

'I'm a detective,' said Maureen. 'It's my job to find things out. Does either of you want to tell me anything else?'

It was only the briefest of glances between the boys, but she noticed it.

'Tell the lady, Ryan,' urged Chris, but he shook his head. 'You can't make him tell you anything,' she said smugly to Maureen. 'He's underage.'

Maureen studied the other woman, who'd been eye-catching once, without the overdone make-up and dyed black hair with fading roots. 'Boys,' she said, 'Could you wait in the kitchen with your dad for a moment? I just want a word with your mum, OK?' They shuffled out. She stepped across and closed the door, leaning against it, smiling.

'Christine Baines,' she said. 'Well, well. It's been a long time.'

Chris stared back defiantly, then looked down. 'You remember, don't you?'

Maureen went on. 'I was just a young copper then. Let's see… fifteen years ago? No, more. You must have been about eighteen. Quite a gang of you that hung around together, wasn't there?'

Chris nodded, but said nothing. She pulled a hankie from her pocket and twisted it between her fingers.

Maureen made her tone a little softer. 'You must have been just a kid when you had David.'

'Nineteen,' said Chris.

'And now you've got Ryan. Not with the same bloke?'

Chris shook her head. She looked up at Maureen. 'Don't tell Harry you know me. He doesn't know anything about…' She hesitated. 'You know, what happened back then.'

Maureen looked hard at her. 'Do you think I would? Well, let's be clear how this has to work. If a kid goes missing, we do anything – *anything*, you understand – to find out what we need to know. You'd expect that, if it was your child, right?' Chris nodded. 'Well, this is the Heslops' child. Can you imagine what they're going through right now?'

Chris looked out of the window, her face sallow in the orange light from the streetlight.

'So, I'm going to need your help,' Maureen went on. 'If the boys have something to tell me, they might want to hide it from you. No one's accusing your children of anything. But they know something, those two, and I want it… OK?'

Chris nodded.

Maureen raised her voice. 'Come back in, please, boys. And Mr Strong, do you want to join us? Only take a few minutes.'

David pushed Ryan back into the room, and Harry followed them as far as the door. He was smoking a cigarette and had a bottle of beer in his hand. Chris said quickly, 'Boys, if you know anything about this, about Helen, you have to tell the lady. You're not in trouble. You've said you go down the café after school. I did too, when I was your age. It's OK, isn't it, Harry?'

He shrugged.

Maureen sat the boys next to each other on the sofa and looked down at them. Then she sat down herself on the big chair and pulled it a little closer. 'I'd like to speak to them alone for a few minutes,' she said to their parents. 'Can you wait in the kitchen until I call you?'

Harry said, 'Make up your bloody mind! And don't put words in their mouths, right?' He stomped out of the room. Chris began to protest until she noticed Maureen's expression. 'I'll wait outside,' she said to the boys.

'Mum,' Ryan whispered.

'It's OK, pet. You just tell the truth.' Chris squeezed her younger son's shoulder before she went out, closing the door softly behind her.

In the silent room, Maureen looked slowly at one boy and then the other, before turning her attention to David. As she did so, she heard Ryan breathe out.

'David, you've told me what Emma said, and we can check that of course. Now, has Helen ever said anything to you about going home this weekend, or up to Carlisle to her gran's?'

He shook his head.

'Who else does she talk to?'

David said quickly, 'She doesn't talk to us much.' Then he reeled off a list of names.

'Are they all Helen's friends?' Maureen asked, writing fast in her notebook.

'No, they're just people in her year. She doesn't have friends, only Emma. Helen's… you know… shy, like. Farm kid. They're always a bit strange, the girls 'specially. Quiet, like. Never hang around after school, have to rush off for the bus.'

'Now, Ryan,' Maureen said, turning towards the younger boy, who sat wide-eyed, watching her. 'You go to a different school, don't you? But you see Helen here at home.'

'She took my room,' he said.

'And how did you feel about that?'

'I don't want her in it.'

'I can understand that,' said Maureen. 'So you're pleased that she's not here?'

'I still won't get my room back,' he said. 'Not until she's gone for good.'

He sounded a lot less childish with his mum off the scene, she noticed.

'Where do you think she might be?'

Ryan shrugged. 'Don't know.' He was still looking at Maureen, like a mouse watching a snake. 'It wasn't all bad, having her here. We had some fun.'

'The whole family?'

David began to fidget, but Maureen didn't shift her attention from Ryan. 'Just us kids,' said the youngest boy. 'And…' His voice broke off.

David interrupted. 'Sometimes we have mates round, when Mum and Dad are out.'

'Do they know about that?'

David shook his head. 'That's why we didn't say before.'

'And who are these mates? From school? Do you have some names for me? I need to hear about everything Helen was doing while she lived here, to help us find her.'

David shook his head again. 'No one special.'

Maureen leaned back so that the boys couldn't see what she was scribbling in her notebook, and continued to write while they both watched her. Out of the corner of her eye she noticed that David was frowning at Ryan.

'There's something you're not telling me, isn't there?' she said loudly, looking up. 'You can tell me now or I'll ask you again in front of your parents.'

Ryan began to sniffle.

Chapter 3

Anna stopped by the side of the road and checked the map she kept in the glove box. She hated not being sure where she was, especially as everyone else seemed to know every road and lane, and how they all connected together. It was dark, and she'd felt rain in the air when she left Workington. Now low cloud blocked any light from the rising moon and she needed her torch to check the map. There it was, Brinfell Farm, perched above the valley that ran south towards Loweswater. The roads were unfamiliar but the fells always reminded her of Mark. He'd been gone nearly two years, and she knew it was time for her to move on. Leaving the army had diluted some of the memories, and she tried to focus on the happy times, not the mangled body in an overturned jeep so far away.

At least she might have this case to herself for a while. Bell had already started his usual Friday night beer-fest by the time she'd reached him on the phone. She'd been quite relieved by his unwillingness to get involved in the case before morning. The army had given her a sphere of responsibility, but here it was different: no matter what HQ said, she was sure Bell believed a woman couldn't be trusted to conduct a major investigation.

Dealing with Helen Heslop's family could be tricky. Anna had no farming experience at all and wasn't sure what kind of reaction she'd get from them. Most of the farmers in this part of West Cumbria were keeping their animals close, if they still had any, and had barricaded themselves on their properties against the threat of the disease. Anna would need to put on the crime-scene gear she carried in the back of the car: not to protect vital evidence, but to convince the family that she wouldn't be contaminating their land. 'Don't surprise them,' Bell had said. 'Tell them you're coming.' She'd rung the farm once and now she pulled over to call them again before the phone signal died completely.

'It's DS Penrose again, Mrs Heslop. I'm close by, about five minutes away. Can you meet me at the farm gate? I know you'll have concerns about me coming onto the farm.'

A man's voice came on the line. 'I'll meet you. If I'm not there, just wait, don't come down the lane. Have you got protective clothing, boots, all that?'

'I have, and I understand that we have to be careful. I take it there's been no word from your daughter? No news from her grandmother?'

'Nothing,' said Eric Heslop.

As Anna pulled up at the farm gate, she saw the 'Keep Out' signs and smelled the disinfectant from the mat that spread across the lane immediately behind it. Beams of torchlight were swinging down the lane. She waited, pulling on her overalls and boots. She eased her ponytail under the hood of her protective suit and blinked into the damp wind. Eric and Rose Heslop appeared on the other side of the gate and Eric shone the torch beam onto Anna's clothing and then up at her face, making her blink before he moved the light away.

Anna introduced herself. 'You did the right thing to tell someone that your daughter was missing, Mrs Heslop.' she said. 'You and your husband must be worried sick. My team are doing all we can to locate her. Someone is with Mr and Mrs Strong in Cockermouth right now. Have you talked to Helen's friends, just to check that she's not with one of them?'

Eric looked at his wife. 'Have you?'

Anna noticed the antagonism between them. Parents often blamed each other when a child went missing.

'I don't know who her school friends are,' Rose said, 'not now she's gone to the big school.'

Anna intervened. 'We can check that. What about the children who live round here, the ones she used to get the bus home with?'

Eric said, 'Aidan will know. We'll ring them.'

'Yes,' Rose agreed, staring at her feet.

Must be the shock that's making this woman so passive, Anna thought. Rose looked up. 'We thought she'd be safe there, with Harry and Chris,' she said. 'They're family. But we shouldn't have let her go. She's only twelve.'

'Just a kid,' said the father. 'Knows nowt about the world.' He put an arm around his wife, but Anna could sense the distance between the two of them.

'Are you both absolutely certain that Helen has not tried to come back to the farm today after school? She seemed to think she would be coming home this weekend. Did she have any reason to believe that?'

'No,' said Eric. 'She can't keep coming and going. It's like a plague out there. We have to keep the herd safe for as long as we can.'

'So neither of you gave Helen the idea that she would be coming home?'

Eric turned to his wife accusingly. He was a small man, wiry, with narrow brown eyes and a weathered face. 'Did you tell her that?'

'No, no!' Rose insisted. 'She'd already had one weekend with her gran, and it'll be Easter soon. We might work something out for the school holidays. Now the army's involved, it could all, you know, clear up.'

Eric raised his voice. 'Clear up?' Frustration bubbled in him. 'Nobody knows how long it's going to last, or else they're not saying. They tell us nowt. All we know is what we hear on't radio.'

He turned his anger on Anna. 'Due respect and all that, love, but you're not from round 'ere, are you? You have no idea what we're dealing with.'

She decided to ignore the man's rudeness. 'For the time being we're concentrating on the Cockermouth area,' she said, 'where Helen was last seen. And you need to make a thorough search of the farm too, the house obviously, and all the outbuildings. Look for any sign that she might have been here. And before it gets too late, ask all your neighbours, people in the area, anyone you can think of. Was anyone in Cockermouth today who might have given Helen a lift, or been asked to do so?' She struggled through the layers of clothing to find a pocket. 'Here's my card, with the direct number. If you find out anything that could help us, ring me any time. I'm in charge of this search for the time being. If my Inspector, DI Bell, thinks it necessary, he'll take over in the morning.'

Rose and Eric said nothing, standing close together but far apart. Anna went on, 'We're based in Workington, but I live just up the hill towards Whinlatter. You have that number and my mobile number too, although the signal is poor around here.'

'No mobile signal around the farm,' said Rose. 'Our son Aidan told me that,' she added quickly.

'Do you have mobile phones?' Anna asked.

'No point, is there?' said Eric.

Rose shook her head. A single tear slid down her cheek. She reached into her pocket and held something out for Anna to take. 'It's an old photo,' she said. Anna looked at the photo in the edge of the torchlight. It was black and white and creased, and the child's face staring back at her looked too young. Rose sobbed suddenly, 'Where is she? What's happened to her?'

Anna reached over the gate and proffered her hand, but neither of them responded. 'We'll do everything we can,' she said. 'Too soon to panic yet. We'll get a list of all her school friends and my colleague DC Pritchard will be gathering information about what happened today. We'll find her.'

'Well, while you're at it,' Eric said, 'tell that bastard Harry Strong that's the last time we trust him and his useless wife with anything. We're done with 'em. Just find our Helen. Come on, love.'

He turned to go, taking his wife with him by the arm. Anna thought Rose was going to say something more, but the moment passed and she watched as the two of them tramped back towards the farm, the torchlight sweeping before them in steady arcs across the muddy lane.

When Anna pulled into the car park that she'd left only a couple of hours before, Maureen's car was already there. The air smelled of earth after the rain. Anna breathed it in and stood for a moment, eyes raised to the sky, watching shreds of cloud pass over the moon. Workington docks and the Irish Sea were not far away, and there was a slight tang of salt on the breeze. She rummaged for a cigarette in her bag, lit it and took a few guilty drags before stubbing it out. She would stop smoking, she told herself again, but not yet.

The old police station was well past its 'use by' date, and plans were afoot for a smart new building on the edge of town, but in the meantime the place had an air of neglected grandeur, cold and grubby, with an internet connection that was painfully slow. When she arrived, Anna had wondered what the point was of investing in new technology when you wasted so much time trying to make it work. Carrier pigeons might be faster. She hadn't mentioned it though, not yet.

In the CID room, Anna put her bag down and went to look at the big display that Maureen was already working on. Anna handed over the picture of Helen that Rose had given her, which was pinned in the centre of the board. 'Pretty poor image,' she said. 'We'll need a more recent one.' Various dates and details were already visible, and a map of the area with pins marking the school, Pond Street and the farm.

Anna pointed at one of the pins. 'What's this one, in the town?'

Maureen peered at the board. 'That's the café where the Strong kids and Helen hang out after school, near the supermarket. When they open up tomorrow we need to check it out, and any CCTV.'

'Tell me what we know so far,' said Anna. Maureen scanned her notes, picking out the details that her boss didn't already have.

'Well, Harry Strong is Eric Heslop's cousin, but no love lost as far as I can judge.'

Anna laughed. 'You're right there,' she said, relaying Eric's parting words.

'Helen's been with them for two weeks.' Maureen looked up at her sergeant. 'Actually the wife, Christine Strong, is already known to us. It took me a while to remember, but then it came back to me. It's on record: Christine Baines she was then, drug possession and soliciting, 1984. Soliciting was dropped, drug stuff was first offence, suspended sentence. Nothing since, but she's terrified that Harry will find out.'

Anna said nothing. It was typical of Pritchard to know all this: typical, and irritating.

Maureen looked back at the board. 'Harry looks like a drinker. Didn't want police in his house, he said. Wouldn't be surprised if he knocks his wife around. Two lads, David and Ryan. They both said they hadn't seen Helen since school, but they're not telling me the whole story, I'm sure of that.' She flipped through her notes. 'Got some names of Helen's school friends and I've been calling round those while I waited for you. Nothing so far. One of us may have to go into school on Monday and talk to the staff and kids. Someone must have seen something.'

She checked her watch. 'Shall I try the friend? Emma Talbot, lives at Redhouse B&B. Bit late now, but I can do it first thing. One of the Strong lads, David, told me that he'd heard from Emma about Helen's plan to go home. When I checked with the Talbots earlier, they said they'd offered to have Helen to stay but the Heslops refused.' She closed her notebook. 'The Heslops might be regretting that decision now. They'll probably blame the Strongs whatever happens, family or not.'

Anna thought back to the conversation at the gate. 'Helen's dad was angry, but the mum seemed really passive. I don't think she's done anything since she found out Helen was in the wind, except get her husband to phone her mother, and cry into her hankie.'

'Takes people different ways, doesn't it?' said Maureen. 'Some go running around like headless chickens and others just sit there, overwhelmed.'

'Well, Rose Heslop is in the overwhelmed group. I wanted to lean over the gate and shake her.'

Maureen looked surprised. 'They didn't let you past the gate? Dinger will have words to say about that. He doesn't like farmers.'

It was nearly midnight when they ran out of things that could be done through the night. There was just a chance, diminishing as time went by, that Helen would turn up, having been with a friend they didn't know about, or fallen asleep on a bus or a train somewhere. All the routine enquiries were put in motion: hospitals, police across the county, transport authorities. Mrs Haile from Carlisle rang for news, and even Maureen's dad, but there were no enquiries from the two families most closely concerned.

When she got home, Maureen climbed into bed beside her patient husband and put her cold arms around him. 'What's on?' Paddy mumbled. 'Missing kid,' said Maureen, and he turned and held her close until they both fell asleep.

At seven-thirty the next morning, DI Bell was already in the office and looking intently at the big whiteboard with all the details of the case so far when Maureen and Anna arrived almost simultaneously.

'Here they are, the two Ps,' he announced. 'Penrose and Pritchard, Queens of the West. What time do you call this?'

Anna ignored the habitual provocation and began her round-up of the circumstances and developments so far.

Dinger listened carefully. 'Friends and other relatives?' he asked.

'Checked. Nothing.'

'All the details circulated?'

'Done, but we could do with a better photo. I'll get back to the mother about that.'

'What about a search of the farm?'

'Parents said they'd do that last night.'

DI Bell shook his head. 'Not good enough,' he said. 'Can't rule anything out yet. The kid's more likely to have come to harm from within the family than from a stranger, we know that, right? So we'll start close to home. Full search.'

'What about the FMD? Farmer Heslop wouldn't let me past the gate last night.'

'Well, Farmer Heslop can sod off,' said Dinger. 'If we want access to his farm we get it. Something for those cadets to do instead of hanging around getting in the way. They've all got crime-scene suits, and wellies, and the farmer can hose them down if he has to, but get half a dozen up there and go over the whole place. If the family are holding back on anything it could scare them into coughing it up.'

He turned to Maureen. 'This job's for you, Pritchard. Let them deal with someone different. You can do the school friend after that. Penrose can have a go at the foster family. Push those lads that Maureen reckons know summat. Lean on them if you have to, Penrose. And the café, the one the kids go to. Knock them up, check out who else hangs out there.'

'What'll you do, boss?' Anna asked.

'Army liaison,' said DI Bell. 'They've got people all over the place shifting animal carcasses. Bet they wouldn't mind a break from that to get a briefing from me. No stone unturned, and all that.'

'If you're doing a briefing, can I come?' Anna said.

'One soldier to another, eh?' said Dinger. 'Nay. Don't need my hand holding, thanks very much.' He pointed a fat finger at them. 'Our revered Superintendent has chewed me out already this month about too much overtime and his financial bloody targets. I'm not going back to him for another dose of crap until I've got something concrete. Right? So get on with it, chop-chop.'

DI Bell eased out of the chair that had wrapped around him a little too tightly, yelled for DC Carruthers who had been keeping well out of the way, and headed off to the new Army HQ near Carlisle.

Eric Heslop's reaction on the phone to the planned search was even more furious than Anna had expected.

'You lot don't get it, do you? I have to protect this place from anything coming in from outside – on the air, on the cars, on boots, everything. And you want to bring a bunch of baby coppers up here… for what? What are you saying… that we know where she is, that we're hiding something?'

Anna had been holding the phone away from her ear and breathed out slowly before she answered. 'I understand your concern Mr Heslop. We will take every precaution, but we must be able to do our jobs. We can't start a countywide search for your daughter if there's any possibility she can be found closer to home. None of us knows what might have happened, but if she said she was coming home it's just possible that she did, and that something happened to her there.'

'Like what, for God's sake?'

'Mr Heslop,' said Anna, as calmly as she could muster. 'As I said, we will take every precaution. DC Pritchard and her team will be there within the hour, if you'd like to make arrangements to receive them.'

She called across to Maureen. 'Did you hear all that? Good luck with Heslop, he's not a happy chap. I'll take a run at those two lads in Cockermouth and see if they can remember any more, and I'll do the café as well. And can you check the B&B girl when you get back from the farm?'

❖ ❖ ❖

Clearly the Strong family were not early risers on a Saturday morning. It took several minutes and a few shouts through the letterbox before the front door opened a crack and half a stubbled face appeared, growling, 'Who the hell are you?'

'Police, Mr Strong. DS Anna Penrose.' She waved her ID in front of the man's eyes.

'More police? Have you found 'er yet?'

'No, and there are one or two more questions for your sons, if you can let me in, please. I'd rather not conduct our business on the doorstep.'

The front door opened a little further and Anna pushed her way into the narrow hall. A young boy stood on the stairs in his underpants and a tee shirt. 'Ryan, is it?' said Anna, and the boy's mouth dropped open.

'I'm Sergeant Penrose. You might want to get dressed, or we could talk like this. Are you coming down?'

Ryan turned and ran back up the stairs.

'That's my son you're giving orders to,' Harry weighed in.

'So I gather, Mr Strong. I've had a full report from my DC who was here yesterday, but we believe there's still more information to come.'

'Ryan, David, get down 'ere,' Harry yelled up the stairs. 'Tell this copper whatever she wants.' He smirked at Anna. 'All right, love?'

He pointed towards the front room, waited by the door until both boys appeared and then stood at the entrance to the room, watching. 'Go on then,' he said. 'Get on with it.'

Anna kept it as formal as she could. She'd taken them by surprise and that might be enough. She looked sternly at the two boys standing awkwardly in front of her. 'We have reason to believe there is more you can tell us about Helen and the time you all spend together after school. Is there anything you'd like to say to me?'

Ryan was clearly worried. He looked sidelong at his brother and then at his dad. David stared down at his hands.

'Well?' said Harry. 'What's up with you?'

'He said he knew our mam,' the younger boy blurted, looking up at his father. 'He bought us pizza, when you were out.'

David rolled his eyes. 'You bloody idiot!'

'What the fuck…' said Harry, as he reached out and smacked David on the side of the head.

Anna put out her hand. 'Leave this to me, Mr Strong,' she said. 'David, you keep quiet. Ryan, who was this?'

The child was close to tears. 'The man in the café. He said he was at school with our mam. He brought us a video, and pizza.'

'When?' Anna began to write in her notebook.

Ryan shrugged. 'Last week.'

'Does this man have a name?'

'Alex.'

'Alex what?'

Ryan shrugged again.

David knew there was no point in holding out. He moved a little further away from his father before he added, 'He didn't tell us his other name, just Alex.'

Anna asked, 'And what else can you tell me about him?'

'He was nice… friendly,' David said, glancing anxiously at a glowering Harry.

Anna pressed on. 'Did you eat the pizza at the café?'

Ryan answered brightly, 'No, he came here with it.'

Harry had listened to this brief exchange in silence, looking from one boy to the other, but at this point he yelled at them. 'He *what*? He came here?'

'You were out,' whimpered Ryan. 'There was nowt for tea.'

As Harry advanced, his face red with rage, Anna stood in front of the boys and pulled her phone from her pocket.

Chapter 4

The police search team arrived at the Heslops' farm just after nine on Saturday morning. Eric was waiting at the gate with several buckets and brushes. He watched while the cadets climbed solemnly into their protective suits and pushed their feet into wellington boots. Eric scrubbed and hosed them one at a time until he was as satisfied as he could ever be that they would not carry the plague onto his farm. He watched as they plodded across the mat, sodden with disinfectant, that stretched across the lane. Maureen had introduced herself at the beginning of this ritual, but all Eric did in response was grunt: 'Local?'

She nodded. 'Workington.'

As they filed down the lane Rose Heslop appeared, looking pale and tired. Maureen introduced herself, speaking quietly to the woman about the plan to find Helen, reassuring her that they would not rest until they had done so. Rose said nothing. She held a handkerchief in her hands, twisting it in her fingers as she followed the cadets back along the lane towards the farm.

Maureen searched upstairs in the farmhouse. She needed to see the girl's room and anything that might offer a clue about Helen's behaviour and intentions. She found an up-to-date photo of two girls, one of whom was clearly Helen, although quite different than the old one they already had. She was pretty in an old-fashioned way, clear skin, pale eyes set quite wide, and hair curling round her shoulders. The face might have been that of a young woman but the room was still a child's, either because there was no money to change the babyish curtains and bedspread, or because the mother wanted to keep it that way. When Maureen looked up, Rose was standing in the doorway.

'I always wanted a little girl,' she said. 'They grow up too quickly these days.'

Maureen held up the photo. 'Was this taken recently?'

Rose took it, held it close. 'During the Christmas holidays. The other girl is Emma Talbot, Helen's friend.'

'Can I keep it?'

Rose thought about this, nodded.

'I think I've finished in here, thanks,' Maureen said, watching as Rose looked round the room as if seeing it for the first time. 'Is there anything else that you feel I need to see? Helen doesn't keep a diary, does she?'

'I don't think so. But…'

Maureen waited.

Rose was looking down at the worn grey carpet, speaking quietly, as if to herself. 'When they grow up, we lose part of them, don't you think? Aidan's so wrapped up in his own world, I hardly know him these days. Brian's still a baby, but for how much longer?'

Maureen said quietly, 'Mrs Heslop, do you have any idea what might have happened to your daughter?'

Rose covered her eyes with her hand. For a moment she said nothing, gazing across the room to the window and the wintry brown fells beyond. 'No,' she said, finally. 'But I wonder if she's trying to scare us.'

'Scare you? What for?'

'Sometimes I think she doesn't like the way we live on the farm. Being so tied to it. So isolated.'

'You think she might have run away intentionally, to push you into moving?'

Rose lowered her hand. 'Doesn't make much sense, does it? But at least that way she might be safe, not – you know – stolen.'

For a few moments there was silence as the two women stood in the bedroom. Specks of dust drifted in a sudden shaft of sunlight that pierced the dark space, and voices drifted up from the yard below.

'Mrs Heslop,' Maureen said in a more formal tone, 'we will need to have something of Helen's: a hairbrush or toothbrush. Just in case.'

Rose looked at her sharply. 'Just in case she's dead, you mean. But that's not going to happen. It won't.'

'I understand your feelings, but I will need something we can check for DNA anyway. It's routine.'

'I got her a new toothbrush for going away,' said Rose, 'but the old one's still in the bathroom. Will that do?'

'Ma'am?' a young man's voice shouted outside below the window. Maureen left Rose still standing in Helen's bedroom and went along the dark landing towards the stairs. Downstairs one of the cadets stood at the back door. 'We searched all the sheds and outhouses. Plenty of muck and cows and sheep and that, but no sign of the kid.'

'The kid?' Maureen interrupted. 'Would you like to rephrase that?'

The cadet reddened. 'Sorry, ma'am. No trace of the missing girl. But we did find something. Can you come?'

Maureen followed him towards a barn full of hay bales, on the outer edge of the farmyard behind the milking parlour. He walked round to the far side and stopped. They were out of sight of the farmhouse. 'Here,' he said, pointing to his feet. Something small and shiny glinted among the weeds and mud. Maureen bent closer: it looked like an earring.

'Just one?' she said. 'Have you looked for the other one?'

'Yes, ma'am,' said the young man. 'No sign of it.'

Maureen held it in her gloved hand. It was in the shape of a rose, about a centimetre across, with a clip that fastened onto the ear rather than pierced it. She pulled a clear plastic evidence bag from her pocket and dropped it in.

'Well spotted,' she said to the cadet, who beamed. 'Anything else of interest round here?'

'No, ma'am.'

'OK, go and wait for me by the gate. Mr Heslop will help us decontaminate. Can't be too careful.'

Back in the farmhouse kitchen Rose and Eric were sitting disconsolately by the Aga. Aidan, the elder brother, was leaning in the pantry doorway and Brian stood by his mother's knee. They all looked at Maureen when she knocked and went in.

'Well?' Eric said. 'Find what you're looking for?'

'Thanks for your patience,' said Maureen. 'Does anyone recognise this?' She held up the plastic bag so that they could all see it.

Aidan leaned forward to peer at the bag in the dim light. 'It's yours, isn't it, Mam?' he said, looking at his mother.

Rose looked flustered. 'Is it?' she said, her face close to the bag that Maureen was still holding. 'Oh, yes. Not seen that for a long time. Where did you find it?'

'Behind the hay barn. Do you have the other one?'

Rose shrugged. 'I might, I suppose, somewhere.'

Eric looked at it. 'Never seen it before,' he said.

'You don't notice things like that, do you?' said Rose. She took Brian's hand and held it tight.

Maureen looked at each member of the unhappy group, but nothing more was forthcoming. 'Right,' she said, 'we've searched the premises carefully, Mr Heslop, and found nothing else of note, but it had to be done. We have a recent photo of Helen, which will be very useful, and Mrs Heslop has given us a toothbrush that Helen had been using.'

Eric looked up. 'What do you want those for?'

'We need to check Helen's DNA, Mr Heslop, and our labs can do that from these items. You understand?'

Eric stared at her momentarily, then looked away. They all knew what he was thinking, but nothing was said.

Maureen pulled her coat around her. 'If you hear anything, from Helen or anyone else, you have my card and details, and my sergeant's too. Ring any time, day or night. Thanks for your cooperation. We could do with your help scrubbing down before we leave, if you wouldn't mind.'

'Bloody waste of time, all of it,' said Eric, getting to his feet. 'You should be out there looking for our Helen, not treating us like criminals.'

Rose stayed in the kitchen, holding Brian close, while Eric and Aidan pulled on their boots and followed Maureen to the gate, where the cadets were waiting huddled together against the wind, like sheep in the corner of a field.

Before she left Pond Street Anna had arranged for a Photofit technician to come to the local police station later in the morning. She'd offered to come back and pick up the boys, but Harry seemed determined to reassert his control over the household by insisting that he would deliver them personally at the appointed time. Anna wondered what kind of punishment he would be meting out to his sons for embarrassing him in his own home.

After leaving the house, Anna parked at the entrance to the school, which was quiet on this raw Saturday morning, and walked slowly down into the town, following the route that the children would have taken when they went to the Market Café. She was looking for CCTV cameras but found none. She'd expected this routine surveillance to be a normal tool of UK policing when she transferred from the military, but that had been another disappointed assumption. There were more cameras every year in Carlisle and Barrow, but not many here, at least not in the outlying streets. Sometimes Cumbria felt like the land that time forgot.

At the café, someone was already at work. The door was locked and Anna knocked on it, holding her ID card up to the window. A woman came to open the door. It was warm inside. Anna thought fleetingly of Maureen up on the farm in this cold wind and was glad that Bell had swapped them around. The café owner, Mrs Edna Taylor, offered coffee, which was immediately accepted.

'We need your help,' Anna began, as the smell of the coffee teased her nostrils. 'A young girl went missing yesterday and we believe that she and her cousins often came here after school.' She felt in her inside pocket for the photo of Helen. 'It's quite an old picture, I'm afraid. The girl is twelve now and will look more grown up than this.'

As she handed over the photo the phone in her pocket buzzed and she reached to answer it. It was Maureen. Anna listened and responded.

'Yes, I called you earlier. No response… No signal, right. I'm in the café now… Can you get the cadets back and then join me at the nick here in Cockermouth at ten? Photofit bloke's coming in, with the two lads. Tell you more then. OK.'

Mrs Taylor was holding the photo out to her. 'Yes, I know this girl. Gone missing, has she? How dreadful, her poor mam.'

‘Did you see her after school yesterday?’

‘No, but earlier in the week they were in, and last week too. Not every day, but regular. Her and two lads. One of them’s called David.’

‘Did they ever meet anyone else here that you recall?’

‘Yes, just recently,’ said Mrs Taylor. ‘He came in once or twice on his own, and then one afternoon he started talking to them. Just, you know, being friendly.’ She hesitated. ‘I think he was lonely. Never saw him with anyone else.’

‘Do you have a name for this man. Did he pay by card?’

Mrs Taylor shook her head. ‘No, always cash. I don’t know him. Sounded local, you know, not one of those Poles or whatever they are.’

‘Can you describe this man for me?’

She thought for a moment. ‘Maybe forty-odd, hard to tell. Quite tall, about your height. Pale-coloured hair, almost like it was dyed. Funny colour for a man. He looked a bit pale too, not red in the face like a farmer.’ She screwed up her own face and hunched her shoulders. ‘As if he was feeling the cold… sort of pinched. Anyway, the kids seemed to like him. The girl came and sat with them, and she usually sat on her own.’

Anna was making notes. ‘Did they leave together?’

‘Oh, no. The kids went home, I suppose, and he stayed a while longer till we were closing up. Half-five.’

‘Did you see where he went after that, to a car maybe?’

Edna Taylor shook her head. ‘He looked as if he hadn’t much money. Bit scruffy, you know. But you can get a car cheap these days, can’t you?’

Anna asked, ‘Do you think you saw him well enough to describe him to someone, to make a Photofit picture?’

‘Aye, I reckon. Does that… do you think he had something to do with…’

'Just routine, Mrs Taylor. I know it's a busy day here, but could you find someone to look after the café for an hour or so, later in the morning? Time is precious when there's a child missing. Say about eleven, at the police station here in town?'

In an interview room at Cockermouth police station the Photofit technician worked patiently with the two boys, adapting the image of the man they called Alex gradually, one nuance at a time. Anna waited until the technician finally handed over the picture he'd created. 'This is the best they could do,' he said. 'They seemed pretty happy with it. I've got a copy, this one's for you.'

Anna looked at the image carefully. It always astonished her how unique the features of the human face could be, even in two-dimensional representation. Juries loved images, more than the dazzling DNA data that forensics could now provide.

'We'll send the boys home,' she said. 'The next witness, Mrs Taylor, is due in ten minutes. Don't show her this at first. Just start from scratch and see where it goes.' As he left the room, Maureen came in. Anna held out the image. 'This is what the boys produced.' Maureen took it from her and held it closer to the desk lamp that glowed in the gloom of mid-morning.

'Is this the man you told me about, the one from the café?'

'The boys said he's called Alex, that's all they had.'

Maureen stared at the image for a while. 'I think I know him, from when I was with the Drug Squad. If it's who I think it is... cannabis grower, dealer, small-time but persistent. The druggies called him "Mr Green". We called him Alex Wetherall. We put him away. Four years.'

Anna was first astonished, and then annoyed. 'You can't be sure it's him.'

As if to prove her point, Maureen logged on to the computer and tapped while Anna watched. In the background they both heard the technician begin his procedure, but their eyes were on the screen. It only took a few minutes. On the left a scroll of text, on the right a face and two profiles. Alexander Wetherall, aka 'Mr Green'. Anna held the Photofit image to the side. The hair was different. Glasses made a difference too, but it was him, no doubt about that, or else someone extraordinarily similar. Release date from Durham Jail, October 2000, nearly six months before.

Anna was deflated. Pritchard was right, again. If Maureen felt vindicated, it didn't show in her voice. 'What's he up to?' she said, puzzled. 'Snatching a kid? Not like him. What happened?'

Anna looked at her. 'And where is he now?'

Alex Wetherall looked out through the windscreen at the open doors of the barn in which he'd parked the van. It was raining and one of the big doors creaked in the draught. He pulled the last dregs from his roll-up and pinched it, savouring the sweet smell. Behind his seat was a metal grille, the kind you use when there are dogs in transit. And behind the grille, snug in a sleeping bag, lay the girl. She seemed restless this morning, but it was just the drugs that made her fidget. She wouldn't wake, he was sure of that.

It had all been so easy. Before she'd realised the direction he was heading, she'd taken the proffered cake and hot drink, both laced with enough to put her to sleep within minutes. He'd used this trick before, but not on a body as small as hers, and he'd had to be careful. Later, in a quiet lay-by, it had been a matter of seconds to carry her round to the van's back doors and stow her safely in the dark interior. For once in his life, he'd planned something well, and followed through. And this was just the beginning.

Chapter 5

'What's a small-time druggie doing taking a kid?' DI Bell leaned back in his chair. 'You know him,' he said to Maureen. 'What do you make of it?'

She shook her head. 'Kidnap for ransom doesn't make sense. Heslops are small farmers. They haven't got any money. No rich relations.'

Bell looked at the piece of paper in his hand that Maureen had printed out for him: he still didn't trust anything he read off a screen. 'How long's he been inside?'

'Four-year sentence, got out in three. Kept his nose clean. He's not really a hard case. Probably scared stiff most of the time and desperate to get out.'

'And you're absolutely sure it's him?' Anna asked. She was finding this new direction hard to believe. First Maureen recognised Chris Strong, and now the likely abductor: local knowledge was all very well, but this was stretching it, and they needed to be sure. 'Could he have a brother, someone who looks just like him? It's not an exact likeness, is it? You said the hair's different and the mug shot on file has him wearing glasses that the boys didn't mention. Is there anyone else who would recognise him?'

'His mother?' said Maureen.

Bell laughed. 'You don't know her as well, surely?'

'My dad probably will.'

'You and your bloody father,' Bell went on. 'That place of his must be crawling with criminals' mothers getting their perms done.'

Maureen grinned. It wasn't the first time that comment had been made. 'It's like a back door to the police,' she said. 'Less obvious than going to the nick, but folk know that what they tell Dad will get back to me.'

Bell went on, 'So where does this bloke's mam fit in?'

'Not sure, but I've met her in the salon, I'll swear to that. We had a funny conversation about Alex once without mentioning him. Do you want me to question her?'

DI Bell ran his stubby fingers over his face. Anna knew he would be thinking about more people, more overtime.

'We do need more officers on this case, sir,' she said, trying to capitalise on his uncertainty. 'We're no further forward and Helen's been in the wind for nearly eighteen hours already. This man is the main suspect obviously, if she's been taken, but we still can't be sure of that. If she's not found pretty soon we have to start a full search with no idea where to begin. Overtime'll go through the roof then.'

Bell rolled his eyes, but Anna ploughed on. 'Surely we don't have to wait till Monday to see if there've been any reports of someone hanging around the school? Kids tell teachers stuff like that. The school staff won't even know yet that she's missing. Until they know there's a problem, they'll have no reason to pass anything on. We need more people to handle all this quickly.'

'We need more people, do we?' he said, imitating her educated accent. Anna turned away. She wasn't sure how much more of Bell she could take. He checked his watch. 'I promised a progress report to the Super by lunchtime so we'd better get on with it. Penrose, get on to the Head at the school. Tell him we need help.

Pritchard, get on to Carlisle. Get them to track this con's mam down. You put him away, right?'

'The Drug Squad did, yes,' Maureen replied.

'Well, you know more than the rest of us about him, so get over there and lean on his mam. She'll do all the usual stuff, but push her. She'll have some idea where he is and we need to know, now, before we waste any more time.' He glared at Anna. 'You're the sergeant, right? So get this organised and stop fannying around.'

Bell stomped out of the office. Anna sagged against her desk.

'He's like that with everybody,' Maureen said. 'Don't let him wind you up.'

Anna wasn't easily placated. 'But it's not everybody he goes for,' she said. 'Just me, as far as I can see. You don't catch it, not the same way.'

'I did to start with,' Maureen said. 'All the time. It's not as bad now as it was back then. You just have to let things slide off you.'

DC Bob Carruthers had put his head up on the other side of the room, following the conversation with interest. Anna went on, as if talking to herself, 'I'm used to hierarchies and rank and so on, and we all tease the juniors, but I'm *not* a bloody junior. I've done stuff and seen things DI Bell couldn't stomach while he…' Her voice tailed away.

Bob caught Maureen's eye and winked. He knew that she had gone for the sergeant's job and been turned down, and now he took pleasure in watching the two women trying to get along, and not managing it. There was nothing Bob liked better than a good catfight.

For an hour they all sat at their respective phones, checking facts, following leads, checking again. By the end of it they had very little new, except the address of Alex Wetherall's mother, Margaret, in Carlisle.

‘I’m off to see that friend of Helen’s from school, Emma Talbot, at the B&B, then I’ll go and lean on Wetherall’s Mam, as instructed,’ Maureen said. ‘You’ll do all the school stuff?’ Anna nodded, the phone already in her hand.

The school’s head teacher, Brian Hellibone, didn’t pick up, but responded to Anna’s message almost immediately. He was horrified to learn that one of his pupils was missing, and seemed to take it personally. ‘She’s one of ours,’ he said. ‘What can I do to help, now, not just wait till Monday?’

Anna knew what needed doing. ‘Is there any way you could contact your teachers, by phone, email, text, whatever works, as soon as possible? Ask them for any information they might have, rumours, anything odd reported by their students about strangers seen near the school. And if any of them is close to Helen we need to hear from them. Can you do that? How many teachers are we talking about?’

‘Teachers and all the other support people,’ he paused, ‘over a hundred in all. But leave it with me. We have a telephone tree system for emergencies, and this is an emergency. I’ll get back to you as soon as I can.’

He rang off before Anna could thank him. That one call could save her team hours of work.

Someone knocked on the open door. Anna looked up. A man was standing in the doorway, holding a crash helmet in his hand. He had a pale square-jawed face and very dark eyes. Black hair hung quite long over one eye and he pushed it back impatiently. A slender body in motorcycle leathers. Anna found him undeniably attractive and hoped it didn’t show. The man stepped into the room and held out his hand to her. ‘Tony Wong,’ he said. ‘I’m the new SOCO. Desk sergeant told me to come straight through.’ The voice was north Cumbrian, with the usual hint of Newcastle.

'Anna – Anna Penrose,' she said, taking his hand, which was warm and dry. 'How come I didn't know you were coming?'

'Your DI does. At least the memo went out last week. Could still be on his desk.'

Anna knew Bell's desk, where information could be sorted by carbon dating. 'He's just left,' she said. 'He'll be pleased you're here. The last SOCO was moved out somewhere pretty quick and we're one down. Where have you been working?'

'Seven years in the Met.' He smiled. 'Bit different up here. You?'

'MP,' she said. His smile was making things worse. She felt almost light-headed.

'Parliament?' he queried, smiling a little wider.

Anna smiled too. 'Military Police... army. Just started here.'

'Oh, another off-comer,' he said. 'But at least I was born here.'

Anna struggled to mask her surprise, although his accent was a give-away. 'Carlisle, born and bred,' he said. 'Would you believe my dad has a chippy? He wanted me to do law or medicine, but here I am. Hands-on science plus solving real problems, that's what I wanted, and as far from Carlisle as I could get.'

'So why come back?' Anna asked.

'Mam died,' said Wong. 'Dad's not good on his own. I've got a sister, but she's in Manchester with two young kids so she couldn't help much. I saw this job and went for it. Feels OK so far. Friendly. London's a mess.'

'Their loss, our gain,' said Anna. 'Hope our boss feels the same. He's old school. Too many women around for his liking.'

'And too many foreigners too, probably.'

'Probably,' she said, hoping that didn't sound unprofessional.

Tony Wong smiled again. 'Just have to prove myself then, won't I?'

Keen as well as tasty, she thought. The last SOCO had been on the job for two years, and been as much use as a chocolate teapot, according to Bell. She picked up the file from her desk and pointed at the big whiteboard. 'This is what we're working on – missing child case. No clear crime scene as yet. We're still pinpointing the girl's last movements yesterday, should have something firmer by the end of today.' She handed over the file. 'Have a look through this, and at the board. I'll make sure DI Bell knows you're here.'

She was already looking forward to seeing Bell's reaction to a new and definitely unfamiliar face.

Wong had been gone only a few minutes when another young man appeared in the office. Anna found him attractive too in a sporty, clean-cut sort of way and wondered what was going on: not a flicker for months and then two men who strongly appealed to her in one day. Could be her hormones, she thought, as the man stretched out his hand.

'Mark Fletcher,' he said, 'from the school. I got a call about Helen Heslop. Have you found her yet?'

'Nothing so far. Have you got something for us?'

'Could be nothing, but the phone call I got said you were looking for any information at all, so I came straight down here.'

Anna asked him to sit and got out her notebook.

He leaned forward, as if he was about to make a very important point. 'You see, I take Year Seven for Personal and Social Development.'

Anna looked puzzled and Mark explained: 'Year Seven are first years at secondary school, same as Helen. The course is just one lesson a week, covers all sorts of stuff.' He gathered his thoughts, seemed to be enjoying her attention. 'Anyway,' he went on, 'we were talking about their journeys to and from school, getting around in this area with not much public transport.

Then the discussion moved on to the perils of hitchhiking, "Stranger danger", all that. One of the girls, Carol Ingram, lives further up the hill from the school gate.' Mark pointed vaguely over his shoulder. 'Well, she walks home. She mentioned that there'd been a van parked just up the hill with a man sitting in it, and said he looked at her funny. She's a bit of a drama queen and I didn't want the discussion sliding off into stuff about bogeymen snatching girls off the street…' His voice tailed off. 'Oh, God, that's not what happened, is it?'

'We don't yet know what's happened,' Anna said. 'Except that Helen hasn't been seen since the end of school on Friday. She could have gone off somewhere by herself. She could be fine. We just don't know. Her family's very worried, as you can imagine.'

The young teacher nodded.

'Can you recall exactly what this girl…' Anna looked at her notes '… what Carol said?'

'Just that it was a van, parked at the roadside, and a man was sitting alone in it. She said he looked as if he was going to speak to her the first time she saw him, but he didn't.'

'And this was more than once? When?'

'This past week, so she said.' He looked at Anna, clearly upset. 'Should I have said something about it earlier, reported it or something?'

Anna shook her head. 'You had no reason to, did you? The man didn't get out or follow her, or anything more sinister?'

'She'd have certainly mentioned anything like that.'

'Well, you've told us now, and it could be very helpful.' Anna reached for a card off her desk. 'If you recall anything else, ring me on this number, any time. And thanks for coming in.'

Within half an hour she was sitting in the Ingrams' front room with a cup of tea, while the young girl huddled next to her mother was clearly enjoying being the centre of attention.

'Tell me as much as you can remember about the van,' said Anna.

Carol closed her eyes. 'It was a dark colour, and a bit dirty, you know, muddy.'

'Dark… d'you mean black?'

'Could be, or dark blue. Or green maybe?' Carol looked up at Anna, who tried not to let the frustration show. It was no good nagging. She tried another tack. 'Did the van have four windows, or just two at the front?'

Carol half shut her eyes. 'Two at the front, then nothing behind. Quite big, you know.'

'Now this is a hard one, Carol. Do you remember if it had a sliding door at the side, like some vans do?'

'I don't think so. I looked back after I'd passed it, to see if the driver was watching me in his side mirror.'

'And was he?'

'No, but the van had two big doors at the back, you know, like a delivery van.'

'Well done, pet,' said Mrs Ingram, squeezing her daughter's hand. Anna smiled brightly, although there was really precious little useful information so far.

'You didn't look at the number plate, did you?'

Carol shook her head. 'Well, you wouldn't, would you?' chimed in her mother.

'Not to worry,' said Anna quickly. She wanted to keep Carol relaxed, to allow more details to surface.

'Just one person in the van? Did you see what he looked like? Young… old?'

'Middling, you know. Mum and Dad's age. Longish hair, quite a pale face. He looked right at me.' Mrs Ingram held her daughter's hand tightly. Anna opened her bag and took out the Photofit that David and Ryan had produced. 'Do you recognise this man?' she asked, holding the photo out for the girl to see.

Carol put her hand to her mouth and looked at her mother. 'That's him, I'm sure it is.' She leaned towards her mother. 'Mam,' she whispered, 'he might come after me.'

Anna got to her feet. 'Nothing to worry about, I'm sure,' she said. 'We have no evidence that this man was responsible for anything that may have happened to Helen. But it's very helpful information, thank you, Carol.'

Mrs Ingram saw her to the door. 'You're just trying to reassure us, aren't you?' she whispered.

'Not at all,' said Anna. 'It's a routine enquiry. It'll be fine, but if you're worried at all, call me any time.' She handed over her card.

As she drove back to the station, she told herself to follow the evidence, not a hunch, and there was no tangible evidence, not yet. Even so, by the time she was adding information to the big board in the CID room back in Workington she was sure in her own mind that the man in the van, whoever he was, was involved in Helen's disappearance and they needed to find him. Someone would need to check the police computer for any record of stolen vans, or rentals. That would take a while... just the job for DC Carruthers, snug in his corner, tapping away.

A note lay on her desk, with a Keswick phone number. 'Call Miss Williams, Helen Heslop's tutor.' More information from the school. Anna dialled the number but it just rang and rang. Whatever it was would have to wait, and meanwhile the hours were ticking by.

It was quiet in the Redhouse Bed and Breakfast now that the only two guests had checked out for the day. Emma Talbot's mother was organising the cleaner, and it was Mr Talbot who brought his daughter into the front lounge overlooking the quiet street and sat with her on the big sofa by the window.

Maureen could see that the girl was nervous and upset.

'I'm Maureen… DC Pritchard,' she said, 'one of the team that's looking for your friend Helen. We're going to find her. I don't want you to worry too much about it. You're safe here with your parents, and you can help us find your friend.'

Emma nodded. She'd been crying.

'Do you think you're Helen's closest friend, Emma? Someone to share secrets with?'

Emma nodded. 'I think she had a big friend at primary, but she went to another school. So now it's me.'

'I'm going to ask you some questions, to make sure we get to know everything we need. Is that all right?'

Emma nodded again.

'Now, before we get to Friday afternoon and what happened then, tell me a bit about Helen. What's she like?'

Emma thought for a moment. 'Well, she's funny. Sometimes she's really grown up, going to her gran's in Carlisle on her own and all that, and sometimes she's not.'

'In what way?'

Emma looked at her dad, who nodded encouragement.

'She has some funny ideas. You can tell her all sorts of rubbish, and she'll believe you. And she doesn't know much about… you know, boys and things.'

'She has two brothers, doesn't she?'

'Yes. I mean, she knows about boys being different, you know,' Emma pointed vaguely towards her legs, 'but when we were doing Sex Ed last term, she didn't know the other stuff, about babies and that. And when she started her periods, I had to explain it to her. My mum gave her the stuff she needed.'

Emma hesitated. 'And she gets breathless sometimes. Maybe it's the asthma.'

Maureen interrupted. 'Helen has asthma?'

'Yes, she has a puffer. Doesn't use it much.'

Maureen's mind raced. She didn't know much about childhood asthma, but she knew this wasn't good.

At about the same time, in the Workington office, Anna was on the phone. 'When did Helen mention this, Miss Williams?' she said, and the woman responded. 'It was last term, quite early on. I was surprised that she was willing to talk about it so soon, you know, before she knew me very well.'

'Do you think she's a trusting sort of girl?'

'She must be. Some children are very reluctant to talk about what happens at home, even when they really should.'

'And what exactly did Helen tell you?'

'Well, it was clear that she was upset about something, and I asked her to stay behind, so we could have some privacy. She just blurted out about her mum and dad arguing, at night, when Helen was in her bedroom. She could hear them through the wall. Her mum had been crying, apparently, but in the morning nothing was said. Helen asked me if I thought her parents were going to divorce. As if I would know.'

'It is an odd thing for a child to ask a teacher, isn't it?'

'Well, Helen's a funny little thing,' Miss Williams added. 'Very childish in some respects. Anyway, I said that I was sure it would be OK, and not to worry. And perhaps she could talk to her mother, you know, without stirring things up too much.'

'And did she?'

'No idea,' said Miss Williams. 'She didn't mention it again, and since then all this Foot and Mouth stuff has blown up. I guess family troubles take a back seat, don't they, especially on a farm.'

'Of course,' said Anna. Bob Carruthers was standing with the other phone, waving at her. 'Can you hang on just a moment?' She put her hand over the mouthpiece. 'What's up?

'Pritchard wants a word, something to do with Helen having asthma.'

Anna spoke again. 'Miss Williams? Sorry to keep you waiting. Do you know if Helen suffers from asthma?'

'Yes, it's in her notes at school. She had her puffer with her every day when she started in Year Seven, but I've not seen it recently. Maybe she's better now.' Anna thanked her and rang off. She picked up the phone that Bob was holding. 'Asthma confirmed, it's in her medical notes at school.'

Maureen's annoyance was unmistakeable. 'Helen has a potentially fatal illness,' she said, 'and this is the first we've heard of it?' Anna felt there was implied criticism of her in this outburst and tried to fend it off, but Maureen wasn't finished. 'We need to talk to the parents,' she went on. 'How can they not tell us something like this? And we need to check with the GP, whoever he is.'

Who's in charge of this investigation? Anna asked herself, hoping that Bob couldn't hear Maureen laying down the law. 'And there's another thing,' Maureen went on. 'When I was talking to Rose Heslop in Helen's bedroom, she said that Helen might have run away to scare them into moving away from the farm. What's the matter with the woman?'

Anna didn't rise to it. 'Mother's in shock, isn't she? It doesn't mean much.'

'Well, one of us needs to talk to her, and that miserable husband.'

'OK, OK,' said Anna. 'I'll circulate the information about Helen's asthma. And we need to know whether she has a puffer with her. Things could go missing at the Strongs' house in that mess. I'll check with them and with the Heslops.'

Maureen asked, 'What if she hasn't got a puffer with her? Anything could set off an asthma attack. Stress, fear, smoke.'

'Leave it with me,' Anna managed to interrupt through the tirade. 'You're going to Carlisle now, aren't you? Leave the rest with me, right?'

Anna didn't have the chance to mention Tony Wong, but what was the point of a Scene of Crime Officer without a crime scene? They were no further forward, had no idea where, when or how the child had been abducted, and only supposition about who had done so. And to crown it all, Maureen was stamping around as if she were the one in charge. Anna was seriously worried: this was her case, not Maureen's. If she failed and the child died, she would carry that guilt for the rest of her life.

When Rose was asked about Helen's asthma she said that Helen took her puffer away with her, so she would be alright, wouldn't she? Anna rang the house in Pond Street. Christine Strong sounded half asleep but Anna left her in no doubt about the urgency of the search for Helen's puffer. Minutes later the phone rang. 'We found it,' Christine said, sounding worried. 'In the drawer in her bedroom. It's blue.' Anna sat with her head resting on her fist for a moment. If Helen had an attack and didn't have her puffer… it didn't bear thinking about.

Chapter 6

'Too many chiefs, not enough Indians,' said DI Dinger Bell, looking round the table. 'Where's DC Evans?'

'Off sick, sir,' said Bob Carruthers. 'That's twice he's been off since the FMD thing started. Someone needs to tell 'im he won't catch the plague as soon as he leaves the house.'

It was seven o'clock on Saturday evening, more than twenty-four hours since Helen Heslop had been reported missing. Bell had called the team together to review progress and the next steps.

'We do need more people on this, sir,' said Anna. She already knew how he would react, but had to keep saying it, in case someone asked questions later. 'This child's been missing for too long.'

'All right, all right, don't nag, I'll get on to it,' Bell said, tapping his pen in irritation. 'OK, how far have we got?'

Anna was gathering her papers and about to start her report when Maureen spoke up ahead of her. Anna frowned at the interruption but Maureen either didn't see her reaction or saw it and was too frustrated to take any notice.

'I went up to Carlisle for Wetherall's mam. Traffic was awful, again. Bloody waste of time. No response, but the place looks occupied. Knocked up a neighbour who only wanted to tell me what a grumpy old sod Mrs Wetherall is. I could have hung around but there was no saying where she was or when she'd get back. I put a note through the door with the phone number, said it was urgent. If we hear nothing I'll try again in the morning.'

Anna was about to start her report, but Maureen clearly wasn't finished. 'The mother's obviously on medication, sir,' she went on, addressing herself to Bell, 'but even so, not telling us that the child has asthma – well, that's life-threatening. I checked with the GP, Dr Jennings. He told me that Helen could be in serious difficulties without the right amount of the right inhaler, the one he prescribed for her.'

'What kind of difficulties?' Carruthers asked.

Maureen checked her notes. 'He said she could feel sick, dizzy, pass out. If there was no one to help her, it could be fatal.'

'Asthma could kill her?' Bell asked.

'Children die of asthma, sir, yes,' said Anna. Now that Maureen had opened this door, they had to go through it. 'If the child has an inhaler, the right inhaler, that should keep the airways open. But if she takes too much of it, that could harm her as well.'

'Does she have the right inhaler?' Bell asked.

'The one the GP prescribed was found at the home of Mr and Mrs Strong, where Helen's been staying. There may be a spare at the farm, but it's never been mentioned.'

Carruthers said, 'If the bloke who's got her knows she needs a puffer, what would he do?'

Bell was thinking. 'Let's assume he wants to keep her alive: he could buy one, or steal it? Depends whether he can find a pharmacy open now. Might have to wait until Monday morning, if the kid's in trouble. We don't even know why he took her.' He hesitated. 'Perhaps he wanted her dead anyway.'

'Whatever his motivation, sir, I've circulated the details,' said Anna. 'All officers have been asked to keep an eye on pharmacies, right across the county. We need some information about where they might be. Cumbria's a big place.'

'Well, well, is that right?' said Bell, with heavy sarcasm. Maureen hid a smile by looking at her notes. He went on, 'Any details about the car?'

Anna shook her head. 'We know a dark-coloured van was seen near the school last week, and the ID on the driver resembles our Photofit of Alex Wetherall, but that's all we have until I can check with all the kids and teachers about Friday afternoon. Someone will have seen something.'

Maureen had more to say and deliberately avoided looking at Anna, who was still waiting for Bell to tell the junior officer to wait her turn. But he carried on listening as if everything was fine, and Maureen kept going. 'Sir,' she said, 'I'm sure Rose Heslop knows more than she's letting on, even if she is drugged up. She said something about Helen trying to scare them, to get them to leave the farm. And when Sarge checked with her about the asthma, she said that Helen always carried her puffer, so it wouldn't be a problem. I ask you! I'd have been frantic if that girl was one of mine, but the mother seems too calm about it. I think she must be on something… tranquillisers probably.'

Yet again Anna was about to speak, but this time it was Bob Carruthers who interrupted and she sat back in her chair, furious that Bell was letting this happen. 'She said the kid was trying to scare them?' Bob said. 'Bit drastic, isn't it? And how long would she stay away if that's what it's about? One night's enough, surely, even for a mixed-up teenager.'

'But it's not just that,' Maureen insisted. 'Neither of the parents told us about the asthma.'

Carruthers wasn't going to let her win the point. 'Each one thought the other had said summat. Easily done, especially when they're in shock, unless someone asks a direct question.'

'OK, that's enough,' said Bell.

Anna waited for both Maureen and Bob to be reprimanded, but instead DI Bell said, 'This sounds like another of your gut feelings, Pritchard, and you know how I feel about those. We need some hard evidence for our new SOCO to get his hands on. Don't even have a name for him, by the way. Anyone met him yet?'

'Could be a woman, sir,' said Maureen, just to wind him up.

'He's called Tony Wong,' said Anna.

Bell stared. 'You're kidding, right?'

'Born in Carlisle, dad owns a chippy,' Anna added, glad that for once Maureen wasn't the only source of local information.

DI Bell leaned back in his chair and rolled his eyes. 'God help us,' he said. 'Women all over the place and now some Chink? What's the job coming to?'

Maureen refused to be diverted and persisted with her suspicions of Helen's mother. 'I think we need to get Rose Heslop in, sir. I could get her to talk, given the chance. Getting information out of her now could save us time.'

'What's the grounds for bringing her in?' Bell asked. He and Penrose were both frowning, surprised by Pritchard's faith in her own interviewing abilities.

Anna had a decision to make. She needed to make it look as if the strategy were her idea. 'Worth a try, sir,' she said. 'It could save a lot of time and manpower.'

Bell looked exasperated. 'Oh, for God's sake. All this feminine intuition stuff gets on my wick. Get her in if you must. And good luck with that husband of hers. Is he in on this too, by the way?'

Maureen shook her head. 'Doubt it. We know they're having problems.'

'Hell hath no fury, et cetera, et cetera,' Bob Carruthers stuck his oar in. He shrugged as the others looked at him disparagingly.

'OK,' said Bell. 'Pritchard's doorstepping Wetherall's mam, Rose Heslop's coming in, Penrose is checking pharmacies and the school kids, and I'll push the search along and keep the Super and the army in the loop. We need enough to tie him to this case. All we know for sure is that he's been hanging round the school.'

'Pervy git,' Carruthers interrupted again.

'Too right, Bob,' Bell went on, 'and the van description is pretty tight. Army have as many blokes on the road as we do.' He leaned back in his chair. 'That's a real operation they're running up there. No messing around.' He looked at Anna. 'You were army, weren't you? You'd 'ave been better off sticking with it.'

She stared back at him, poker-faced. 'Thank you, sir,' was all she managed to say.

When Bell and Carruthers had gone, Anna's escalating anger spilled over. 'DC Pritchard,' she began, 'don't you dare do that again – undermining me like that in front of Dinger and his dog. Bell asked for my report and you jumped in without even asking.' Maureen looked away, but Anna wasn't done. 'And then you did it *again*, banging on about Rose.'

'But you agreed with me,' Maureen responded, taken aback by Anna's reaction.

'I had to, didn't I?' she said, still standing, leaning towards Maureen. 'And anyway, that's not the point. The point is that you seem to be ignoring me and encouraging our beloved leader to do the same. I won't have it. I may be new here but I expect my officers to respect the proper order of business.'

Now Maureen was angry. 'Oh, that's it, the good old "chain of command". Well, that was the army, and this is the

Cumbria police. I've been in it a long time – long enough to understand how it works.'

Anna snorted. 'How it works? Not much evidence of anything working up to now.' She picked up various papers and arranged them quite unnecessarily into a pile. 'We need some evidence, real hard evidence. You know that. It could take you hours to get anything out of Rose, even if there's anything there. We're one man down already, and you'll be in here playing mind games with a woman who's so drugged up she can hardly remember her own name.' She stopped and stared hard at Maureen, who stared back.

There was a tentative knock on the open door. Both women looked towards it, making the young PC wish he'd waited. He waved a piece of paper. 'Thought you'd want to see this,' he said. 'Report of an attempted break-in at a pharmacy near Silloth. Neighbours reported the noise.'

Maureen had sat down at her desk, fuming. Anna held out her hand for the paper. 'Anything taken?'

'Not by the look of it,' said PC Edwards. These angry women were making him very nervous. Anna snatched the paper and PC Edwards left as quickly as he could.

'Silloth,' she said. 'It could be him.'

Maureen shrugged. She'd had enough for one day.

'Now, look,' said Anna. The interruption had cooled her down a bit. 'I know I'm new here, OK, but we can't be running around like headless chickens and contradicting each other in front of DI Bell. Things have to be prioritised when we're so short of people.' She hesitated. Maureen didn't respond.

Anna tried another tack. 'OK, if that's the way it has to be. I'm *suggesting*, right, that you check with Rose's GP about her medication. He'll mumble on about patient confidentiality, but see what you can get. If we want anything useful out of Rose, it will have to be when she's less under the influence of whatever it is she's on. Can't have you wasting time while she's off with the fairies.'

'Right,' Maureen said, without looking up.

Anna went on, checking something on her notepad, 'And get back on to Helen's tutor first thing—'

'Miss Williams,' Maureen interrupted, but Anna let it pass.

'Yes, her. Get anything else you can about what Helen said about life at home before you go for Rose. Might give us some leverage. And try again with Wetherall's mother. I'll take Wong up to Silloth as soon as it's light. Might find something concrete up there, instead of all these…' She waved her hand vaguely.

'Ideas? Suggestions?' Maureen added.

'All that. And I meant what I said before. If you've got something to throw at Bell, throw it at me first, right?'

Maureen hesitated. She'd been relying on 'do it first, apologise later' for twenty years on the job, but she'd had enough. An apology stuck in her throat. She got up without a word and left the office. She needed to check another of the 'ideas' that Bell and the others were so sceptical about.

An hour later, as Christine Strong practically pushed Maureen out of the house in Pond Street, there was a little more to add to the picture. The boys had mentioned that Alex said he knew their mum, and that was way back, in Carlisle where Chris and Rose had known one another too. The links were tenuous, but they were more than just 'ideas'.

Maureen smiled as she drove back home. Forensic evidence was important, she knew that, but sometimes what really mattered was why people do what they do, not just how.

It was only just light on Sunday morning when DS Penrose and the new SOCO turned into the main street of Silloth looking for the pharmacy. Anna was glad to get the chance to see more of Tony Wong. There was definitely something interesting about him.

The weather overnight had been wild and the wind fresh off the sea was sharp with salt. Early sun caught the tops of the cedar trees that lined the road running down to the harbour and the beach. Across the Solway, the Scottish coast looked to have been sketched in with a fine blue pencil.

Tony sniffed the air. 'Used to come here when I was a kid, on the train or the bus, before we had a car. My mum loved it.'

'Ah,' said Anna. 'You told me that she died. Sorry.'

'We miss her. That's one reason I stayed at home for as long as I did, afterwards.'

Anna wanted to ask where he was living now, but it was none of her business.

The key holder was waiting for them at the front door of the pharmacy on the main street, his collar pulled up against the wind.

'Mr Patel?' said Anna. 'Sorry it's so early. Time is precious. Missing person enquiry.'

'So what's that got to do with a break-in here?' Mr Patel seemed irritated to have been dragged from his bed during the only lie-in of his week.

'We believe the person may need medication and be prepared to steal it.' That was less than the truth, but Anna didn't want to start a lot of gossip about the case.

Mr Patel shook his head. 'But they got nothing. Didn't get past the metal grille as far as I can tell. Come and look.'

He led them round the corner and then down an alley that ran behind the row of shops. There was a door in the wall and he stretched his hand towards it before Tony stepped in front of him, barring his way. 'Just tell us, but don't touch anything, please,' he said. 'Just possible there's some traces we might find.'

Mr Patel held up his hands. 'OK, OK.' Anna took his arm and propelled him back out into the alley, then stood back and watched as Wong set about his business with impressive concentration. For fifteen minutes he traced and retraced his steps into the alley, then back, then up to the broken window. Occasionally he kneeled down, checking the ground. Anna felt redundant. He clearly preferred to work alone. She checked the caller's name on the original police report. The noise had been reported from the flat above the café on the far corner of the street.

The sign on the door of the café said it wasn't due to open until nine, almost an hour away, but she hammered on the door and heard a window open above her head.

'Too early,' said a woman's voice. 'Come back at nine.'

Anna pulled out her ID and held it up. 'Police,' she said. 'Can I ask you some questions about an incident last night?'

Through the glass door Anna saw a woman in a housecoat and headscarf shuffle across the floor, between tables still piled with chairs. The door opened, and Anna smiled brightly.

'Yes?' said the woman. She drew on the stub of her cigarette and then lobbed the dimp out into the street.

'The pharmacy was broken into last night, at the back. Someone rang the police from this address, about the noise? After dark, about eleven, we think.'

'Aye, that was me. I was upstairs by then.' She pointed above her head. 'Heard a noise, then an engine revving a bit later. Must have been about half-eleven. Sounded like a motorbike.'

'Are you sure?'

'Cars don't sound like that, except those stupid drag things. Yeah, motorbike, I reckon.' The woman shook her head. 'Is that it? Café opens in a bit… I can't hang around.'

Anna checked the phone number and walked back across the road. As she came towards him Tony paged through his notes, and told her what he'd discovered, which wasn't much.

'Whoever it was came on a motorcycle. Clear impressions in the mud in the alley. The grille is pretty firm and he clearly didn't have the tools to force it. Did his best though. There are other pharmacies around. Did you get anything across the street?'

'Noise of a motorbike around half-eleven last night.'

'I thought you said the suspect was driving a van.'

Anna shrugged. 'Who knows? That case might have nothing to do with all this. Anyway, he might have tried again, like you said. Let me make a call.'

She walked down towards the sea to get a better signal and called in. Maureen answered. Anna ignored their previous disagreement and asked simply, 'Any other pharmacy break-ins reported, before we set off back?'

'Yes, there is. Something from Wigton. They're on Sunday opening and someone called in just a few minutes ago. Proper break-in this time. Made a real mess. Don't know what's missing.'

'We're on it,' said Anna, taking down the details. 'This new SOCO's impressive by the way. Real concentration. And he knows someone at the forensics labs. Very useful, I reckon.'

Maureen sniffed. 'He'll have to walk on water before Dinger gives him any credit.'

'Another pharmacy break-in, Wigton,' Anna said, as she got back to the car. 'You OK with that? Got everything you need?'

'Not much to find. I got a piece of the grille in case there's anything on it. I'll do a report for the owners, although they probably wouldn't notice the missing piece. So, let's go,' he said. 'Great stuff, this. Just the sort of work I like.'

As they drove, she asked, 'None of my business, but do you have your own place now? You're not driving down from Carlisle every day, are you?'

He smiled. 'No, spent enough of my life living over the chippy. Smell gets into everything. I've got a flat in Whitehaven. It'll do for now.' He looked across at her. 'You?'

'I'm renting a little house out towards Keswick, up the Whinlatter Pass road. I love the hills, always have.'

'I did some rock climbing myself,' he said, 'while I was at uni.'

Anna was surprised, but she said nothing more. It could wait.

'You know Pritchard wanted the sergeant's job?' Wong said out of the blue after a few minutes' silence. 'I heard them talking about it in the canteen. She must be pretty pissed off.'

'I didn't know that,' Anna admitted. It figures, she thought.

'People don't mention it when you're around, obviously,' said Wong.

'Well, it's no good her taking it out on me,' she said. 'Not my fault the whole system's screwed.'

He glanced across. 'Someone said the Home Office were kicking up about not enough women in senior posts.'

Anna knew what was being implied. 'So they grabbed the first one that came along, regardless of ability, is that what you mean?'

'Whoah,' he said. 'Just thought you might need to know. You have to work with Pritchard every day.'

More's the pity, Anna thought. Wong made a mental note not to mention it again.

There was more to do at the Wigton pharmacy, and they needed help from the pharmacist to identify what might be missing from the shelves where boxes and bottles had been swept onto the floor.

'Someone had a hissy fit?' Tony Wong said, looking at the chaos in the store room.

'Or else wanted to cover their tracks,' said Anna. 'Are you OK with this for a while?'

Wong nodded, looking intently round the small room. 'You carry on.' He looked up and smiled at her unexpectedly and Anna suddenly realised something. He looks like Mark, she thought. Different face entirely but the same expression, the same smile. And he thinks the same way: rational, straightforward. *That's* why I fancy him. She smiled back, revealing nothing. He was probably younger than her, and she was his senior officer. Tricky.

Anna called for help from the local nick, and she and the young PC they sent went house-to-house along the row of terraced houses that overlooked the back of the pharmacy. Someone had heard a dog barking around midnight, and Anna was taking the details when the young PC called to her. 'Lady at number seventeen, ma'am,' he said. 'Thinks she heard a motorbike, not sure of the time.'

The lady in question was standing on the front step of her house, clearly wanting to know more about what was going on. Anna introduced herself.

'This is a very quiet street,' said the woman. 'Never any trouble, you know, not since they moved out of number nine.' She gestured down the road. 'Brought down the whole neighbourhood, the no-good scum,' she said with a vehemence that left Anna's notebook stippled with spit.

'About last night, Mrs... er...'

'Hobson – Vera Hobson.'

'You heard a motorbike, is that right? Can you give me an idea of the time?'

Vera Hobson clasped her hands together as if in prayer. 'Well, I went up to bed about half-eleven, and I was just dropping off. Maybe midnight? Don't keep a clock in my bedroom, not since

I've been having trouble… you know, in the night, since my husband died. Can't bear watching the hours tick by.'

Anna nodded with as much sympathy as she could muster. 'And you're sure it was a motorbike, not a car?'

'Definitely a motorbike,' Mrs Hobson said with conviction. 'My husband, Gerry, he had one. Couldn't stand it myself, but the noise – well, you can't mistake it, can you? Just like Gerry's, it was.'

'Just like it?'

'Oh, yes. I'd know it anywhere. Gave me quite a turn actually.'

Anna looked up at her. 'You don't remember the model of your husband's bike, do you?'

'Kawasaki,' said Vera. 'He said British bikes were rubbish compared to the Japanese. Maybe that's why I didn't like it. My father was in the war out East. Japanese! Really.' She pursed her lips in disapproval.

When Anna got back to the pharmacy Tony was still busy, and she went to talk to the pharmacist while the shop was quiet.

'Is anything obviously missing, from what you can see back there?'

The young woman went and stood in the doorway, looking into the room. Anna could see her mentally checking where things were and what should have been stored on the empty shelves. 'Looks like quite a gap where the painkillers should be.' She pointed to a low shelf on the right. 'And up there, there's a range of inhalers, or there was. Not much left. Can I get a bit closer?'

Tony explained where it was OK to stand and the woman approached the shelf. She reached down to pick something up and he nodded. 'The smaller boxes at the end are the children's inhalers,' she said. 'We don't have many of those, looks like they're still here.'

She peered at the small printed labels on the front edge of the shelf. 'Yes, the other inhalers have gone. All of them. There are usually half a dozen or so.'

'The other inhalers?'

'Yes,' said the pharmacist. 'The bigger ones have gone, the ones meant for adults.'

Anna winced.

'Is that a problem?' the pharmacist asked.

Chapter 7

On Sunday morning first thing Maureen dialled the number of the farm and waited. The phone rang for a long time before someone picked up. It was a man's voice, one Maureen didn't recognise. She introduced herself and asked to speak to Rose.

'Oh, God,' said the voice. 'Is it about Helen? Have you found her?'

'Who's speaking?' Maureen said.

'Sorry, I'm… my name is Barry Blake. Rose worked with me at the Cockermouth auction. Look, it's a really bad time to call. Rose has sheep, you see, and, well, the slaughter team is on its way. Can you call back later in the day?'

'Mr Blake,' Maureen said, 'must I remind you that Helen Heslop has been missing since Friday afternoon and it's now Sunday morning? This is urgent police business that cannot wait. Now may I speak to Mrs Heslop, please?'

A momentary silence followed before Barry Blake spoke again. 'Yes, sorry. But things are pretty difficult here. Rose… Mrs Heslop… is in a bad way.'

'Tell me exactly what's going on, Mr Blake. Is this to do with Foot and Mouth?'

'Mr Heslop thinks the sheep are a risk because they might bring in the disease and wipe out the dairy herd the farm relies on.

He says the sheep will have to be culled. That's what Mrs Heslop is upset about.'

In the privacy of the CID room Maureen rolled her eyes. The woman's daughter hadn't been seen for two days, but she was too stressed about losing a few sheep to come to the phone. 'I see,' she said. 'Please explain to Mrs Heslop that I need to talk to her urgently, here at the police station in Workington. Do you know where that is?'

'Yes,' he said. 'When do want to see her?'

'As soon as possible.'

There was a brief silence. 'I'll bring her down to you. I've nearly finished here. I think it would be good for her to be off the farm for a while, until the sheep have been… you know, disposed of.'

Maureen was curious. 'What are you doing there, Mr Blake, if you work for the auction mart?'

'Well, the auctions are cancelled for the foreseeable future, of course. I'm currently working as a livestock valuer.' He hesitated, then added, 'We have to advise on compensation for the farmers.'

She was still curious: this man didn't sound like a business acquaintance, more like a close friend. 'If you can bring Mrs Heslop down here, Mr Blake, that would be very helpful.'

'Yes, of course,' Barry said. 'We should be there in an hour or so. Will that be all right?'

Maureen put down the phone, then walked through to speak to the desk sergeant.

'I'm expecting a Mr Blake and Mrs Heslop in an hour or so. When they get here, send them both through, will you? Don't let him leave her and go, OK?'

'Is that the kid's mother?' the sergeant asked.

Maureen nodded. 'And Blake's her friend,' she said.

It was just past noon when the desk sergeant rang through to say that Maureen's visitors had arrived. She went out to meet them. Rose had clearly been crying and looked tired and pale. Barry Blake had his arm round her.

'She's pretty cut up,' he said. 'Can I stay with her?'

Maureen went ahead of them and ushered them into the office. Bob Carruthers looked up from his desk, nose to the wind like a bloodhound, and she changed direction, taking them down the corridor to an empty interview room. It was poorly lit and cheerless, devoid of any furniture except for four chairs and a table set against one wall. A large reel-to-reel tape recorder stood ready. Maureen went into the room ahead of them and Rose stopped in the doorway, eyes wide in alarm. She put a hand to her mouth and tried to turn around. Barry urged her forward into the room, and pulled out a chair for her to sit down.

He looked at Maureen accusingly. 'Is this really necessary?'

'Yes, I'm afraid it is. And if you would take a seat too, Mr Blake. Just a few questions, and then I'll need to speak to Mrs Heslop on her own.'

Barry looked anxiously at his watch.

'I won't keep you long. Can I get you both a drink?'

Rose looked up, then across at Barry, who patted her hand. 'Yes,' he said. 'We both need something. White coffee for me, please. Rose? Drink?'

She nodded, taking a handkerchief from her bag to blow her nose. 'Coffee,' she whispered. 'White, please.'

Maureen left them for a moment, coming back with two plastic cups from which steam curled slowly into the fusty air.

'Sorry about this dismal place,' said Maureen. 'And don't worry about the tape recorder, it's off. This is just a chat, nothing official.' She'd already decided that a softer approach would be best. She took a chair to one side of the table with Rose Heslop and

Barry Blake on the other. Their chairs were quite close together and Barry moved his slightly away.

Maureen smiled reassuringly. 'I know you must be very busy, Mr Blake, and thank you for bringing Mrs Heslop here. Before you have to go, could you explain what's going on at the farm, so that I can understand what Mrs Heslop's been dealing with there, on top of the anxiety about her daughter.'

'Well,' he began, 'Mr Heslop called me early this morning.' Rose sat quietly beside him, leaning forward, one elbow resting on the table, her hand over her eyes. 'He said all the sheep would have to be killed, pregnant ewes, all the lambs, and wanted me to do the valuation.'

'They're not sick then?' Maureen was horrified to hear this and regretted her initial reaction to hearing about the sheep.

Barry shook his head. 'No, but it's like a fire break, you know. There has to be a gap between each farm and the next, and the sheep are a risk when they move around.'

'They're my sheep,' said Rose, looking up. She was clearly angry. 'He doesn't care about them. Just the herd.'

'The dairy herd,' explained Barry. 'That's the farm's main income, you see. He... Mr Heslop... wants to protect his herd.'

'I see,' said Maureen. No wonder Rose was looking ten years older than the last time they'd met. 'So the sheep have been culled?'

Rose looked away, blinking back tears, then put her head down, close to the table, hands clasped together in front of her, as if in prayer.

Barry went on, 'Yes, they were starting the job when I brought her away. Best thing for it. She didn't want to stay.'

Tears dripped onto Rose's fingers and the scratched Formica of the table. Maureen's mind was working furiously: Rose was clearly distressed, but was the cause of it anger, grief or fear?

'Thanks for bringing Mrs Heslop in, Mr Blake,' Maureen said. 'Perhaps it's for the best, as you say. You can leave her here with us, and we'll make sure she gets back to the farm.'

Rose looked up and shook her head, holding Barry's arm tightly.

'I'm not going back there,' she said.

He glanced at Maureen, then bent and said in a low voice into Rose's ear, 'But what about Brian?'

She started to cry again. 'I can't go back there, not yet. Aidan will look after him for now.'

Barry looked at Maureen and explained. 'Brian has a pet lamb – he tried to hide it this morning. We found him with it, in a cupboard. He tried to keep it quiet, but we heard it and found them both. Brian was holding the lamb very tightly, but we had to take it.'

Maureen didn't know much about farming, but she knew about children and their pets. 'Not his lamb too?' she asked.

Barry nodded. 'It had to be all of them for the precaution to be worth anything.'

Maureen felt her own eyes pricking. 'Well,' she said after a moment's pause, 'thanks for the explanation, Mr Blake. Mrs Heslop will be fine here for a while. I'm sure you have things to do.'

'Another farm, another flock,' he said. 'Sometimes it feels like it'll never end.'

Maureen couldn't imagine the passage of the gruesome days, one after another. 'Good luck to you,' she said. They shook hands.

Barry leaned down to Rose, one hand resting on her shoulder. 'You know where I am. Call me if you need to, OK?'

She nodded and held his hand tightly for a moment before he pulled away and left the room.

The interview room door was still open and Maureen was shuffling her notes ready to talk to Rose when Anna Penrose appeared in the doorway and gestured for Maureen to come out. She did so, leaving the door ajar behind her, and walked a few paces away, out of Rose's earshot. 'She's not going anywhere,' she said to Anna. 'They're shooting all the sheep at the farm. She couldn't wait to get away.'

'Christ,' said Anna. 'Who was the man I saw leaving? He looked upset too.'

'I've not quite worked that one out,' admitted Maureen. 'He's Barry Blake, local stock valuer apparently, but he used to be Rose's boss at the auction mart before it closed. The two of them are pretty close, by the look of it.'

'Too close?'

'Not sure. Could be. Our Rose is quite a girl, according to Chris Strong. Anyway, what about the pharmacy jobs?'

'Nothing in Silloth,' said Anna, 'but at Wigton the pharmacist confirmed that the stock of inhalers had disappeared – the adult ones – and a lot of painkillers too. So if this is the person who's got Helen, we can assume the girl's still alive and that her asthma is kicking off.'

'Or she could be OK and this is a precaution?'

'Could be,' said Anna. After all she'd said about assumptions she was already jumping to some of her own. 'Tony Wong says he'll let us know more as soon as he can: any prints, possible blood type, tyres. Looks like they used a motorbike, by the way, not a van.'

'If it's the same person,' Maureen insisted. 'We don't know that.'

Anna insisted on the last word. 'Too much of a coincidence. There's a pretty good chance that whoever stole those inhalers is holding Helen.' Anna gestured towards the interview room. 'What's your interview strategy?' she asked.

Maureen looked up at the ceiling of the corridor they were standing in. 'Interview strategy, ma'am? I haven't been on the interviewing course, have I? It must be sergeant level only.'

'I'm giving you an hour, DC Pritchard,' Anna said, lowering her voice. She didn't want anyone to hear this exchange.

'Fine,' said Maureen. 'Thank you, ma'am.'

But she didn't go straight back to the interview room. She went to the toilet, just to calm down. Penrose was a pompous shit. Maybe it was time to ask for a transfer. Back in the interview room, Maureen found Rose in tears. 'Brian's just a bairn,' she murmured, 'he doesn't understand. Even Eric was upset about the lamb, but there was nothing we could do.'

'Have you eaten, do you want something from the canteen?' Maureen asked.

Rose shook her head. 'Couldn't eat anything, thanks.' She looked up. 'Could I have another coffee?'

'Before I get it, Rose, do you understand why we have to talk to you?'

Rose looked up tearfully, and shook her head. 'I've told you everything I know.'

'Clearly you're upset, but I have to ask you again, do you have any idea where Helen might be, or who might have taken her?' Rose felt for her handkerchief and blew her nose. Then she shook her head again. 'I can't think straight. Can I have another coffee?'

Maureen looked at the weeping woman. She wanted to lean hard on her, but if Penrose and Bell wouldn't back her up there wasn't much she could do. They would be on her back all the time, trying to muscle in. She leaned back in the chair.

'Coffee? OK, back in a minute.'

As soon as she left the room Maureen spotted Anna down the corridor but it was too late to turn around. Anna walked quickly towards her. 'Now what? Maureen, we need to get on with this.

Get some information out of Rose. If it moves us forward, great, otherwise, let her go home and we can move on.'

Maureen shook her head. 'She's still crying about the sheep. Says she doesn't know where Helen is, or who with. She's either too drugged up to think straight, or she doing a good job of pretending. It's like talking to a wall. And she says she's not going back to the farm.'

Anna rolled her eyes. 'Look, where Rose goes is none of our business. If you can't get any relevant information out of her, we can't accuse her of anything, not yet. And *we* can't talk here.' She took a few steps towards the CID room, then turned back. 'Is there any evidence at all that Rose knows where her daughter is, or who she's with?'

Maureen had wanted to keep the substance of Chris Strong's information to herself, but Penrose was forcing her arm.

'I think Rose and Alex Wetherall go back a long way,' she said. 'Chris Strong told me that they were friends twenty years ago, in Carlisle. Possibly more than just friends.'

Anna's expression didn't change. 'It's tenuous at best,' she said. 'Old gossip from Chris Strong, who's desperately trying to shift the blame from herself for not looking after Helen properly. Can you imagine what a lawyer would make of it?'

She kept walking and Maureen had no choice but to follow her back to the office. Bob was not around and Anna could speak freely.

'I told DI Bell that Rose agreed to come in, but he thinks it's just an excuse to get away from the farm and is wasting precious time. Sounds like he's right.' She picked up a file from her desk. 'Before we let Rose go, here's what came back from the SOCO about the pharmacy break-ins. No prints worth using, but he's sent the possible blood sample away for DNA analysis. It was a motorbike, no sign of other fresh tyre tracks at either scene, so no link to the blue van.'

Maureen was silent for a moment, still fuming about Rose, but then she said, 'Wait a minute. Whoever's driving the van could have a motorbike stashed in the back. Or he could have stashed a motorbike somewhere else and is using that to throw us off his trail.'

'But that means the van is still unaccounted for. We've got every copper and army bloke looking for it, and found nothing as yet that doesn't check out OK.'

Maureen had another thought. 'What if he's hidden the van in a garage or shed or something, out of sight?'

Anna groaned inwardly. She should have thought of that herself. 'We could be looking for days. And where's Helen all this time?'

'Same place,' said Maureen. 'She could be confined somehow, under cover, with enough food, water, shelter, while he decides what to do.'

'But why does he want her? If it is the man the kids knew from the café, and if that man is Alex Wetherall – lots of "ifs" – then why did he decide to take Helen? If he wanted money, he'd have been in touch by now surely.'

'Hang on,' said Maureen. She went across to her desk and found her notebook, flicking through it for the recent information from Chris Strong. 'Here,' she said. 'Chris told me that Rose was pretty busy partying when Eric was working away on and off, back in the 1980s. She'd leave the bairn with her mum and hit the town. Blokes were round like flies, Chris said.'

'Catty, but so what?'

'I saw some of that with the bloke who brought her in today, Barry Blake. She wasn't flirting exactly, but she sort of leaned in to him, and he responded. I'd have said they could be, you know, close.'

Anna frowned. 'What if they are? What's that got to do with Helen's disappearance?'

Maureen wondered about Anna's private life: she didn't seem alert to sex as a driving force. 'Maybe the real target here is Rose,' she suggested. 'Someone's trying to get at her through the child, to put pressure on her.'

'Pressure for what?'

'To leave Eric? Looks like their marriage is in trouble anyway.'

Anna sat for a few moments staring at the board and the photos, not wanting to admit that Maureen might be right. She was tired of playing second fiddle to this woman. She stood up, pulling her coat off the back of the chair.

'There's a message from the Head of the school, Hellibone. Says he's heard about a pupil who knows something. If it's not enough, I'll have to go up to the school and talk to the kids all together. We need more details about this van, whether or not Wetherall is involved.' Maureen got to her feet too. 'What about Rose?'

Anna knew she had to assert herself. 'We've wasted enough time on her already. If she refuses to go back to the farm, and she's not being up front with us, for whatever reason, there's not much we can do about it right now. Arrest or discharge. If she insists on going to Carlisle, help her get the train or something, or take her yourself. She might say more when her guard is down. We've had her here too long already. It's enough.' Anna picked up her keys and was gone.

Left alone, when her annoyance had worn off a little, Maureen sat at her desk and began to doodle on her telephone message pad. She scribbled down numbers, adding, subtracting. Then she picked up the phone and dialled. 'Is Tony Wong there?' she asked. When he came to the phone, she told him what she wanted.

There was a pause. Then: 'Is this a formal request?' he said.

'Well, no,' she admitted. 'It's just a hunch.'

Another pause. 'Sorry, I'd need the proper paperwork. Who's the officer in charge?'

It wasn't going to work, Maureen knew that. Bell had said many times that he wanted no more of Pritchard's 'hunches', and this one would cost money. 'Are you still there?' Wong asked.

'Yes,' she said, 'I understand. I'll get back to you, thanks.'

She put the phone down. Bloody procedure again. Just for once, why couldn't intuition count for as much as 'facts'?

Chapter 8

Back in the interview room, Rose was slumped uncomfortably in the chair, sipping her coffee. Maureen softened her demeanour. 'I'm sure you understand, Mrs Heslop,' she said. 'We have to think about every eventuality, every possibility, in a case as serious as this.'

Rose sniffed distractedly. 'The doctor gave me something to help me sleep, but it's like a fog over everything.'

'I'm sure,' said Maureen. She hesitated. 'Will they have finished, up at the farm now?'

Rose shook her head. 'There'll be a lot of, you know, clearing up to do.'

'Well, if you'd like to be away overnight, I'm going to Carlisle. I could drop you off at your mother's.'

Rose looked up, her eyes filling with tears. 'I can't be at the farm, not until they've got rid of the sheep properly. But what about Brian?'

Maureen said, 'Come in the office and ring home. See if your husband will let Brian come to you, just for the night, while he's upset. You can both get a good night's sleep, and then you and your mam can decide what's best for Brian. If you're both going back to the farm tomorrow, I can take you.'

'Are you sure?'

Maureen nodded. 'I'll show you where the phone is.'

She sat at her desk in the CID room, her head down, listening to every word. 'Did you speak to your husband?' she asked when Rose put down the receiver.

'No, to Aidan. He says Brian is all right and shouldn't leave the farm. He may be saying that just to cheer me up, of course.'

'Children are amazingly resilient,' said Maureen. 'What have you decided to do?'

'I think Brian will be all right for tonight,' said Rose. 'If the offer to drive me to Carlisle is still on, I'll take it, please. I can't stay away for long. The family need me, and I can't help you find Helen.'

'Fine,' said Maureen. 'We can talk as we drive.'

Rose shrugged. 'I'm very tired,' was all she said.

The school building was deserted, but there was a lone car in the car park when Anna pulled in. She tried the main glass doors at the front of the building but they were locked. Almost immediately Mr Hellibone approached from the other side with a large bunch of keys. He introduced himself.

'Can't be too careful about school security at the weekend,' he said. 'I thought it best for us to meet here rather than persuade the lad to go to the police station. He seemed very reluctant to do that. Didn't want his dad thinking he was in trouble.' He led Anna down a corridor towards his office. Outside, he paused. 'Just so you know, the lad is called Philip Farthing, he's in Year Eleven – same year as David Strong, Helen's cousin. He spoke to one of my teachers in town this morning, who called me and… well, here he is. I thought it best not to wait.'

Hellibone ushered Anna into his office. A tall boy gangled to his feet.

'Philip, this is Detective Sergeant Penrose,' said the Head. 'I'll leave you to it, shall I? OK, Phil?'

The boy nodded. He was almost as tall as Anna herself. Shorn dark hair clung close to his scalp and a sprinkle of acne reddened the exposed forehead.

'Now then, Philip,' said Anna. 'Thanks for coming to see me. I understand you may have some information about Helen Heslop?'

She sat down on one of the easy chairs in the room but the boy remained standing, legs apart, hands at his sides, like a soldier standing easy.

'Yes, miss. I saw a van, miss,' he said. 'Down the road, Friday afternoon. Looked like me uncle's van, but it wasn't.'

'Who's your uncle?'

'Alan Farthing, miss, but it weren't his van. Different number plate. His is BMG 449P. I remember that because it's P for Phil, like me.'

'What kind of van was it, the one you saw on Friday?'

'Dark blue, two doors at the front, big doors at the back, just like me uncle's delivery van.'

Anna was writing notes and didn't look up. 'And where was this, Phil?'

'Down near the corner. Pond Street.'

She looked up. The boy was still standing, quite relaxed. She didn't think he was making this up. Why would he? 'Was there anyone in the van? Could you see?'

'A man got in the driver's seat, and Helen got in the other side.'

Anna felt her heart jump. 'Say that again,' she said.

'Helen Heslop,' he said. 'Dave Strong's cousin, isn't she? She's living with them. He says she's a pain.'

'Are you sure it was her?'

'Oh, yes, miss.'

'And she got into the van?'

'I saw her. I was sitting on the wall, lower down on t'other side, waiting for someone.' He smiled. 'And I was having a fag on the sly, you know. Me uncle would've given me a bollocking if he'd seen me, but it wasn't 'im, was it? Wrong van.'

Anna was thinking quickly. This was all coming out too easily. She asked, 'Was there anyone else around?'

'Not that I saw. Most of the kids had gone. Friday afternoon, you know.'

'And you say the number plate was different?'

'Aye, wasn't a P at the end. It was GHH 86T.'

Anna stared. 'Are you sure about that?'

'Yes, miss. Good at numbers, me. '86 was the year I was born. Don't know why the letters stuck in me head, but they did. I was sitting there a few minutes, having a smoke, like, then Helen came down the street, and she just walked across and spoke to the bloke. Then she got into the van.'

'Could you hear what they said to each other?'

He shook his head. 'But I thought it was funny when she clapped her hands.'

'What, as if she was applauding something?'

'No, like she was happy… like a baby does.'

Anna closed her eyes for a moment, imagining. 'And then they drove off?'

'Aye, he went down the hill, towards town.'

'Could you see her expression as they passed you, what she was doing?'

'She was smiling,' said Philip. 'They both were.'

As they set off towards Carlisle, Maureen was so preoccupied with nursing her own anger that she didn't talk for a while, concentrating on the traffic. It was only when she noticed the silence that she realised that Rose was sitting with her eyes closed. Was she asleep? Maureen reached across to touch her shoulder. No response. Shit! So much for the second cup of coffee and the offer of a lift to Carlisle. All she'd ended up with was an unresponsive witness and a telling-off from Penrose. What a waste of energy.

The nauseating smell of burning animals that enveloped the car as they approached the city hadn't been enough to wake Rose, but when Maureen pulled up outside Jo Haile's guesthouse Rose suddenly opened her eyes, looked vacantly around, mumbled thanks and got out without another word. Maureen cursed. Another chance missed, and Penrose would sneer even more.

Just as she was about to pull away, Maureen's mobile phone buzzed. What she heard made Maureen want to go straight into the guesthouse, confront Rose, give her a hard slap and shout into her startled face that Helen had been abducted by a man she knew, not a random stranger.

'So the lad is sure it was Helen?' Maureen asked Anna on the phone.

'Certain. He knows David Strong and that Helen is his cousin. And we're pretty certain that the man in the van is Alex Wetherall. Dinger's organising a full-on search for Wetherall, now that we're sure he took Helen.'

Maureen knew what Anna was going to tell her to do, but she held back, waiting for a direct instruction. 'OK, ma'am,' she said, when it came. 'I'll go straight back to Alex's mam's place. I know enough about him to work on her.' She could feel her adrenaline level rising after the disappointments of the morning and set off through the traffic that hissed along wet streets.

The curtains of the terraced house were drawn but Maureen could see light behind them, and as she stood on the doorstep the sound of the TV was audible. She rang the bell, and leaned over to tap on the front window. Judging by the volume of the TV Mrs Wetherall might be hard of hearing. How old would she be, Maureen wondered. Definitely in her sixties, at least.

The front door opened a crack. 'Margaret?' said Maureen. 'It's Maureen Pritchard, Cyril Cornthwaite's lass... you know, from the salon.' She had her police ID in her hand, but the Cornthwaite connection would be more likely to get the door opened. And it did.

'Come in, Maureen,' said Margaret Wetherall. 'Rotten night, isn't it? Go through, it's warmer in there.'

Indeed it was warmer. A wall of heat and sound hit Maureen as she stepped into the small room. Margaret followed her in and mercifully muted the TV so that they could hear each other.

'What brings you here?' she asked.

Maureen held up the necessary ID card. 'I came yesterday, but you were out. Business, Margaret, I'm afraid. It's about your Alex.'

Margaret put a hand to her mouth, her eyes wide. 'He's not...? Is he OK? What's happened?'

Maureen helped the woman into a chair. 'He's fine, as far as we know. But we need to find out where he is.'

'What's he done now?' said Margaret, looking suddenly older. 'He promised me, when he came out this time, no more trouble.'

Maureen needed to slow things down, change gear, relax the woman and then winkle out the information she wanted, piece by piece. 'How about a cuppa, would you mind?' she said, taking off her coat. 'I've not had chance to see Dad yet, and I'm gagging for some tea.'

Tea. The magic word. Margaret got up, glad to have something to do. Maureen followed her through into the small kitchen at the back of the house. 'Could I use the loo while you do that, pet?' she asked.

'Top of the stairs,' said Margaret. 'Help yourself.'

Maureen trod carefully up the steep stairs. There was no sign of anyone else in the house, but she wanted a quick check. Only one toothbrush in the bathroom. She flushed the toilet to cover any noise, and pushed open the door to the left. Margaret's room, by the look of it. Tidy. Cold. The top step creaked and she stepped over it, pushing open the other bedroom door as she did so. This room felt even colder. In the dim light from the hall she could see a narrow bed on the other side of the room, with no sign of recent use. There were various cardboard boxes, an exercise bike, a few clothes hanging up on a rail across one corner.

'In here,' Margaret called as Maureen went back down the stairs. In the front room she had pulled out a small table and a tray of tea things sat on it, a coil of steam rising from the teapot spout. 'Never bother with the pot when I'm on my own, but it's worth it with company,' Margaret said. Maureen realised that the woman was genuinely pleased to see her. She was lonely.

Maureen scoured her memory for details of the family. It was so long ago. 'Alex is your only one, isn't he, Margaret?'

She put down the teapot. 'He is now,' she said. 'Our Sheila, she died, you know. Leukaemia.' She sat down, reaching for the handkerchief in her sleeve. 'It's not right to bury your own child, not right. Our Alex took it very hard. He was away when it happened. He always says he should have been here, but he was a soldier. Army might have let him go for the funeral, but he was too far away.' She looked up. 'Falklands. By the time he got back here, it was all over. And…' She hesitated. 'Well, he were never the same, you know, after the Falklands.'

Maureen sat very still. Images on the muted TV in the corner of the room flashed and jiggled but she didn't want to break the spell, stop the flow of words from a lonely woman to her unexpected guest. 'How old was Sheila?' she asked.

'Nineteen,' said Margaret. She wiped her eyes. 'Just engaged to a lovely lad. They wanted a big family.' She sniffed. 'I've always wanted grandchildren. Ever since Eddie died, that's what I wanted. Otherwise, what's the point? We die, our children die, and that's it. Everything stops.'

'What about Alex? Does he have anyone, a girlfriend?'

Margaret shook her head. 'There was someone, years ago. He told me he was sure about her, but then I think she went off with someone else. He gets these funny ideas sometimes. Bit of a dreamer.'

'Do you remember what this woman was called?'

Margaret shook her head.

Maureen pressed on. 'And then he went in the army?'

'Aye, maybe to get away. But it was too much for him. Don't know what he did out there, but he wouldn't talk about it when he got back. And then he started going out a lot, drinking.'

'When was that?' Maureen was piecing the story together as it spilled out of Margaret's memory.

'He left the army in 1985. They kicked him out. They knew he wasn't right, but they did nowt to help. He turned up here in a right state. Angry. He wasn't like that before. Couldn't get a job.' She hesitated. 'I couldn't have him here.' She looked across at Maureen. 'I didn't feel safe. With my own son.'

The gas fire fizzed. Maureen was desperate to turn it down. She could feel the heat searing her legs but didn't want to do anything to interrupt. Margaret had more to tell her, she was sure of it.

'Did he ever hurt you, Margaret?' she asked. 'You could always come to me or my dad, you know. Nothing official. We could help you.'

Margaret shook her head. 'Not my own son,' she said. 'He's not a bad man.'

'Do you think he might hurt other people?' Maureen asked.

Margaret looked down at her hands. 'He might. Sometimes he just flips. One minute he's nice as pie, then something sets him off. That's what scares me.' She looked at Maureen again. 'Why are you here?' she asked, as if suddenly aware of the line of questioning. 'What do you want?'

Maureen decided to be straight. 'We're looking for Alex,' she said. 'We think he might have taken a child.'

Margaret stood up suddenly, knocking the table as she did so. The teapot wobbled precariously.

'A child? He would never do that. He loves children… always wanted some himself, he said. Who told you that?'

'Someone saw him,' said Maureen. 'Last Friday afternoon, driving away with a child. No trace of him or the child since then. It's Sunday now. We have to find them.'

The woman was standing, looking down at her. 'That's rubbish… bloody rubbish. Your lot, they've got it in for 'im, ever since the drugs thing. But he served 'is time. He's straight now. He told me. Just wants to settle down. He would never hurt a child.'

Maureen didn't react, keeping the same even tone as she replied. 'Do you have any idea where he might have gone, Margaret? We think he has a van, a blue van.'

'He hasn't got the money for a van,' said his mother, as if that settled the matter. 'I told you, it's all rubbish. He's got a place in Cockermouth, he told me that. Looking for a job down there. Just for a change, he said.'

'You've not seen him?'

'Not for weeks. When he came out of the nick he stayed over there for a while, Newcastle way, then he turned up here one day.

Just moved back in, never asked me. Said he was looking for an old mate. I didn't really take much notice.' She hesitated. 'I hoped he would go away again. Anywhere. I didn't really want him here, what with his moods.'

She sat down again. Maureen could see her wondering about her son, about what he might have done.

'Margaret,' she said, leaning forward and taking the woman's hand. 'I want you to promise me something. If Alex gets in touch, or if you can think where he might be, I want you to ring me. The number's on this card. Any time, day or night. OK?'

Margaret nodded.

'It's really important we find him, before he gets into more trouble.'

Too late for that, thought Maureen, but she had to give his mother some hope. 'I'm staying at my dad's tonight. Do you want me to call in again tomorrow, before I go back to Workington?'

Margaret shook her head. 'I know where you are,' she whispered.

Outside in the street it was raining hard and Maureen sheltered in the car to make her phone calls. How did they manage before these new phones came in? She couldn't imagine looking for a call box in this rain, or going down to the police station just to use the phone.

'Bob?' she said when the first call was picked up. 'Is Anna there?'

'She's in with Dinger. Sounds like he's not happy.'

'Can you get her to come and talk to me? Tell her it's important.'

'Is it really important?'

'Just do it, Bob.'

'Maureen?' Anna's voice sounded tired. 'Did you get anything out of Rose?'

'Nothing. She fell asleep in the car.'

'Waste of time, I knew it,' said Anna. 'What about Wetherall's mum?'

'Hasn't seen him, she says, doesn't know where he is. No sign that he's been in the house, but she could be lying. She did say he's not been right since his army days, and that was nearly twenty years ago. And now he has mood swings: nice one minute, violent the next.

I told her we thought Alex had taken a child. She was horrified, said it was impossible, how he loves kids, blah, blah. But it scared her. I think she'll tell me if he turns up.'

'What's the chance of that though?'

'He'd have to be desperate,' Maureen admitted, 'but that might happen.'

'Are you coming back now?'

'No, staying over. I'll be in at eight tomorrow.'

No more was said. Things were still pretty icy. For the first time in years Maureen realised she wasn't looking forward to work the next day. And then her phone rang again. It was Margaret Wetherall.

'There's something else,' she said.

'I'm still right outside,' said Maureen. 'Open the front door so I don't have to stand on the step. It's wet out here!'

In the dark hallway, Margaret said, 'I have seen Alex. It was last week.'

Maureen didn't chide her about lying earlier. There was no point. Instead she asked, 'And how was he then?'

'He seemed, you know, strange. Excited. And there was another thing.'

'Yes?' said Maureen.

'He went in the kitchen and did some baking. He's never done that before. I wanted to help but he wouldn't let me. And…' She hesitated. 'When I went back in the kitchen, afterwards, there was a funny smell.'

'Baking often smells, doesn't it?' Maureen hadn't done any for years, not since the kids left, but she remembered.

'Aye,' said Margaret, 'but this was different – sweet, sickly. I had to open all the windows.'

Maureen didn't respond to the information, but her mind was working busily. 'Is that all you wanted to tell me?' she said mildly.

Margaret nodded.

'Well, thanks, and if you think of anything else, just call me, right? I'd better go. Look after yourself, Margaret.'

Out in the street again, Maureen was sure she understood how Alex had kept Helen quiet.

Chapter 9

Helen stirred. She turned and raised her head, but couldn't move her right arm. The wrist was tied to the side of the van and the thin cord chafed her when it was pulled taut. Now the skin there was bleeding and she moved her body to relieve the pressure on it, pulling the blanket up towards her shoulders with the other hand. Alex wasn't there. Maybe he'd gone outside, before it got light. There was a chemical toilet at the far end of the barn, but he always went outside. He took her to the toilet whenever she needed it, but she hated using it, knowing that he was standing just outside the door.

She tried to work out how long she'd been there. It was Friday afternoon when she'd climbed into the van thinking that he would take her back to the farm. Then she'd eaten some cake, and had some sweet coffee that he'd offered her, and after that there was nothing. When she'd woken she was in the back of the van, and there was an oblong of grey light towards the front, latticed by a grille that stood between her and the seats at the front. She'd pulled at it with her free hand but it held firm. When she tried to raise her head it was heavy and she felt sick. How long ago was that? She screwed up her eyes, trying to remember.

Scraps of memory floated around. She'd drifted in and out of sleep. He'd pulled her out of the van and into the toilet, and he'd heated food on a little stove in the corner of the barn. She remembered the smell of paraffin and the hissing of the blue flame. Oxtail soup. And tinned peaches. Then he'd made her drink something that tasted bitter, and after that her head swam and it went black, until the next waking. She'd lost track of time. Had he spoken to her? She'd tried to talk to him, called him by his name, but he'd laughed at her and slammed the big doors, shutting her in darkness. Why? What had she done? Why was this happening?

Once she'd woken when the sound of an engine was very close by, and the light in the barn suddenly brightened. Then the noise died away. She had shouted out, called his name, but there was no sound in reply. Nothing except the noise of rain on the roof of the barn, and the wind finding cracks in the old walls.

She couldn't work out why she was there. Maybe David and Ryan had told Alex to take her away so that they could have their rooms back. Or Dad had told Alex to keep her away from the farm. Or Aidan and his mates were playing a trick on her, like the ones they played on each other. And now something had gone wrong. She wanted to ask Alex what he was doing, how long they would be here, but the words stuck together and she couldn't break them apart. Only his name escaped her mouth. 'Alex.'

It had been dark when the wheezing started. Helen felt the familiar tightness in her chest and breathed in deeply, fearing the noise that it might make. And it was there, a slight rattle to begin with, but then louder, and soon she was pulling for breath. 'Need a puffer,' she'd said, and Alex looked in her bag but Helen knew it wasn't there. She never took it to school since she'd left the farm. No one would check like Mum did, and she knew that other kids at school would tease her if she used it, or if it was discovered in her bag. 'I need a puffer,' she'd said again.

That was before he'd left. When he'd come back he had a boxful of puffers. They looked different from hers but she didn't care, tearing off the plastic cover and making one work, pulling the stuff into her lungs, waiting until the tightness began to ease. Then she'd felt dizzy and had lain down again while he watched her.

'Alex,' she called now. But she could sense he wasn't there. She pulled her knees underneath her and kneeled by the grille, holding on to it with her free hand. There was a bag on the passenger seat: not her bag, a different one, dark in colour, with big handles that splayed wide. Helen peered through the grille, trying to see what lay inside the bag. There was something dark and shiny, metal. Light filtered though a crack in the wall and shone into the cab, onto the open bag. Helen stared. A gun. There was a gun in the bag, right in front of her. Maybe he meant her to see it. Her stomach turned.

The barn door opened and shut quickly. She slid back, away from the grille, and lay down, her heart thumping, her chest tightening with fear. He opened the big doors and stood looking at her. 'Is it working,' he said, 'the puffer?'

She nodded. She wanted to speak, and 'Thank you' came out. He smiled. More words came to her. 'Why?' Helen asked. 'Why am I here?' She wanted to ask about the gun too, but couldn't.

Alex climbed into the van and sat with his legs out in front of him. He closed the big doors. She was suddenly afraid and shuffled back away from him, as far as she could. The cord on her wrist tightened and she cried out.

'Do you want me to take that off?' he asked.

'Yes, yes,' she said. 'It hurts.'

He didn't move.

'I won't run away,' she said. 'I promise.'

He got to his knees and moved awkwardly towards her. A small torch from his pocket lit up the place where the cord was tied to a handle on the wall of the van. It took both his hands to undo the knot and he held the torch in his teeth so he could see what he was doing. Helen looked at the side of his head as he worked, and smelled him: sweat, and diesel. She held her breath. In a few moments the pressure on her wrist reduced. She held it out to him.

'Please,' she said, 'take it off here too. It's very sore.'

He hesitated, then worked on that knot until the cord fell away. Helen sobbed with relief and held the swollen bloody wrist tight with her other hand.

Alex sat back, as before, looking at her from the other side of the van. The dim light from the front windows caught the side of his face.

'There's no need to be afraid of me,' he said. 'I won't hurt you. I just had to make sure that you stayed here for a while, until… until you got to know me better.'

Helen had no idea what he meant. She knew him already, from the café. She'd liked him, thought he was friendly and treated her like a proper grown-up. But now he was treating her like a dog.

'But why?' she asked. 'I don't understand.'

'Maybe it's time for a talk,' he said. 'Are you feeling better now?'

'Yes, the puffer works. Where did you get it?'

'Doesn't matter,' he said. 'I got it, and there's more. Your mum told me you had asthma, but I didn't know…'

'My mum? When did she tell you that?'

Alex looked at her for a moment, then turned towards the big doors and pushed them open. 'We need to talk,' he said. 'But let's have something to eat first. I'm hungry, are you?'

Helen sat with her back to the grille, nursing her wrist, still wondering about what he'd said. Maybe he knew Mum from the auction, like many other people did. She was hungry, she realised. 'Not that cake,' she said. 'There's something wrong with it. Makes me feel sick.'

'No more cake. I bought some sausage rolls this morning. Would you like one? And some coffee?'

She shook her head. 'No coffee.'

He smiled again. 'This coffee's OK,' he said. 'Really.'

Nothing more was said and Alex disappeared from sight while Helen listened to the hiss of the Primus stove. The coffee was hot and sweet, without milk, just how she liked it. Maybe her mum had told him that too. And the sausage roll was delicious. Crumbs of pastry escaped her mouth and she brushed them off her jumper. Her wrist was feeling better. He's going to take me home now, she thought.

'I can't let you go yet, Helen,' he said, looking at her over the rim of the tin mug in his hand. 'We have to wait a bit longer.'

'What for?'

'She must have had some trouble, or else her phone's not working.'

'Who? What phone?'

'She hasn't said anything to you?'

Helen didn't know what he meant. Nothing was making sense. Alex put down his mug and wiped his mouth with the back of his hand. 'She always was secretive like that,' he said. 'Years ago, when we first got together, I never really knew what she was thinking. But I do now. It's different now.'

'My mum?' guessed Helen.

'Yes, your mum,' he replied. 'Rose. My Rose.'

Helen bristled at this. 'She's not your Rose.'

'Oh, but she is,' he said quietly. 'She always has been. And now I have you.' He took another sip of coffee, not taking his eyes off her. 'Who decided to call you Helen?'

She shrugged. 'I don't know. My dad's mum was called Helen. Maybe that's why.' He didn't respond. Helen continued, 'Why am I here?'

He put down the mug. 'Are you warm enough? It's freezing out tonight. Do you want another blanket?'

'I'm OK. Why am I here? When can I go home?'

He sighed. 'OK. Too many questions.' He pulled a blanket towards him and put it round his shoulders. His hair looked shorter than before, and he'd stopped wearing the glasses that he usually wore when he was driving. It made him look quite different. He hadn't shaved, and a dark shadow changed the shape of his face.

'What's your other name?' she asked, but he ignored the question. He was speaking slowly, and looking away, as if she wasn't there. She kept quiet, hoping he would talk some more.

'It was years ago, when your mum and I met. She wasn't much older than you, but younger than me. I always liked her, but I didn't ask her out until later, just before she left school.'

Helen listened. She couldn't imagine her mother being with this man. It must be a mistake.

'I thought we were OK,' he said, 'but she wanted more. You know, more money. Bit of a snob, your mum, isn't she?' Helen didn't react. He went on, still not looking at her. 'She said she didn't want to see me, and then this other bloke was all over her. Worked at Sellafield, good prospects, all that stuff. Bastard! I knew she'd made a mistake. I told her that but she wouldn't have it. That's when I went thieving, after the army, to get the money to win her back. And then I met her again.'

Helen interrupted, 'What did you take?' She was still trying to imagine her mother having boyfriends. It didn't seem right.

'Cars mainly, bikes sometimes. Then I got into tellies, videos, anything you could carry away.' He laughed. 'Never got caught, too clever.'

That makes sense, Helen thought. When he'd talked to her and the boys in the café, she'd thought he was clever. Different.

'What happened next?' she asked.

He shrugged. 'Want something else to eat? Biscuits?'

'No. I want to know what happened next.'

'Got in with the wrong people, didn't I? They said I could make bigger money. And I did. Really big money. It was OK. Told me mam I was on the rigs. She liked the money, didn't ask questions.'

'Did you get caught?' Helen pictured him with his hands up, surrendering to a crowd of policemen, like in the films.

He nodded. 'They sold me out. Police picked me up with some of the stuff.'

'What stuff?'

'Heroin. More money than weed. More jail time too.'

'You went to jail?' Helen was astounded. She'd never met anyone who'd been in jail. 'What was it like?'

'Easy, most of the time. Bit like the army. Four years, but I only did three.'

'When did you get out?'

'About six months ago. Went back to Carlisle after a bit, then came down to Cockermouth.'

'What about your job?'

He snorted. 'Job? Who needs a job? That's for mugs.'

'But what do you live on?'

Alex Wetherall tapped the side of his nose. 'That'd be telling, wouldn't it? You'll see, soon enough.'

'See what?'

'Questions, questions,' he said. 'No more, right? Not yet. Got to keep some secrets, haven't I?'

He picked up her coffee mug and his own and pushed his way out of the back of the van, closing it firmly behind him. Helen knew it was locked, and there was no handle on the inside. Then he opened it again, and looked in at her. 'Nearly forgot to put that cord back. Can't have you running away.'

'I won't,' she said. 'Anyway, where would I go? I don't know where we are, do I? It's cold, and you've got the food.'

He laughed. 'Very practical,' he said, 'just like your mam.'

He's making it all up, Helen said to herself. I'll get him to drop me off somewhere so I can go home. But then she remembered the gun, and suddenly felt sick. She called out, 'Alex?'

He looked in at one of the front windows of the van. 'Keep your voice down,' he said. 'What now?'

'Why have you got a gun?' she asked. 'I saw it in your bag.'

He smiled. 'I have to protect us,' he said. 'People might not understand. I have to keep you safe, don't I? There are soldiers out there, I saw them. They're rounding up people who are out in the open, taking them to camps, locking them up.'

'Why?' said Helen. More things she didn't understand.

He looked hard at her. 'They think people are spreading the disease, so they have to be locked up. That's what would happen if they caught us, or if you tried to run away from me. You'd be locked away from everyone, like a leper. That's not what you want, is it?'

Helen shook her head, imagining the disease eating away her lips.

'That's why I have this gun,' he said. 'To stop us from being captured by the soldiers or the police.'

'Really? Is this true?'

'True,' he said. 'Now go to sleep.'

Helen lay back, wondering about it all. She remembered what her dad had said about how the disease spread and must be stopped. Mum had said they needed the army to sort it out. That's why Alex and she had to stay hidden and be so careful. Tomorrow she would have another sausage roll and persuade him to take her home, back to the farm. If he knew her mum, he'd do that. Mum must be worrying a lot by now. Helen was thinking about Brian as she drifted off to sleep.

When the big doors of the van opened suddenly, Helen woke with a start. It was still dark. Alex was lifting up one end of a big board, which formed a ramp running to the floor of the barn. 'Move over to one side,' he said. 'Shift all that stuff too. The bike needs plenty of room.'

She did as she was told, and watched as he wheeled a motorbike to the base of the ramp and then pushed it up, into the back of the van. Helen had to hold the heavy machine upright while he climbed in and secured it with a chain looped through the wheels and round the handles that he'd tied her to. The bike was big and she worried that it might squash her if it fell.

'What's happening?' she asked. He didn't answer, moving around the barn picking up various things and putting them either in the back of the van or in the well of the passenger seat. Then he hung a brown curtain over the grille, fixing it quickly with plastic ties.

'Are you taking me home now? What about the soldiers?'

He stood with both hands on the open doors, looking in at her.

'We're not going straight home, not yet. Something I have to do first. Something I need.'

'Money?' she guessed.

'Bright little bugger, aren't you?' he said. 'Yes, money. Always useful, and I know where we can find some. We'll be on the road for a while. Stay back here, don't mess with this curtain. I've got a few things to do and then we're off.'

A few minutes later she heard him banging something, first at the front of the van, then at the back, and then he got into the driver's seat and the engine stuttered and roared into life. They moved slowly backwards, then he got out, and she heard the barn doors creak as he closed them. Then they bounced over the rough ground for a few minutes before the smoother surface of a road, or at least a track. The van stopped again for a few minutes and then started off.

Helen was confused. She didn't know why all this was happening but she'd had enough now. The van gathered speed, then slowed as it turned, but the rear slid to one side and the motorbike wobbled, the chain clanking as it slackened and tightened again. Alex swore. Helen hung onto the grille, but he shouted at her to leave it alone, and she locked her fingers into one of the handles at shoulder-height and braced her feet to keep herself steady. Then they were going down a hill, and again the back of the van swung to one side, but this time it didn't stop, and Helen felt it sliding sideways. They didn't slow down. She hung on, watching the heavy bike strain against the chains.

Suddenly the van lurched the other way and began to tip. Helen slid towards the bike, her knee scraping painfully against the footrest. She couldn't hold on. Her fingers slipped away from the handle and she fell heavily on top of the bike as the van shook. There was a sound of splintering wood and another lurch before they stopped dead.

For a few minutes Helen couldn't move, her left foot twisted under her and sharp pain in her knee and shoulder. She breathed in slowly to steady herself and heard the wheeze in her chest. Her bag had dropped onto the wall holding the bike, which was now the floor of the van as it lay on its side. The engine noise had stopped and there was no sound except for the rattle of her breathing. Slowly, she pulled away from where she had fallen and tried to stretch out. The brown curtain hung to one side and she pushed it away to look through the grille. Alex was lying quite still, his head against the door, the upper part of his body wrapped over the steering wheel.

Helen found her voice. 'Alex,' she said. There was no response. The van tipped again, and Alex fell further towards the door, his head now down on his chest, but he made no sound. Is he dead? Helen wondered. Will I be able to get away? The wheezing was coming again, and she looked around for the puffer that she'd been using. There it was, in her bag, just within reach. She groped for it and took a deep pull, then another until her head swam.

She raised her head and sniffed. A needle of sharp air, smelling of earth and cold, pierced her senses. Looking to her left, she could see a sliver of light across the back of the van. The doors had sprung open with the impact. Slowly, painfully, she pulled herself across towards the light. Her feet reached it first and she pushed with them. One of the doors creaked and swung open a few inches before it stopped. Twigs and earth were visible where it was stuck fast in a bank.

The other door gave way as she kicked on it, and the gap between them was just wide enough. She could crawl out, if she could just get her body to do what she wanted. For a few minutes she lay still, gripping the puffer tightly in her right hand. Both legs worked, but her left shoulder throbbed. She wiggled her fingers, but that hurt and she stopped. The cold flooded in through the open doors and wrapped itself around her. She turned her head and pulled a blanket towards her, but the shivering didn't stop. There was no sound except for the chattering of sparrows in the hedge outside.

Chapter 10

The blue van lay on its side at the bottom of a bank. The lane at the top was icy, not yet thawed by the morning air, and the van had smashed through a gate onto a farm road and then down again into a field. Helen crawled through the narrow space that had opened up between the back doors, breathing in the cold air to clear her head. Her left knee was bruised and scraped from the fall against the motorbike. She pushed the precious inhaler deep into her school bag and pulled the strap up over her shoulder. The corner of the grey blanket was dangling from the back of the van and she pulled that out too, using a corner to dab her knee and then wrapping it round herself and over her head like a shawl. Then she sat down heavily on the hard earth, crying with shock and pain. Her mind was focussed only on survival. She knew that Alex had a phone, but he also had a gun, and she didn't want to risk going through his things.

There was no movement in the cab. Peeping round the side of the van, she could see Alex's head reflected in the side mirror but he was motionless. The sky was getting lighter by the minute. She had to get away, now, before he realised she had gone. No time to go back to get some water, although her mouth was dry. She pulled the blanket tight and tucked the ends into the waistband of her trousers so that she could move her arms freely, then pulled herself upright on her good leg. The left leg was stiff and sore: she flexed it carefully, pushing through the pain to see that it would take her weight. Using her arms and her right leg she hauled herself up the bank on the far side of the van, out of his sight if he opened his eyes. A few steps along the track to the shattered gate and then out onto the road.

She listened for the sound of traffic, but there was nothing. The road might have been closed, as many were because of the Foot and Mouth. Alex wouldn't have cared about that. He had been intent on going somewhere, but she didn't know where that might be, or even where she was now. Pale pink streaks in the dawn sky told her which way was east. The road she was standing on ran roughly north to south. On either side were empty fields, no animals anywhere. To the north Helen could see a plume of smoke. One of the pyres for burning animal carcasses, like she'd seen from the train to Carlisle when she'd visited Granny Jo last week, but there were many such pyres scattered across the ravaged land.

She had to move. There was no sign of habitation in either direction, and she made an arbitrary decision to head south, to her left. Something told her that home lay to the south, and that was all she wanted, to be home, in the dark farmhouse kitchen by the red Aga, playing with Brian and his toy farm.

As she turned, the sound of creaking metal reached her. It could be the van, tipping into a more stable position, or maybe it was Alex, moving, clawing his way out, reaching for the gun. Helen began to run, whimpering with pain, gasping for air against the tightness in her chest. Again the sound: she looked back but there was nothing to see except the high hedges on either side of the narrow road.

She struggled on. Her knee ached to start with but gradually the pain eased and she could walk more quickly. The sharp eastern pink had spread and faded as if someone had added water and smeared it across the sky. To her left, a long way off, a line of orange light burnished a distant fell top. The puddles under her feet were hard with ice. She wondered how far she'd come, and she wondered whether Alex would come after her if he was still alive. She'd never seen anyone dead, and wasn't sure how she would know if they were.

A faint buzz grew louder. Was it behind her or ahead? She stopped, her head raised, listening. It was louder now, but still the sound swirled and she couldn't place its origin. An engine, it was an engine. He was alive, and coming after her!

She looked around, desperate to find a place to hide. The grey blanket would be a camouflage: she could pull it over herself and disappear, but where to go? The hedge on the right was thicker, with a line of trees behind it. She hobbled across, pulled the blanket round her face for protection and pushed through the hedge, then stumbled headlong into a ditch. It was damp and muddy at the bottom, but deep enough to crouch down. On the other side, beyond the trees, stretched a large field with the outline of a farm at the far end. She pushed back the blanket and listened. The engine sound had stopped. Was it him, on the motorbike that he'd pulled from the back of the van? Was he looking for her?

As she watched, hardly daring to breathe, she noticed the cows. Black and white cows in the field, grazing, just like the cows at home, but why weren't they hidden away in a barn, fretted over by an anxious farmer looking for the drooling mouth or lame foot? Three cows were within a few feet of where she crouched in the ditch, but they took no notice of her or anything else. She could hear them chewing, smell the fresh dung that steamed in the cold air.

The noise began again. This time she could see where it was coming from as a Land Rover nosed through a gate on the far side of the field, near the farm buildings. It stopped and waited while a man fastened the gate and then climbed into the back seat. He was carrying something long, hooked over his arm. It looked like a shotgun. Helen's chest heaved and she reached for the puffer, taking a long pull, then another. She wanted to crawl away, back through the hedge to the road, but dared not move.

The Land Rover began to move very slowly along the far side of the field. Just ahead of it a cow dropped to the ground, not gradually as an animal settles itself, but suddenly. All four legs gave way at once and it dropped. The other cows continued to graze. The Land Rover stood motionless. Another cow, a few yards from the first, dropped silently to the ground in the same way, and a slight movement of the air brought with it a faint sound, like the popping of a distant cork. Helen wanted to look away, to move back and further down the road, far from the wrecked van and the man who knew her mother, but she was rooted, staring at what was happening as the Land Rover moved remorselessly across the field, closer and closer, and the cows dropped one by one. The animals lay where they fell, and still the beasts that remained standing did not look up or move away.

The Land Rover was heading towards her. She could see the barrel of the gun protruding from the back window, and the driver's face with a flat cap pulled down against the cold. She heard the pop at the same time as the legs of the cow nearest to her buckled and it fell heavily to the earth. Then one of its legs began to move. There was another pop and the movement stopped. They were very close now. Another cow dropped and still the remaining one took no notice, its head still down, chewing its last mouthful before it too was killed with a single muffled shot. The driver stared straight ahead. He's seen me, she thought for a terrified moment. He's going to turn and they'll shoot me because I've seen what they're doing. But then the vehicle turned away and continued its murderous progress round the field while the bodies of dead cattle littered the ground like small boats on the ocean.

Tears ran down Helen's face, tears of terror and fear and sadness for the cows slaughtered as they stood harmlessly in their familiar field. Suddenly the tightness in her chest turned to steel and she couldn't breathe. Panic-stricken, she sucked at the puffer until her head swam, the light faded, and she collapsed, head down, in the ditch just as the heavy rain began, big drops pattering through the branches of the trees overhead and onto the blanket that shrouded her body. The Land Rover finished its deadly round and disappeared again through the far gate. Helen lay motionless, her lungs overwhelmed by too much medication. Slowly, the ditch began to fill with water.

Back down the road that Helen had stumbled along, a motorbike emerged through the shattered remnants of a farm gate and onto the road. Alex leaned on it for a moment. He drew a bloody hand across his face and blinked into the early light. The engine of the bike roared but Helen didn't hear it.

When she came round she knew that she had to get away from Alex and the van and the men with guns and the dead cows, to the only safe place she could be sure of. She lay for a while, breathing in slowly, pulling air into her tight lungs. She felt sick but the dizziness had passed and she sat up. The sun was higher in the sky and she worked out which way was south by looking at the shadows. She'd picked up a chocolate bar from the van before she left and now tore into it, tasting the sweetness in her dry mouth. She wanted water too. Somewhere there would be a stream she could drink out of, if she was careful. Apart from the dead cows, there were no animals around in any of the fields that stretched away to either side of the lane, so the streams should be clean. The chocolate wrapper was stuffed back into the school bag she was carrying over her shoulder. She had to make sure that no one could follow her trail. If the soldiers found her, they would lock her away.

The food made her feel better and she stood up. Walking on the lane was easy. Soon she reached a junction where another lane led off to the left. Just like their lane at Brinfell, there was a gate in front of this, with a mail box on a post next to it. A wide pad loaded with disinfectant stretched right across the road in front of the gate. To one side was an old sink with more disinfectant in it and a brush. The gate was locked but she climbed over it, padded to and fro across the soggy mat a few times to clean the soles of her shoes and then scrubbed at them with the brush. Now if the soldiers picked her up she could show them that she was clean, and she wouldn't be spreading the disease. Maybe they'd believe her, but Alex had said they would lock people up just to be sure.

The lane wound away down a slope and then round a corner. There was no farm or house in sight, but the line of bushes at the bottom of the slope told her there might be a stream in the dip and she walked towards it, stopping every few paces to look around and listen. She was exposed out here. Someone might see her. The bag pulled on her shoulders and she hitched it up.

A small concrete bridge carried the lane over the stream. She stepped carefully down the bank and bent to scoop water into her hand and to her mouth. It was cold and fresh. She stood on the pebbles by the bubbling water and thought again about what to do. Above the noise of the stream a sound came to her. An engine. She ran along the bank for a few paces to the shelter of some gorse bushes and hid behind them. Keeping her head down, she heard the vehicle go over the bridge. Stay hidden, she said to herself. Whoever it is will be going to the gate and back to check the box where anything for the farm would be left. Sure enough, within a few minutes the engine noise was back. It was a quad bike, she recognised the sound now, and waited until it faded to nothing.

Behind the gorse bushes the faint marks of a sheep trod continued to a point where the beasts obviously crossed to the other side of the stream. Helen did the same. The chocolate and water had made her feel less dizzy, and the sun was bright through the bare trees that lined the banks, although there was not much warmth in it. The trees thinned and a dry-stone wall barred her way after a little while, the stream running under it. The gap for the stream was too small for her to squeeze through without getting very wet, but she found enough protruding stones in the wall to help her climb over.

Standing on top, she looked around. Sunlight was gleaming on the high fells to the east and south, but there were rain clouds coming too. Something about the landscape looked familiar. The gurgling of the stream as it found its way under the wall was the first sound that struck her, but there were others. Somewhere above her in the pale sky was a rhythmic thudding, and from a different direction the unmistakable sound of a siren. Helen dropped her bag onto the grass in the empty field on the other side and climbed down after it, backing down the bank to lie flat with her head down, listening and waiting. The thudding was getting louder and she turned to see a helicopter clattering high above, its front end dipped like a speeding bird, heading north. The siren sound changed as it drew nearer and then it too receded. There must be a major road somewhere off to the right.

Why did the lie of the land look familiar? Leaving her bag on the ground, Helen clambered back onto the wall. Ahead of her, in the far corner of the next field to the south, was an old barn. Without seeing its far side she knew that there were big double doors that creaked when they opened. She'd seen the barn and the fields around it in a quick look through a gap in the curtain as they'd pulled away, before he'd shouted at her to stay out of sight. Was that hours ago, or days? It didn't matter. The barn would protect her, and she stumbled towards it.

Chapter 11

Dinger Bell looked at the exhausted faces gathered round the big table in Workington CID room on Monday morning. 'I've got HQ on the phone demanding action,' he said, 'and nowt to tell them. What the 'ell's going on with you lot? Bloody kid can't just disappear off the face of the earth. We've got a description of the van, we're pretty sure there's a motorbike involved, we know our man and there are police and army all over the place, so why are we still sitting here like a bunch of lemons two and a half days after she disappeared?'

Anna searched for some reason to interrupt this tirade, something positive. 'We're pretty sure the mother knows more than she's giving us. She's too certain the girl won't come to harm.'

'And?' said Bell. 'Does she know where her daughter is?'

Maureen butted in. 'Don't think so, sir. She was a real mess, but I pushed her and Wetherall's mother too. The only thing I did get was a strong feeling that Alex had used drugs in some form to keep Helen quiet after he took her. You can put hash in cake, and he'd been baking apparently. Pretty weird thing to do if there's no ulterior reason.'

Dinger looked at Carruthers. 'Bob, anything to add?'

Bob Carruthers hadn't expected the question, but he couldn't let the women do all the talking. 'They must have holed up somewhere or we'd have spotted them by now.'

Bell waited, but Bob had no more to offer.

'What have we got on this bloke so far?' the DI asked.

Maureen shuffled her notes and glanced at Anna, who nodded. 'Brought up in Carlisle, there was a sister who died young. Usual adolescent stuff, then off to the army. Served in the Falklands. Sounds as if he had a bad time. Discharged in '85. Drifted around… his mam says he was drinking, out a lot. I came across him when I was with the Drug Squad. We thought he was growing cannabis up on the fells, or at least dealing in it, then he graduated to the harder stuff. That was early '90s. Disappeared for a while, possibly in Holland. Back on our radar,' she checked her notes, 'July 1994, on the edge of some pretty big deals but we couldn't pin him to anything. Finally got him in '96. We picked up one of the heroin shippers and swept Wetherall up after that.'

'Bloody CPS,' Bell muttered. 'We could've had villains like this off the street years ago if not for them whingeing on about having every last i dotted before we went to court. So when did he go down, finally?'

Maureen went on, 'November 1996, four years, Durham. Kept his nose clean, out in October 1999.'

'And now this,' said Bell. 'Where was he after he came out?'

'From what the mother said he stayed over in the north-east for a while, then back to Carlisle to see his mam.'

'Ah, bless,' sad Bob, 'came to look after his old mother. What a treasure.'

Maureen waited for the sarcasm to fade. 'She says he seemed excited about something. Didn't get a job, said he didn't need to. Mam said she wasn't sorry to see him go. She was afraid of him.'

Dinger looked up. 'Why?'

Maureen said, 'I reckon he knocked her around. She said he would just go off, no warning. She blamed the army experience, but he's clearly a violent man.'

'Great,' sighed Dinger, 'that's all we need.'

'Could be looking for a body,' put in Bob, helpfully.

'And we still don't know where. Could be anywhere.' Dinger looked round. Anna could see he was rattled, but suspected that it was the prospect of looking bad in front of his superiors that bothered him most.

Maureen decided to ask the question that had been bugging her since the very beginning. She might get slapped down again, but it had to be said.

'There's one other thing, sir,' she ventured, deliberately avoiding looking at Anna. 'I haven't checked this with you, Sarge, sorry, and Wong couldn't check it without authority from a senior officer, because of the cost.'

They stared at her. 'What are you on about now?' Bell asked. 'Another gut feeling?'

Maureen nodded. 'You could call it that. What if Helen were Alex Wetherall's child?'

'Him and Rose Heslop?' said Anna.

'I'm sure they've been, you know, more than just friends in the past. I looked at the dates, when Eric was working away and Rose was out on the town. Then I asked Tony Wong to check the DNA, but he said he couldn't do that without permission.'

'Too right,' said Dinger. 'Paternity tests don't come cheap.'

'We'll have Wetherall's DNA on record,' Maureen pushed on. 'And we have a toothbrush from Helen, in case we find a body.'

Anna listened. If Alex believed that Helen was his child, that might explain him tracking her down, and using her to get to Rose. She wanted to disagree with Maureen, but thought it was worth checking and she had to say so.

'Could be worth a try,' she said to Bell. 'Yes, it'll cost a bit, but a positive result could explain a lot, and be useful when it comes to court.'

Bell rolled his eyes. 'Gets more tabloid press every bloody day. "He kidnapped our love child," says farmer's wife. I can see it on the front page of *The Sun*.'

Maureen looked down. There was a lengthy pause.

'OK,' said Dinger finally. 'Sounds mad, but what the hell? Get Wong to use his contacts, have the checks done. Right? Happy now, Pritchard?'

Maureen smiled. 'How long will it take?'

The DI shrugged. 'Depends what else they have to do. I'll not be holding my breath.'

Anna's attempt to say something was interrupted by the office door opening. The desk sergeant put his head round. 'Call at the front desk, sir, about a van in a ditch. Want me to put it through?'

'Bugger all going on in here, George. Give us something to chew on.'

When the phone rang Bell picked up. The rest of the group watched his face as he listened, hardly daring to hope that it might prove useful. Bell gestured for a pen and began to scribble. 'Blue van, off the road. Where? Tallentire? Where the 'ell's that? Anyone in it? Shit. OK, get it taped off, no one touches anything, right?' He looked at the team. 'How long to get up there, wherever it is?'

Maureen said, 'From here, half an hour, max. Ask him where exactly. So many lanes round there.'

Bell listened again, scribbled and slammed down the phone. 'At last!'

He was all action, Maureen noticed, as soon as there was something potentially newsworthy to do. On his feet now, directing operations. 'Bob, you stay here. Call Carlisle, we need more men to get a search started. And find Wong and get him out there, chop-chop.' Bob scuttled away. Bell pointed at Maureen. 'Pritchard, you know your way around, you're with me. Penrose, you follow on. Oh, and Bob – call DCI Tognarelli, tell him we've got a lead and I'll fill him in when we know more. Stop him pestering me all the bloody time.' He looked around. 'Come on then,' he shouted, crushing his cigarette into the overflowing ashtray.

Maureen expected they would be the first to reach the site, but when they turned the final corner of the narrow lane an army car was already parked at the side of the road. 'Told you,' said Bell. 'They're organised, these buggers. Let's hope they 'aven't been clomping around.' He peered out at the bank of heavy cloud that seemed to be moving away to the east. 'Bloody rain. Could've washed out some of the details we need. I've got wellies, you'll just get muddy.'

For a few minutes he and the two soldiers chatted about the case. They'd been in the area checking reports of a vehicle seen on a closed road when the call came through from the brigadier about assisting the police. Even Maureen was impressed that the top brass seemed to be talking to each other about a case like this, which was well beyond the army's original remit. Must make a change, she thought, from spending all their time disposing of stinking carcasses. She peered through the gap where the gate had been and down to the wide-open doors of the blue van. The number plate bore no resemblance to the one offered so confidently by the Farthing boy at the school, but she noted it down anyway.

'We're sure there's no one still in there?' Bell said.

'We had a good look, sir,' said one of the soldiers. 'Tried not to get too close, but the back of the van is clearly empty, and the cab too, unless there's someone right down on the floor. No sign of movement in the ten minutes we've been here.'

'Map here, sir,' said the other man, who looked to be no more than a lad. He spread it out on the bonnet of the car, pointing out exactly where they were. Then he indicated another spot, about half a mile to the south. 'Load of dead cattle in a field here. Blokes who were picking up the carcasses told us they were shot this morning. Had to kill them in the field because they couldn't get them into the barn. The guys were out doing that earlier on.' He checked his watch. 'About three hours ago. It was the vet leaving the site who saw the van and called it in.'

'Three hours? What took him so long?'

'Paperwork at the farm, I guess. And he called it in when he got back to the office. No signal out here.'

'And where's this paragon of civic duty now?' asked Bell.

'Back at HQ in Carlisle. Said he couldn't wait. We've got his details.'

Bell swore. 'Three bloody hours. They could be anywhere.'

Anna joined them, nodding to the two soldiers. Bell said, 'Penrose, can you take these two and sort out a search of the immediate area? They're probably long gone by now, but worth a try. It's possible the girl could be on her own. And it's possible he'll cut up rough if he's cornered, so watch out. We don't know if he's armed.' He turned to Maureen. 'Does he have any history with firearms apart from in the military?'

'Not that I can recall, sir,' she said, 'but from what his mam said, that's possible too.'

Bell pointed to his car. 'There's full kit in the back, Pritchard. Tape, plastic shoe covers, gloves. Let's get this scene prepped for forensics. Where's that Wong bloke when you need him?'

Right on cue, Tony Wong's car pulled up behind Bell's and the SOCO stepped out. A bit young and looks foreign, Maureen thought to herself, hoping Bell wouldn't antagonise him straight away. Almost immediately she realised that Wong had all the confidence he would need to withstand the DI's innate scepticism. He knew exactly what he was doing, and got on with his work with minimal direction from anyone else.

Bell's radio crackled and he held it close to his face. 'When?' he said. 'About bloody time! Get a move on.' He explained their position as carefully as he could and the radio stopped crackling. 'Dog and handler,' he called to Anna. 'On their way. Better get an ambulance down here too, just in case. Hope to God we won't need a child-sized body bag.'

After Anna had made the call, Bell had another idea, and walked her a few paces away down the road where it was quieter.

'Let's have another think about the girl's mother,' he said. 'Up to now you don't think she has been upset enough, is that right?' Anna put her head on one side, wondering which line to take – speculation, or hard evidence.

'It's a tricky judgement,' she said. 'Mother's been sedated by her doctor, so her real feelings might be deadened. And it was Prichard's feeling that the mother might know more than she's telling us.'

'And you feel that too?'

Anna hesitated. 'I'm not so sure. I'm waiting for the DNA.'

Bell stepped back, delved in his pocket for a cigarette and lit up. He offered one to Anna, but she shook her head. 'How are you two getting on?' he asked.

'Fine,' Anna replied, too quickly. She'd been afraid for a while that the mutual antagonism between herself and the female DC might be noticed, and probably blamed on her.

'Pritchard's a good copper,' said Bell, 'but she was in the Drug Squad for a long time.' He drew on his cigarette. 'Picked up some bad habits. They're a bit of a law unto themselves, county-wide, different command structure.'

Anna wondered what he was trying to convey. 'Are you saying she's used to having her own way?'

'Aye, that's about right. So how do you deal with that?'

Another choice. Anna could come clean about the difficulties or gloss over them. 'Not really noticed it,' she said, but didn't look at Bell while she said it.

'OK,' he said. 'So who's the best person to tell the mother about this new development and see how she takes it?'

'You reckon Pritchard should do that?'

'I do, but I'm checking with you.'

Anna was still trying to work out what he was up to with this unexpected show of respect for her judgement. He wants Maureen to deal with Rose, but he wants that to be my decision, she concluded.

'I was thinking the same myself,' she said. She knew what Bell was hinting at: Rose is a mother, Maureen is a mother. Real women, not like me. She smiled at Bell, although she felt like kicking him where it hurt.

'OK,' said Bell. 'Let's split the work up. I'll take charge of the pursuit of Wetherall, who may or may not still have the girl with him. We won't be sure about that until the crime-scene mob have finished and we get the dogs to work. We'll send Pritchard and Carruthers up to Carlisle, to talk to the mother.'

'And Wetherall's mother too?' said Anna. 'She might have an idea where he might go in a crisis, and probably wants him found as much as we do.'

'Right,' he said. 'You get on to Ma Wetherall, crank it up a bit. If she doesn't want her precious son back, give her the chance to get him put away again – for a bit longer this time.'

Anna nodded, then hesitated. 'Sir, do we have to send Bob with Pritchard?'

'Why not? Good experience for him.'

'That's true,' she began, wondering how loyal Bell would be to his preferred sidekick and fellow Mason. 'But Pritchard doesn't need him, you know, hanging around.'

'Hanging around? Is that what you think of DC Carruthers?'

Anna said nothing but her expression did. Bell put back his head and laughed. 'Fair enough. I take it you don't want him either, so he can hang around with me instead, right?'

'Yes, sir,' said Anna. If she could glean some useful information from Margaret Wetherall about where Alex might have gone, that would do her reputation no harm at all.

'You go, I'll brief Pritchard,' said Bell.

'You off then?' Tony Wong asked as Anna set off for the road. She turned back to speak to him. 'Pritchard and I are going to see the two mothers, Wetherall's and Mrs Heslop.'

'Well,' Wong said, 'from what I can see so far, someone's taken a motorbike from here. Wetherall might have been able to hide a kid in the back of a van, but not much chance of hiding her on the back of a bike.'

'You mean, he could have left her alone and gone off?'

'Or the kid escaped. Looks like blood by the driver's door, probably banged his head. If the girl was OK, she might have taken her chance and legged it.'

'But where?' Anna said. 'Why didn't she just wait till we turned up and let us find her?'

Wong shook his head. 'She could have been injured herself. Panicked. Tried to run, collapsed somewhere.'

'Or had an asthma attack,' said Anna. 'Poor kid.'

He watched as she turned away and ran towards the car. DS Penrose was very like women he'd seen and admired in senior posts in the Met, and he wondered what she did when she wasn't working.

In the barn where she and Alex had been only a few hours before, Helen closed the big doors and used the toilet in the corner that she'd hated when she'd been here earlier. At least Alex wasn't standing outside, listening. She felt safe for now, out of sight.

Fine lines of sunlight pierced the gaps in the old barn's walls and caught the dust and shreds of hay that danced in the draught as Helen moved around. They caught in her throat and irritated her itching lungs. Already wheezing, Helen found a tarpaulin that Alex hadn't thrown into the van and made herself a place to lie down. She was overwhelmed almost at once by exhaustion and the after-effects of medication, and didn't hear or see the convoy of white trucks that rumbled along the lane a few yards away, heading for the pyres and leaking fluids as they passed. It was only when she woke that the smell of rotting flesh made her retch. She had to get out of this place.

Chapter 12

Maureen pulled over on the outskirts of Carlisle and rang Jo Haile's guesthouse, where she'd dropped off Rose Heslop the night before. Rose sounded breathless when she finally got to the phone.

'I'm ready,' she said.

'Ready?' Maureen repeated.

'To go back to the farm. Is it still OK for you to take me? You said last night…'

Maureen cut her off. 'There's been a development, Mrs Heslop. I need to talk to you. I wanted to check you're still in the city.'

'What is it? What kind of development?'

'I'll be there in a few minutes,' said Maureen, and pressed the red button on her phone before Rose could ask any more. The more anxious Rose was, the more likely she was to talk.

Rose was waiting at the front door and ushered Maureen into the empty dining room. Jo Haile hovered anxiously at the door offering coffee. She was a striking woman, and Maureen could see where Rose's good looks came from: a hint of grey in Jo's dark hair, but the face was unlined despite the tension she must be feeling. Maureen shook Jo's hand and introduced herself, but declined the coffee. Jo waited, but she could see Maureen didn't want her to stay. She closed the door as she left.

'Well,' Rose demanded. 'What is it?'

'Please sit down, Rose,' said Maureen. 'An hour or so ago we found the blue van that was last seen in Cockermouth on Friday. We have reason to believe that this van belonged to Alex Wetherall, an old friend of yours. And we also understand that your daughter got into this van on Friday afternoon after school, apparently of her own free will.'

Rose sat down, her face suddenly pale. 'What about Helen? Have you found her?'

'No, the van was empty.'

Rose looked away. Maureen could see that she was struggling to know what to say. 'Where is she? Where's Helen now?'

'The full search has already started,' said Maureen.

Rose turned on her, face furious. 'So what are you doing here pestering me? Get back out there and find her.' She put her hand to her mouth after this outburst.

Maureen persisted. 'We have reason to believe that you may know more about your daughter's abduction than you have told us.'

Rose flared up again. '"Reason to believe?" What does that mean? Someone's been talking, haven't they?'

Maureen said nothing. She wanted Rose's anger and fear to loosen her tongue.

'It's that bitch Christine, isn't it? What's she said?'

'I'm not at liberty…' Maureen began, sounding just pompous enough to goad Rose a little more.

'Well, Chris is no better than she ought to be! Just trying to dump the blame on me, when she and that useless man of hers…'

'Blame for what?' Maureen asked mildly.

'For Helen going missing. They're blaming me.'

Rose was crying now and Maureen sat patiently while she found a hankie and wiped her eyes.

Finally Maureen said, 'Can you explain to me why you might be to blame, exactly?'

Rose said nothing, but she was obviously thinking hard. Maureen waited. 'Maybe I can help,' she suggested. Rose looked up. 'You and Alex Wetherall know each other.'

'Years ago we did,' Rose broke in.

'So you say. You can't blame us for wondering why this man has apparently deliberately sought out your daughter in Cockermouth, got to know her well enough that she would feel safe with him, and then invited her into his van and taken her away. How could that have happened? You tell me, Rose.'

The room was silent, save for the occasional sound of a passing car in the street outside and the buzzing of a vacuum cleaner elsewhere in the boarding house. Every room was occupied, and in the evenings the place hummed with workers summoned to deal with the FMD outbreak from all over the country and beyond, like soldiers billeted during wartime.

Rose patted at her eyes with the handkerchief while she spoke.

'I bumped into him in town, last year sometime. I was coming out of work and he was just there. It was a shock, he looked different.'

'And after that?'

'Nothing,' she said. 'We had a coffee, I think. He told me he'd been in the army, then away working on the rigs for a while. That was it.'

'And you've not seen him since?'

Rose shook her head.

'If this man took Helen, what reason would he have?'

'Money, I suppose,' said Rose.

'Has he been in touch with you or your husband since Helen went?

'No, but…'

'Well,' said Maureen, 'it doesn't look like a kidnap for ransom, does it?'

'Maybe he's just crazy.'

'So if the man who took your daughter is crazy, why have you been so calm about it?'

Rose shook her head. 'It's these pills the doctor gave me, they make my head spin. When they wear off, I…' She began to sob. 'I just want her back! Where are they now?'

There was a slight tap on the door and it opened to reveal Jo, looking upset. 'Have you found Helen?' she asked. 'Please tell me what's going on. I could hear Rose crying.'

'Come in, Mrs Haile,' said Maureen. 'I'm explaining to Rose that the van we believe Helen was in was found near Tallentire, off the road and empty. No sign of Helen or the man who appears to have taken her.'

'So where can they be?' Jo asked.

'That's the problem, Mrs Haile. It's highly likely that Helen is no longer with the man who took her.'

Rose stopped crying abruptly. 'You mean, she's out there on her own?'

Maureen nodded. 'It's more than likely.'

Rose let out a howl of despair. Jo Haile went to her, looking back reproachfully at Maureen. 'For God's sake, do something,' she said. 'You have to find Helen. She's just a child. Anything could happen to her. Rose can't help you… look at her, she's in bits.'

Maureen knew there was no further she could go now. She was absolutely sure Rose had known all along that Helen was with Alex, and that he wouldn't harm her. Now that she'd heard her twelve-year-old daughter might be alone in the stricken countryside, the full dread of what might happen to her next had suddenly struck home.

'I have to go home,' Rose said plaintively. 'I have to be with Brian.'

'I'll take her,' said Jo. 'Please don't ask her any more questions, Maureen. It's not fair, none of this is her fault.'

But Maureen wasn't quite done. 'There's just one more question, Rose, and then I'll leave you alone. Do you have any idea at all where Alex might go if he needed a place to hide?'

Rose didn't look at her, merely shook her head.

'OK,' said Jo. 'That's enough.' She took Maureen's arm and steered her towards the door and out into the dark hall, closing it behind them. 'You can see how upset she is.' As Maureen put out her hand to open the front door, Jo pulled her back with a hand on her arm. 'Now look,' she whispered, 'you need to find that bastard and lock him up properly this time. Don't ask me what's been going on, but something has. And that's just between us, right?'

Maureen smiled. 'Thank you,' she whispered. She took a card from her bag and handed it to Jo. 'Call me any time, if you need to. OK?'

When she got to Mrs Wetherall's door Anna sat in the car for a few minutes, wondering what Maureen would do in this situation to get the woman to talk. The local accent probably helped, but there wasn't much Anna could do about her voice. Maybe it was more about softening the tone, and slowing down, and being prepared sometimes to say nothing and let the silence stretch. Anna's natural style, if she had one, was to pull rank and get heavy with people, but it didn't work here. Most people got annoyed and clammed up.

The door opened after a long delay and Anna smiled at the anxious face that appeared in the crack. She raised her ID card, smiled again and asked if she could come in for a few minutes. 'Pretty cold out here,' she said as the woman hesitated. The door opened further and Margaret Wetherall stepped back, just as Anna had begun to wonder whether Alex was actually in the house. Surely not, but the picture they were forming of him was of a desperate man who was prepared to take irrational risks.

'Have you found him?' the woman said.

Anna shook her head. 'No, not yet. We need to, Mrs Wetherall, for his own sake, before he gets into even more trouble.'

'I told Maureen about him,' said Margaret. They were still standing in the dark hall. 'He's not a bad man.'

Anna pushed on a door to her left. 'Can we go in here? Bit more light.'

The room was evidently rarely used. Anna sat down on a hard sofa near the window but Margaret Wetherall stood, hands clasped in front of her, holding a string of black rosary beads. She looked as tired and grey as the net curtains that drooped in the winter light.

'I told Maureen that he was in the Falklands,' she said, 'and what that did to him.'

Anna brightened. Here was her chance to make a connection. 'I was in the army too,' she said. 'In Bosnia. Only came out a short while ago.'

'Fancy,' said Margaret.

'What regiment was Alex in?'

'2 Para,' Margaret replied. 'He was at Goose Green.'

'That was a tough one.'

Margaret didn't respond and didn't look up. Anna wondered what to say next. Suddenly the older woman started to speak. 'He wasn't the same when he came back. Wouldn't talk. He wanted to leave the army, but they made him wait. Then they kicked him out, so he came home.'

Stay quiet, Anna said to herself. Just let her tell you. People were passing the window but Margaret didn't seem to be aware of them, or even of Anna. 'He kept the drugs upstairs,' she said. 'When I asked him about them, he hit me.' Margaret blew her nose. 'He hit me a lot.'

'Did you ever report him?' Anna ventured. Any record of violence would help their case.

'My own son?' Margaret said with unexpected force. 'How could I?'

Silence fell again, broken only by the noise from the street and Margaret's regular sniffing. Anna needed to refocus the woman's attention on where Alex might be now. There might even be some light to shed on his relationship with Rose.

'Did he live with you when he was a young man, before the army?' she began.

'Joined up when he was nineteen,' Margaret responded. The rosary beads clacked quietly between her fingers. 'He had a few jobs before that, but mostly he hung about.'

'Any special friends?'

'A gang of them, can't remember who they all were. Some lasses.'

'Serious girlfriend?'

'Not that he told me. But when he was back from the army he was different, wild like. I told Maureen, he was out a lot. Mrs Henderson, next door, she said he had someone back here more than once when I was away at me sister's.' Sniff. 'Bloody nerve! In my house.'

'Would Mrs Henderson recall anything more about that, do you think?'

Margaret looked at Anna for an instant. 'Dead, isn't she? Last year.'

'Oh,' said Anna. 'I'm sorry to hear that.'

'She were a nosy cow.'

Anna tried to collect her thoughts. Every path she went down seemed to be blocked. 'Mrs Wetherall,' she began again. 'When Alex was young, was there anywhere he would go, somewhere he really liked?'

'Apart from the pub, you mean?'

'Yes, out of town perhaps, somewhere quiet?'

There was no response and Anna went on, trying to fill the silence. 'We all have some quiet places we like, don't we? Where I live, it's in the middle of a forest... Whinlatter, do you know where that is?' Still no response. 'A little cottage behind an old guesthouse, but that's empty now so there's no one around but me.' What else could she say to gain the silent woman's attention? She'd tried everything.

Margaret stared out of the window. 'If you catch him, what will happen?' she asked.

'He'll probably be charged with kidnapping the child. That's up to the lawyers to decide.'

'But he'll go back to jail?'

Anna understood. His mother wanted to be free of him. 'That would be up to a judge and jury,' she said, 'but it's highly likely.'

Still without looking at her directly, Margaret Wetherall said quietly, 'He used to go fishing. Somewhere on the Solway, where there was a pier that stuck out into the tide. I think it had some thing to do with an old train line, way back. Don't know what it's called. Big fishing spot. Him and his mates went there a lot.'

'And you don't know the name of this place? Are you sure?'

Margaret shook her head. 'If you do catch him, don't say anything about me telling you that, will you? Because...' She broke off and looked at Anna. 'He's not a bad man,' she repeated. 'That's all I've got to say.'

Anna left Mrs Wetherall to her rosary beads, her fear and her guilt. She and Maureen had arranged to meet at a café near the police station in Carlisle to share what they'd gathered from the two mothers. As she had a few minutes to spare, Anna went into the station, introduced herself, and asked for a map of the Solway. 'Going fishing, are you?' asked the desk sergeant.

'Where would I go, for the best fishing?' Anna asked.

He laughed. 'Don't ask me, Sarge. Football man, me. Fishing's like watching paint dry.'

When Maureen found her, Anna had spread out the relevant part of the map on the table in the café and was examining it carefully. It was a large-scale map and all sorts of lumps and bumps were visible on the southern shore of the Solway Firth as it ran westwards towards the Irish Sea. Anna explained what Margaret had told her.

Maureen took off her glasses, pulled the map towards her and peered at it. She traced slowly along the southern shoreline of the estuary with her finger, then stopped and looked even closer. 'Your eyes are younger than mine,' she said to Anna. 'Where my finger is, what's that?'

Anna took the map to the window to get more light and came back smiling. 'Look,' she said. 'On both sides, south and north, there's a pier or something sticking out. Margaret said something about a train line.'

Maureen looked again. 'That's it! The old railway line that used to run across to Annan. Demolished ages ago, but both ends of the viaduct are still there. You can walk out and fish from it, right into the tide. That must be the place.'

As they left the café Maureen pulled her phone from her pocket. 'Get the Solway Firth maps out, Bob,' she said to DC Carruthers. 'Anna and I are on our way back.' In separate cars, they didn't have a chance to share what they had learned. When they got back to Workington the team reconvened in the CID room.

At last there was some hard information to work on.

Bell said, 'SOCO reckons that Alex had a motorbike in the back of the van. Same one he used for the pharmacy thefts. He'd clearly pushed it up to the road and presumably driven off on it. Tyre tracks look as if he was heading north.'

'What about Helen?' Anna asked.

'He could have her on the back of the bike, but that looks highly unlikely. Too noticeable, too risky. So he either dumped her or she got away on her own. Either way, the dog didn't get very far when they set it off. There's some stuff all over the road that must stink to high heaven. The handler reckons the dog was too distracted by it.'

Maureen chipped in, 'Some of those white trucks are around today, the ones that pick up carcasses. They leak all over the place… locals are always complaining about it.'

'Aye, could be that,' Bell agreed. 'Anyway, the handler pulled the dog on a bit further, as far as the next lane end, to the south, but there was a big disinfectant pad across it, and the dog got stuck again.'

There was a brief silence while they all wondered the same thing.

Anna said, 'I don't get it. Why would a girl running away from the man who'd kidnapped her stop to disinfect her shoes, if that's what she did?'

They all nodded.

'Well, the dog gave up,' said Bell. 'But we've got those cadets again, the ones who searched the farm. Army blokes got them organised pretty quick and they're fanning out. It's a big area. Nothing so far.'

The door opened and an older man came into the office. Anna recognised the uniform of a Detective Chief Inspector, although the man looked hardly tall enough to be a policeman.

His face was softer than Anna expected, more thoughtful, and it was familiar: maybe he'd been on her interview panel. All the people at the table got to their feet.

'Don't get up,' he said, waving his hand. 'Any more news about the girl? I heard you found the van you've been looking for.'

Bell responded immediately. 'No sign of her yet, sir. Search dog was confused by there being too many powerful smells around: white truck leakage, disinfectant. No news from the search team yet. Looks like the girl may have tried to get as far away as possible, although it's hard to figure out why. Not much daylight left now, so they'll keep going as long as they can and start again at first light.'

'What's the weather forecast, do we know?' DCI Tognarelli asked.

Bob had already checked. 'Dry tonight, but looks pretty rough tomorrow. High winds, rain. Not good for anyone out on their own, never mind a young 'un.'

No one spoke for a moment. They were all wondering about Helen. Bell broke the silence. 'We're just catching up on Penrose and Pritchard's enquiries in Carlisle.'

'I'll stay for that then,' said the newcomer. He turned to Anna. 'DCI Sam Tognarelli,' he said, extending his hand. 'We have met, at your interview. It's probably a bit of a blur.'

So she was right about that. And unlike others she could mention, he'd seemed genuinely pleased to see a woman in a promoted post in CID. There was some story about him tangling with the IRA in Whitehaven years before. He must be close to retirement, but recent rumour was that he'd decided to stay on after his wife had died suddenly. If Bell had his eye on the DCI job he might have to wait a bit longer.

Bob had found a way of projecting the map of the Solway on to a screen and Maureen pointed out the old viaduct that was apparently a favourite spot for fishing. 'From what Wetherall's mother said, it's possible that he's gone to ground somewhere in this area.'

'And we think he's armed?' Tognarelli asked.

'SOCO found a cartridge case on the floor of the van, under a seat. No sign of a firearm, but if he does have one he's a trained soldier and would know how to use it.'

Tognarelli sat for a moment, thinking. 'OK, DI Bell, what do you need?'

Bell had his list ready. More men, some of them armed, dogs, a mobile incident unit to coordinate the operation in such a remote location. Tognarelli was making notes. Anna guessed he was thinking about the cost. He looked up.

'OK,' he said. 'Leave that with me. This man's pretty desperate by the sound of it. Possibly armed and potentially violent if he's cornered. We need him in custody before any more damage is done.' He turned to Bell. 'Keep me in touch, right?'

The DCI was almost at the door when he turned and said to Anna, 'DI Penrose, how are you getting on?'

Anna was surprised. 'Fine, thank you, sir,' she replied.

When the office door closed there was silence for a moment. All eyes were on Anna, who blushed. Then Bob Carruthers spoke up, mimicking his superior. 'And what about you, DC Pritchard, after twenty years on the job, how are you getting on?'

Maureen glared at him.

'Shut up, Bob,' Bell growled. 'OK, everyone, that's enough. Let's get on with it.'

They were gathering coats and bags when the phone rang. Bell picked up. 'What?' he growled. 'Hang on a minute.' He put down the handset. 'Pritchard!' he yelled. Maureen came back into the office.

'Wong on the phone,' said Bell. He flicked a switch and the voice on the other end of the line was suddenly audible across the room. 'Say that again,' he ordered.

'Test results on Wetherall and Helen's DNA,' he said. Maureen's heart bumped. 'No match. Alex Wetherall is not related to Helen Heslop.'

Maureen sank down in a chair. She'd been so sure… But almost instantly she had another thought. It didn't matter. All that did was that Alex believed he was Helen's father, and there was only one person who could have led him to do so.

Chapter 13

In the barn, Helen searched in vain for a bottle of water or any food that Alex might have left, but there was nothing and she was very hungry. The tarpaulin she'd used to lie on might be useful, though, and she folded it up carefully and put it in the school bag she'd been carrying since Friday. What day was it now? she wondered. She went back over things in her mind. Alex had said something about getting her puffer on a Sunday, and that had been the day before. Early this morning she'd watched the cows being killed, and now it was getting dark again. So this was still Monday. Tomorrow would be Tuesday and by the evening she would be back at the farm. Her leg wasn't painful now. She could walk to the main road that she could hear a few fields away, and there would be a bus.

At the bottom of her bag she'd found a five-pound note that Granny Jo had given her. Alex had said Mum knew where she was and that she was safe, but that was before. Now he might be dead and Helen would need to get home on her own. For a few minutes her mind was very clear, but then things clouded over. All she knew was that she needed to go to the main road to wait for the bus, and that it was getting dark. Dark was good, she thought, because the soldiers wouldn't be able to find her and arrest her for spreading the disease.

There was just enough light left in the sky for her to find her way alongside a wall that seemed to be running in the right direction. To the right, which Helen reckoned must be the west, there was a pink glow in the sky and she could see enough to walk without stumbling. She came to another wall, but there was a gate a little further along to the left that was easy to climb over. Another field. This time there was barbed wire fencing and it took her a while to work out the best way over it. In the end she laid the tarpaulin over the top and managed to push the wire down enough to get over the fence without being scratched.

By now the pink glow in the sky had faded, and the wind was stronger, but the noise from the road was louder and she could see car headlights. One last wall, one last gate, and Helen dropped her bag onto the ground on the far side, waiting until a car had passed before she climbed over and stood still. Her chest was wheezing from exertion and she pulled air into her lungs. She had the puffer but didn't want to use it unless she had to, in case it made her feel worse.

As far as she could work out, if west was to her right, then she should go left. She hitched up the bag and set off, walking along the grass verge by the side of the road. There were lights ahead, and she passed a sign. 'Govenbry,' it read. There might be a phone box in the village, but she had no change. A bus driver would take her money. There must be a bus stop here.

And there it was. A little shelter, with a bench inside. Helen put down her bag and sat down. The awful smell wafted around her again. Suddenly she felt sick and terribly tired. She had to lie down. She lifted her legs onto the bench and put her head down on her bag. She heard the occasional car or lorry when it passed by but was too dizzy to raise her head. Ten minutes later the bus driver slowed down as he approached Govenbry, but there was no one standing at the bus stop, no arm raised, and he put his foot down again to drive on towards Cockermouth and the end of his shift.

Helen woke. Her neck was stiff and she still felt sick. She had no idea what time it was, but when she stood up and looked out of the bus shelter there were pale shadows visible. The moon had risen. It was still very windy. She leaned against the entrance to the shelter, trying to clear her head. The road was quiet. How long would she have to wait for a bus to Cockermouth, she wondered. And if she could get there, what then? She didn't want to see anyone except Mum and Brian, or go anywhere but home.

A car was approaching, going the way she wanted to go. She looked up and watched as it slowed and then stopped in front of the shelter. The passenger window rolled down and a face appeared quite low down, as the driver leaned across to speak to her.

Helen saw a man's face, and a woollen hat pulled down to the eyebrows. 'The last bus has gone, pet,' he said. 'Do you want a lift somewhere? Jump in.' Helen didn't know what to say. 'I'm waiting for my dad,' she said finally. 'He's coming to pick me up.'

The man hesitated, frowning at her. 'Are you sure you're all right? It's quite late.'

'Yes, I'm fine,' said Helen. She took a step back. Who could she trust? She tried to smile, but she was thinking about the men in the field with the cows. The man shook his head, the window rolled back up and the car pulled away, disappearing round the bend in the road.

Helen watched the lights recede. The air outside the shelter had helped to clear her head and she felt safer on her own. She wouldn't get a bus, not tonight. She would walk until she needed to stop and find herself a place to sleep. When the new day came she would keep away from anyone she didn't know, and then when it was dark again she would walk the last of the way home. She would get there all on her own, and her mum would be there, and Brian. Mum would make sure that the soldiers didn't come for her, that Dad and Aidan didn't give her away. She would eat and sleep and then she would go back to school and see Emma again and all this would be over.

Helen walked through the quiet village as if she knew exactly where she was and where she was going. There was no one around.

She passed a junction where the main street appeared to go off to the right. The sign at the junction said Cockermouth was just two miles away. That wasn't far at all, but she did want some food first. Up ahead there was a sign high up, a garage. Helen wondered if she could stop there, tell them she was lost and get help, but she wasn't lost, and they might report her. Instead she decided to go in and buy some chocolate. She still felt sick. Chocolate was the only thing she could face.

The man behind the counter was reading a newspaper and hardly looked up when Helen put the chocolate bars, a bottle of water and the five-pound note on the high counter. He gave her the change and she walked out, feeling relieved. Outside the wind seemed suddenly stronger, pushing into her as she left the shelter of the garage building. She stood on the empty forecourt for a few moments. Sometimes there were toilets behind petrol stations. She walked round the back and tried a door. It opened. There was the toilet, but it was smelly and she didn't want to use it. She closed the door again.

A little further away from the back of the petrol station was a low fence, and beyond it a patch of grass and an overgrown garden. A passing car's headlights lit up the area for a second and Helen noticed a shed in the far corner. There was no one around. She stepped over the fence and carefully across the uneven ground to the door of the shed. If this is open, she said to herself, I shall stay here, eat my chocolate and rest.

The door was unlocked. Inside was a jumble of old garden tools, bags of compost and empty sacks. Air whistled through the side of a small window, but it was dry. This is my little house, Helen said to herself. She used what energy she had left to heave bags and old sacks around until there was space for her to lie down. In the last few minutes before she fell asleep she thought about Alex. He'd been lying to her about knowing her mum, just to get her to stay with him, she was sure of that now. Mum was going to be cross with her for accepting a lift from a man, but at least she'd known better than to do it for a second time.

Alex had been standing in the village shop for a few minutes, looking for any news in the local paper about Helen or him. He had no idea where she might be, whether she'd been found. If she had, and she'd talked, the police would know everything. He had to get back to Rose. It couldn't wait any longer. Once he had the money, everything was in place. It was almost dark outside. He wasn't looking forward to going back to the damp abandoned building where he'd stashed the goods, but it had served its purpose. He was off the grid, out of sight, on his way to a new life.

The shop door tinkled as someone came in. Alex pulled his hat further down and pushed the glasses higher. He turned towards the shop window to check that his appearance was reassuringly unlike the Photofit picture he'd seen in a newspaper earlier in the day. Beyond his reflection he saw the police car standing outside. The urge to run was strong, but he kept very still and listened, out of sight of the counter, where a conversation was taking place.

‘Na’ then,’ said the shopkeeper. ‘Cigs, is it?’

‘Given up,’ said the unseen person. ‘Wife nagging were bad enough, then the kids started. This is business, Arthur. Any sign of this bloke?’

There was a rustling sound. Alex held his breath.

‘Nay, mate, can’t help with that,’ said the shopkeeper, after an interminable pause. ‘What’s ’e done?’

‘Can’t tell you that, mate, but it involves a kiddie.’

‘One of those, eh? Bastard.’ There was a pause. Alex kept as still as he could.

The shopkeeper said, ‘Couple of blokes come for the fishing, but that’s all. Been quiet all week. Too bloody quiet. Takings are way down.’

‘Well, brace yourself, mate,’ said the unseen voice that Alex guessed belonged to the policeman from the car outside. ‘Could be a lot of folk around wanting sarnies and coffee and stuff tomorrow, early on like.’

‘What’s up then?’ said the shopkeeper.

Alex couldn’t see the local constable smile and tap the side of his nose with his finger. ‘Can’t tell you that either,’ said the policeman, ‘but it could be a good day for you. Summat’s definitely up.’

‘Come on, what kind of summat?’ The shopkeeper was curious now. Alex’s heart was racing.

‘Could be a chopper around, dogs, all sorts,’ said the policeman, ‘but you didn’t hear that from me, right?’

‘Lips are sealed,’ said the shopkeeper. ‘Sure you don’t want some cigs? I won’t tell your missus.’

‘Oh, hell, just a pack of ten, Arthur. Might need these tomorrow.’

Transaction complete, the shop door tinkled again, and Alex watched as the police car pulled away into the night. He put down the magazine he'd been pretending to read and began gathering chocolate bars and some bottled water. Then he walked as casually as he could manage round to the counter. 'Long day tomorrow,' he said, as Arthur counted the items into the till. 'But there's a good tide running so we'll make the most of it.'

'Come with some mates, have you?' asked Arthur. 'Could be noisy round 'ere tomorrow, from what I hear.'

'We're heading west,' said Alex.

'Good idea,' said Arthur.

Money was handed over, and Alex picked up his purchases and left the shop.

Outside in the darkness he leaned against the wall and breathed slowly, digesting what he'd heard and what it meant.

A chopper, dogs? Must be a search planned, and probably for him. But how did they figure out where he was? He'd hidden the bike so thoroughly that he doubted it had been found, and anyway it was miles away and he'd hiked the rest of the way here along hedgerows and beside walls, avoiding the empty fields where a walking figure might have looked conspicuous. Helen couldn't have told them anything as he'd never said where he was going. Or had he? Surely he'd been careful, even after those shots of whisky.

He checked that the police car was gone and then walked slowly back towards his place. It had to be him they were looking for. If Helen didn't know, who else might have told the police? Rose wouldn't have said anything, she had too much to lose. Suddenly it dawned on him and he groaned. His mother! Stupid cow. Never could keep her mouth shut. They'd given her some sob story about the danger her precious son was in and she'd blabbed. It made no difference now. For whatever reason a shit load of police would be crawling over this place tomorrow and he had to get out.

It was just gone six in the evening. They wouldn't come before first light. He had time to decide what to do and disappear ahead of them. Might even have time to slow them down a little. Despite his anxiety, perhaps because of it, he smiled. It felt like being back in the Paras, with enemy action expected in the morning, but this time there were no fuckwit officers giving orders. He was on his own. Adrenaline bounced round his body as he walked. By the time he got back to the abandoned house where he'd been hiding out he had a plan, and the smile had broadened.

The motorbike would have to stay where it was. They knew it was his and roadblocks could be in place already. Army HQ was not far away on the outskirts of Carlisle and the area to the east was heaving with them, all the blokes and vehicles collecting carcasses for the huge pyres at Great Orton. Heading south wasn't much better. He needed to break out overnight and be well away in a stolen car by the time they moved in. There was one way out. Dangerous but possible. What was that motto in 2 Para? *Utrinque Paratus* – 'Ready for anything', and he was.

Packing what he needed into his rucksack took only a few minutes. Accomplishing the rest of his plan took a little longer. The moon was full and bright, but the black balaclava pulled up over his mouth and down his forehead left only a small area of pale skin and he rubbed dirt onto his face, just like they'd done in the Falklands. That's what this reminded him of: the cold, the danger, the challenge of pitting yourself against the landscape.

He'd worked out the tide times and knew how long it might take him to reach the shore at the right place, a few miles to the east, before starting to head north out into the wasteland of the Solway Firth. He'd been lucky with the tip-off in the shop, and would need to be lucky again, but no more than he deserved.

This was his time. The rivers were low, and the spring tides meant high tide would be very high and low tide very low. He'd only ever walked halfway across the firth before, to the sand banks between the Eden and the Esk, but he knew what to expect. Finding a way across without getting stuck fast in the mud would be mostly trial and error, with only limited time before the tide turned and water would rush in from the west, pulled by the strength of the moon. He could die there, but he wasn't going to die, not now. He knew it. Rose was waiting for him and he couldn't let her down. She couldn't contact him, but that changed nothing. She'd said they would be together, and he would make it happen.

Chapter 14

He had what he needed. The first part of the journey he could do in regular clothes and boots, heading for the old monument on the edge of Burgh Marsh, close to the beach where he would start across the Eden. He would change into his wetsuit there, with waders over the top, and ford the river, carrying the long strong stick that he'd used before and kept in the old place for a future fishing trip. But this was no fishing trip. He was crossing the firth to save his skin.

He set off across deserted fields, keeping low, avoiding the lanes as much as he could. Within sight of the monument he turned left towards the beach. Looking down, he could see the River Eden sliding westwards, moonlight gleaming off its black surface. He didn't hesitate for long, wading out into the stream. Using the stick he probed ahead, searching for the firmest footing on the sandy bed of the river. The water deepened as he strode out, almost to the top of the waders. Halfway across he hit a deeper hole and had to retreat, taking a different line, with the lights of Gretna on the other side of the firth directly ahead of him. Rising in the east, the full moon lit the wasteland all around, and the beam from his head torch swung from side to side as he moved. The precious cargo in his rucksack weighed him down, but it was all he had in the world now and could not be abandoned. Without the money he might survive, but for what?

Cold water topped his waders and began to trickle into the boot, weighing down his legs even further. This could be it, he thought, pinned to the river bottom and drowned in the rising tide, but as he pushed forward the water level began to drop a little and no more leaked into his boots. He pulled with all his strength, one foot, then the other, as the bank rose gradually. With one final heave on his stick he was out, and sank on to the muddy riverside, gasping.

For a few minutes Alex made himself think carefully, checking everything one more time. In the rucksack the waterproof inner lining had served its purpose and the contents, clothes, shoes, and the precious package, were all dry. He wriggled out of the waders and emptied the water from the boots. Suddenly his feet slipped from under him and he slid helplessly down the bank into the water, but without the weight of the rucksack on his shoulders, crawling up the bank was easier. Covered in mud, he struggled back into the waders and had to sit again for a few minutes, to regain his breath and check the time. He was behind schedule. He got to his feet, breathing hard still, but he had to move on.

Ahead of him lay the flat expanse of mud and sand known as Rockcliffe Marsh. Some of it was exposed even at high tide and he'd seen cattle out here before, but now it was deserted. Any animals that had escaped the bolt gun were under cover, locked away from the pestilence while anxious farmers checked for limps and drool and dreamed of an end to it all.

There were paths across parts of the marsh, and little bridges across some of the channels, but these were for farmers coming out from Rockcliffe and led in directions that were no use to him. The lights on the other side of the firth were his best guide.

In his head he held the image of the course of the Esk on the far side of the marsh. To find the best spot to cross, he needed the lights of Gretna ahead and to the left of him. When he was close to his crossing place, the lights and sound of traffic on the bridge that carried the motorway into Scotland would be on his right. But all that was to come. First he had to cross the marsh.

The first two channels were narrow enough for him to jump across, although to manage the second he had to take off the rucksack and throw it ahead of him. The third channel was too wide to be jumped. He looked to right and left but there was no sign of a point where crossing from bank to bank would be possible. He peered down, dropping his chin so that the head torch would light the water at the bottom of the slope. The sides of the channel were slick and grey, and the water below it a murky brown. Alex walked a hundred paces to his left, but there was no obvious fording place. He tried to his right, with growing desperation. Every time he turned back he was losing his advantage. He had to keep ahead of the tide and of the men and dogs that would soon come looking for him. Above all he must be safely across and under cover before there was light enough for a helicopter to track him down.

Calculations blurred in his mind as he stood, breathing slowly, trying to think. Sometimes he just wanted it all to be over, to go back to jail where at least he could eat and sleep and turn off his mind. But he had things to do before that. There were scores to settle and a prize to claim.

A thin layer of cloud that had slid across the moon sailed on a little further. In the stronger light, just within sight, he could see the faintest traces of disturbance on the near bank to his right, as if something or somebody had found a way down without sinking irretrievably into the mud. He scoured the further bank for signs that whatever it was had found a way up. Nothing.

There was no sign that whatever had gone down the bank had got out on the far side. But it was still his best chance, possibly his only one in the time he had left.

Far to the west, the breeze was stirring and the tide had begun to creep towards the shore. Soon it would start to surge into the lower reaches of the two rivers, pushing back the flow, nosing into the creeks. And to the east, beyond and below the line of Cumbrian hills etched in silver against the dark sky, he could see the faintest tinge of the new day.

In the pre-dawn glow, as a full moon slipped towards the horizon, Anna Penrose was leading the group of police surrounding an old gatekeeper's hut, one of two sites identified as places where Alex Wetherall could be hiding out. The other was an abandoned hotel, a few hundred yards closer to the coast, where the fishing fraternity were known to hang out and store some of their equipment. These two possible needles in the proverbial haystack had been identified by DI Bell, after much scouring of the maps and consultation with the local policeman. Anna had her doubts, but, as Bell had made clear, he wouldn't accept advice from anyone without the precious 'local knowledge'.

At least, to Anna's relief, this was one occasion when the omniscient DC Pritchard couldn't help, first because her local knowledge didn't extend to fishing on the Solway, and second because she had been assigned to help with the search for Helen and keep an eye on Rose. With Pritchard out of the way, Anna felt more at ease, and this realisation bothered her.

Whatever Anna's scepticism about Bell's confident predictions, she and her group would be first in when both locations were covered. She felt a surge of adrenaline more intense than at any time since she'd left the army, a mix of exhilaration and fear that reminded her of those days, and how much she missed them. Nothing had mattered then except staying safe, supporting your people and achieving a righteous goal.

Keeping low, they slowly closed the circle round the gatekeeper's hut, watching for signs of movement, hearing the wind in their ears and the crunch of boots on hard ground. Anna's radio crackled.

'Any sign?' Bell asked.

'Nothing yet,' she whispered. 'Can't believe he's asleep, but it's possible.'

As they came within twenty yards of the hut she stopped and raised her hand. Within a few seconds the signal had passed round the circle of men and they had all stopped, waiting. Anna raised the loudhailer to her mouth.

'Police! You're surrounded. Come out slowly, hands over your head.'

They crouched down, waiting for movement or the flash of a bullet. Nothing. She shouted again. 'OK. Keep low. Move in – fast. Now!'

Shouting figures ran the last few yards, and the door of the hut thudded inwards.

'Clear,' came a voice as men surged inside. 'Nothing, Sarge.'

Anna stood by the broken door and shone a torch into the gloom of the hut. No sign of occupation, just a couple of empty bottles, two rotting fishing rods and a net propped behind the door. The pile of dirt in one corner could have been human waste, but it was old and frozen. Anna spoke into the radio.

'Rabbit 2. No sign.'

The radio squawked. 'Rabbit 1, no movement here either. We'll hang fire. Get the dog in. See if it picks anything up.'

The group stood back, breathing returned to normal. The handler pulled his dog into every corner of the hut and then outside where he lengthened the lead and followed at a trot as the dog sniffed frantically round the building, this way and that, before setting off eastwards to where pink light outlined low hills. Anna waited. Furious barking. Her radio crackled again. 'Badgers,' said the dog handler. She heard him speak to the dog and the barking stopped. 'Nowt,' came his voice. 'Sorry, ma'am.'

'Clear here,' said Anna into her radio. 'We'll head down to you.'

She gestured and the men fell in behind her, the dog and the handler bringing up the rear. When they came within fifty yards of the old house they stopped and fanned out, crouching behind sparse gorse bushes and a low wall. The place was bigger than she had expected and in a worse state of repair. Two storeys, Victorian brick incongruous in the grey landscape, large windows boarded up in places and sometimes not. Anna was facing the back of the building. The lower half of one window had lost its boarding and could have been used for access. Bell and his team were on the other side, looking towards the main door and the strip of weedy asphalt that ran towards the lane.

Bell shouted a warning, his words bouncing off the walls into the air. No response or sign of movement. Then the flicker of a white plastic bag caught Anna's eye in the hedge to her left, and simultaneously a gun shot cracked from the other side of the building. They dropped to the cold ground. Anna's heart thudded in her chest and dogs barked frantically.

Someone shouted, 'Gun shot. Stay down!' They waited, expecting a second report, but nothing happened. Anna groped for her radio. Before she could speak, Bell's voice emerged from it.

'He's in there, or someone is. You lot stay where you are, and keep well down.' Anna heard the warnings given through the loudhailer. What now? she wondered. Was he alone? Was he expecting them? Too many questions.

'Any movement round the back?' Bell asked.

'Nothing,' she said.

'Fire a shot, over the roof, see if we can draw him out.'

Anna drew her newly issued pistol, positioned herself behind the wall for protection, signalled to the men behind her to stay down, and fired a shot into the air. The report was loud, bouncing off the brick walls.

There was no response.

Bell's voice again. 'OK, any protection back there?'

Anna considered. 'This wall runs down to the left, and closer to the house.'

'Stay behind it, and when you're close, get up to the house wall. Can you do that?'

'Roger,' said Anna. Was this just Alex's ploy to get them nearer, to save ammunition? Or was it her chance to show that army experience trumped local expertise?

When the crack and the flash came less than a second after Anna began to move, she dropped flat to the ground and stayed there. No pain. Whoever had fired had missed, but where had they fired from? The flash seemed to come from the ground below the half-boarded window, not from the window itself. It didn't make sense.

Bell's voice came direct this time, not through the radio.

'We've found a tripwire. Have a look on your side.'

Anna swung her torch over the path she'd taken and there it was, a thin wire glinting in the light. 'One here too,' she called back.

'Stay there,' he called. 'We're going in.'

'Clear, clear!' came the cries as the vanguard hunted through the rooms of the littered building. Then another voice, 'Sir, in here.' Anna pulled herself up to the open rear window of the house and over the sill to stand by Bell in the back room where moonlight seeped into the small space. Their torches scoured the floor and found a pile of dark material. Dinger pushed at it with his foot. A sleeping bag. In the corner a single-burner stove, a tiny kettle and a couple of empty cans and a bottle. Something pale fluttered in the draught. Anna picked it up. It was a bank note. She whistled. 'Fifty.'

'OK, OK,' said Dinger. 'He's been here. Get forensics.'

He turned away. 'Dog!' he yelled.

The moon faded as the daylight strengthened, revealing the browns and greens of the land, gleaming on the river that wound down tidal channels to the open sea. They watched and listened as the dog pulled his handler down the lane, not towards the shore but south for a few yards and then through a gap in the hedge.

'Where's he gone now?' Bell asked in exasperation. He was being led a dance and he knew it. 'Follow the dog,' he said to Anna. 'You're a bloody sight fitter than me.'

She ran, revelling in the chance to do so after the tension of the past hour. Across the field they went, then over a stile into another field and on again. Anna's radio crackled. It was Bell. 'We'll follow on the road. Keep flashing the torch, right?'

Anna heard the car engines start up and saw the headlights following on a parallel track. The dog was still pulling, field after field. Twenty minutes passed, thirty, as the sky gradually lightened. Suddenly the handler pulled the dog back and stopped.

'I know where he could have gone,' he said. 'There's a way across the firth, starts out there, north of Burgh. People have used it for years, centuries. They call it the Sulewath.'

'The what?'

'It's the name of the crossing. Probably the old name for the Solway.'

'How far from here?'

'Maybe five miles, east and north. There's a monument by the shore, the crossing starts near there.'

Anna relayed the information over the radio, and heard the flood of cursing that greeted it. 'Across the Solway? He'll kill himself.'

'Maybe that's what he wants,' said Anna. 'Blaze of glory and all that.'

More cursing.

The handler interrupted. 'If that's the way he's gone, he's well ahead of us. Low tide was two hours ago. If he's not across by now, he'll drown out there.'

They stood, waiting, as the light grew. Anna realised how little she knew about the man they were following. Who was he? Where was he?

On the far side of the firth, Alex Wetherall looked to the west and the line of lights winking along the shore. He'd hoped to hear the crack of his booby traps as they went off but by that time he was well away. He'd already found and taken the first car, left unlocked by a careless rural driver living on the edge of nowhere. The fuel gauge had soon registered empty, though, and it was the second car he sat in now, easing his hunger with a stash of chocolate, watching the dawn. The discarded waders and wetsuit were buried in a deep hole by the shore, where a rising wind was shredding the waves of the incoming tide.

He was alive, in another country, with money in his bag and ready for anything. For a few moments out there in the mud and the darkness he'd thought he might never see the sun again. But he had unfinished business to settle.

Chapter 15

After Maureen had left the guesthouse in Carlisle, Rose was inconsolable. Her mother had insisted that she take some of her pills and went to rest for a while and now Rose woke not knowing whether it was day or night. For a few minutes the desperate dream she'd been having froze in her mind. She was in a crowded street. Hundreds of people were walking the other way and she had to push against them. Helen was somewhere ahead but Rose couldn't see her. She called out, but the people took no notice and pushed her backwards, pulling at her clothes.

She woke, sweating and terrified. All the bedclothes were on the floor and suddenly she was very cold. She realised that someone was knocking on the door. It was her mother. 'Aidan rang,' said Jo, 'looking for you. He wants to speak to you, pet, says it's very urgent.' A few minutes later Rose was standing in Jo's tiny office, making the call. It was answered almost immediately and Rose recognised her elder son's voice. 'Aidan, it's Mum.'

She heard him sob as he answered. 'You've got to come home,' he said. 'Dad's going mental. I can't handle him and Brian.'

'Has something happened?

'One of the cows,' said Aidan. 'Drooling, sores on her mouth. Dad found her this morning, after the sheep went.' Rose closed her eyes at the memory. 'He says this is it. He's called the vet in again.'

'Which vet?'

'Any vet. They just send someone. Should be here soon. You've got to come back.'

'I will,' she said. 'Is Brian all right?'

'He knows there's something up. He's been hiding in that cupboard, where we found him… you know.'

Rose closed her eyes against the memory of Brian's lamb being pulled from his sobbing grasp.

'I'm coming, Aidan. As soon as I can.'

'When?' Her normally taciturn son sounded desperate.

'Now. I'll be there as fast as I can. Mum will bring me. Tell Dad and Brian. I'll see you all soon.'

In the car Jo drove in silence for a while, glancing occasionally at her daughter, who slumped in her seat, eyes closed. Whatever pills the doctor had prescribed, Jo thought, they're just making things worse.

'You all right, pet?' she asked after a while. Rose needed to wake up, face up to what was happening, for the children's sake. Jo pulled up at the farm gate. 'I won't come in,' she said. 'Eric doesn't want people coming on the farm, does he?'

Rose rubbed her hands over her face and breathed deeply, trying to rouse herself. 'It may not matter any more,' she said. 'If the cows go, then we won't have any animals left to worry about, will we?'

'That might not happen,' said Jo. 'Try not to be too down. The boys need you to be strong, and Eric too.'

Rose shook her head. 'We need Helen home.'

'Well, that's not in your power, is it?' said her mother. 'The police will do their jobs, and you have to do yours.'

'A job, is it?'

'Yes,' said Jo, firmly. 'You can do it, Rose. I know you can.'

Rose heaved herself wearily out of the car. 'Thanks,' she said.

'Call me,' said her mother, 'as soon as you know anything. Promise?'

Rose nodded and turned to walk across the disinfectant pad and down the lane towards the place she couldn't wait to get away from. She found her wellington boots under a bucket where she guessed Aidan would have left them for her. A small figure emerged from the house and stood quite still for a moment before it ran towards her. Brian was encased in overalls, hat and boots, and dashed with his arms outstretched towards his mother, shouting, 'Mam, Mam!' Tears arrived too, as she bent to scoop her boy into her arms.

In the kitchen of the farmhouse Aidan was standing leaning over the Aga. Rose put Brian down and he stood beside her, clinging to her legs. Her eldest child turned around. He'd been crying too and looked exhausted, more like his father than Rose had ever noticed before. He came towards Rose and hugged her for the first time in months.

'The vet's here,' he said. 'Looks bad. Dad's with him. He's in a terrible state, Mam.' He lowered his voice. 'Drinking, hard.' He pulled his brother's hat off and ruffled his matted hair. 'Brian and I did some cooking, didn't we, eh?' He sniffed and wiped his nose on his sleeve. 'But it's no good without you here, Mam. We need you.'

'I'm here now,' she said, looking round. Dirty dishes were piled in the sink and the floor was sticky.

'Where's Helen?' Aidan asked. 'Have they found her?'

Rose shook her head. She looked down at Brian. 'I'll tell you later,' she said. Aidan understood. 'Go and get those drawings you did yesterday,' he said to Brian, 'to show Mum.' The little boy scampered off. Aidan sat down at the table next to his mother. 'I had to hide the shotgun,' he said, keeping his voice low. 'One of Dad's mates, Keswick way, did himself in over the weekend and I thought… well, I've hidden it.' He moved his chair sideways, closer to his mother. 'You won't leave us, will you? Please, Mam. He'll go under if you do.'

Neither of them ventured out into the yard, waiting in the kitchen while the vet did his checks. It wasn't long before the back door opened and a young man came in and asked to use the phone. Aidan disappeared outside and Rose took Brian upstairs out of the way. She heard the vet on the phone. His accent was quite noticeable, one of the overseas vets who had been drafted in to help out in the emergency. Suddenly the fog in Rose's head cleared a little and she thought of something she could do. She waited until the vet was finished, then she picked up the phone.

'Mr Vincent's line,' said a woman's voice, crisp and efficient.

'Can I speak to him?' asked Rose.

'No, 'fraid not. He's in a meeting. Might I ask where you got this number?'

Rose would not be fobbed off. 'Steve's our regular vet. He gave us it when the outbreak started – said to call him if it was urgent. It's urgent. Can you give him a message, to call Brinfell Farm? This is Rose Heslop speaking. I have to reach him.'

The woman reluctantly agreed, but gave no guarantee about how long it would take.

Eric Heslop looked to have aged ten years when he came back to the house and Rose couldn't find the words to say to him. Instead she held out her arms and he stood dumbly in front of her, arms rigid by his sides. He looked and smelled unwashed, like a tramp.

'That's it,' he said in a dull voice. 'Vet's called in the bolt-gun gang. Nothing we can do but wait.'

'Where is he now?'

'Checking the barns, thinking about how they'll do it. Aidan's with him.' Eric stared at her. His eyes were red-rimmed and dull. 'Vet's just a kid... called Matias he says. French or summat? Don't seem to know much about Foot and Mouth.'

'That's Spanish, I think,' said Rose. 'I've called Steve Vincent. We need a second opinion.'

Her husband sat down heavily as if his legs had just given way and rubbed his face with a dirty hand. 'We're finished, love,' he said. 'If not this time, then very soon. It's going on and on... Nowt we can do to escape it.' He looked up at her. 'What about Helen?'

Rose shook her head. 'The police still don't know whether she's with the man who took her. They found the van, but there was no one in it.'

'So where is she? Are they out looking for her?'

'Of course. They think she might have got away, on her own. I'm sure they'll find her soon.'

Rose was far from sure about anything, but she didn't know how much more Eric could cope with. He looked defeated. She felt desperately sorry for him, but detached, as if he were a stranger or someone she'd read about in the paper. Just another wretched farmer whose life had collapsed.

Aidan came in. 'Vet says the slaughtermen are backed up, it'll be tomorrow before they come. Soon as it gets light.'

Eric stood up slowly and stretched his back. 'Cows still need milking. You stay here, lad, talk to your mam. I'll do it.' He walked slowly back into the yard.

'Go and get a proper wash, Aidan,' said Rose. 'Then I'll get Brian in the bath. You both look like refugees. I'll make us a decent meal.'

He looked at his mother for a moment, as if he wanted to say something, but then he turned and trudged off upstairs. Rose looked at the drawings Brian had wanted to show her. In the centre of the page was a red and orange mound. Black smoke rose from it, and the legs and heads of cows and sheep were carefully pencilled in at the edges of the flames.

While Brian was splashing in the bath, Rose went quietly downstairs. She could see that Aidan was asleep in the big chair in his dressing gown. The regular thump of the milking machines was still going, so Eric would be in the parlour. She went back upstairs to her bedroom and shut the door. The place was a tip and she pulled the bed straight before going to the chest of drawers to find what she'd come back for. She couldn't recall which of the two small drawers at the top she'd put the phone in, so when the first one proved fruitless she didn't worry unduly. The second drawer was where she kept her knickers and she rooted through it, feeling for the familiar hard oblong. But she didn't find it. She took everything out of the drawer. Nothing. Then all the other drawers, with the same result. Nothing. No phone.

Rose sat on the bed, her heart thumping, feeling sick. The phone Alex had given her was her only link to him. For months she'd looked after it, charging it secretly at work, keeping it on silent, checking it as soon as she left the farm and could get a signal. Once she'd found a spot behind the barn on the far side of the yard where there was just enough signal to make a call, and she'd tried. That was when she'd lost the earring the police had found. Nothing more had been said about it. Had they forgotten, or was it one more thing that the Pritchard woman would throw at her? And now the phone was missing and Rose's stomach heaved at the thought of what that might mean.

Brian was more than usually clingy. Dealing with him and making their meal occupied her time and her mind. When Eric and Aidan went out to start organising things for what was to come, Rose set about clearing up the house. She baked and read to Brian, longing for the phone to ring. But it stayed silent.

Rose was clearing up their evening meal when she heard the noise outside and glanced at Eric, who was on to his third beer of the night and seemed not to notice.

'Was that the quad bike?' she asked.

He nodded. 'It's Aidan. Can't blame the lad for not wanting to stop here.'

'Where's he going?'

Eric shrugged. 'He wouldn't tell me. Just said he wanted to see his mates.' Eric stared into his glass. 'I've smelled beer and fags on 'im before. But I can't tell him off about that, can I?'

Rose was about to protest, but there was nothing she could say. She'd walked away when the sheep were taken, and would have preferred never to come back.

It was a couple of hours later, after she'd managed to get Eric upstairs to bed rather than letting him slump in the chair, that Rose heard the purr of the quad bike and the double thump as Aidan's boots hit the porch floor. He'd clearly been drinking. Rose had never seen her son drunk before and guilt hit her hard. The boy stood just inside the door, swaying slightly. He unzipped his jacket and threw it into the corner. Rose went to pick it up.

'Leave it,' he growled at her.

'Where have you been?' she began. 'You know you shouldn't take the quad on the road.'

He laughed. 'There's no one around to see. Us lads can get together, have a drink and a ciggie, a few laughs. Not much to stay here for, is there? And by tomorrow there'll be nothing left.'

She looked at him. He seemed taller and older than the last time she'd really noticed him. She didn't like what she saw.

'You shouldn't be drinking,' she said. 'Not at your age.'

'Think I'll end up like me dad, do you?' He took a step towards her and held on to the rail of the Aga to steady himself. 'Fat lot you'd care about that.'

Rose frowned. He'd never been rude to her, not like this. Before she could respond, he looked hard at her. 'Lost summat, have you?'

Suddenly she knew. He'd found her phone. There were messages on it she hadn't known how to erase. She had to lie. 'Not as far as I know,' she said. 'Why?'

He pushed his hand into the pocket of his jeans and pulled out a small black phone. 'This yours?' he said, holding it up. 'It was in your drawer, upstairs. Brian was looking for summat the other day, and he found it, brought it to me. He wanted to use it. I told him it didn't work and I'd throw it away.' He dangled it in front of her. 'But I didn't, did I?'

She stared at him.

'How do you know it's mine?' she said defiantly. 'Could be your dad's.'

He shook his head. 'No chance. We had a look at it tonight, me and the lads. Did no one ever teach you about passwords, Mam?'

Rose felt for a chair and sat down. Aidan stayed on his feet, brandishing the phone, looking down at his mother. 'All sorts on here,' he said, swaying slightly.

'You have to give it back to me,' she whispered. 'It's private.'

'So it bloody should be,' he hissed at her.

Rose found a hankie and dabbed at her nose. 'You seemed so pleased to see me,' she said. 'And now you're… you're horrid.'

'Horrid?' he mocked. 'How do you think it feels, watching your mates leering at stuff on your mam's phone? I was shamed. And who's this "John" anyway? Where d'you know him from?'

Thank God we decided to change names, she thought.

It was time for her to push back. 'You wouldn't understand,' she said. 'Your father and me… it's been bad for years, not just since all this happened. I've been very lonely.'

'And now you've found a friend,' he mocked. 'How sweet.'

Rose still couldn't quite believe they were talking like this. Aidan was just a boy. He had no right to judge her, but he was, and she didn't know what he would do next. She couldn't wrestle the phone off him. She was at the mercy of her own son, her drunk son.

'What are you going to do with it?' she said.

'I'm going to keep it,' he said. 'Otherwise you'll go away again, and if you do…' He gestured towards the ceiling. 'That man upstairs, your husband, he *needs* you. When you went away he just folded up, and if the herd goes tomorrow, that's it for him. I've hidden the shotgun but there are other ways.'

Aidan put the phone back into his pocket. 'You have to stay here, Mam,' he said, more calmly than before. 'Whoever this John bloke is, tell him it's off. You're staying here, with us.' He walked unsteadily towards the stairs. 'I'm going to bed. Tomorrow is going to be shitty.'

He turned back at the bottom of the stairs. 'And don't bother trying to find it,' he said, holding up the phone. 'This stays on me, insurance.'

Rose sat at the big kitchen table and leaned forward to rest her forehead on its solid surface. She was still sitting there, her mind a blur of misery and fears, when the phone rang and jolted her to her feet. It was almost midnight.

'Is that you, Rose?' Steve Vincent asked. 'The office sent your message and I've just picked it up. Only got home ten minutes ago. What's up?'

Rose could have cried with relief. At last, someone she could rely on when everything else seemed to be crumbling.

'One of the cows is drooling… mouth sores. Eric called the vet in, and he's condemned the herd.'

'Who? When?'

'Spanish bloke. Matias something. You'll probably know him.'

There was a long pause. 'Yes, I do.' Another pause. 'Has he called it in?'

'Yes, the crew are coming in the morning, early.'

'Shit! Sorry.' She could hear the exhaustion in his voice. 'Look, Rose, I have to get some sleep. But I'll be with you first thing. I'll tell the office I've been called in for a second opinion. That's what you want, right?'

'I do,' said Rose, 'though Eric seems to have given up. He needs to talk to someone, Steve, that's why I thought of you.'

'How bad is Eric?'

'Hard to tell, I've only just got home from Carlisle… I expect you know about Helen?'

He murmured his commiserations and asked if there was any news.

'There's a full search continuing tomorrow – army are helping. For now, it's Eric we have to think of. Aidan says he's hidden the shotgun.'

'Christ,' said Steve. 'OK, Rose, I'll be there. Try to get some sleep, 'bye.'

Rose couldn't bear climbing into bed with Eric and lay down with Brian instead, but after a few minutes she got up again carefully, to avoid waking the boy. She stretched out under a blanket on the sofa in the sitting room and let the cold air and more of her pills numb her mind until sleep came. She thought of Helen. Why was there no word?

During the night, the wind buffeted the old garden shed that stood behind the petrol station outside Govenbry. It screamed through the gap by the window above Helen's head as she lay on her bed of old sacks and the tarpaulin from the barn. She was cold, and even the chocolate hadn't sated the hunger that now cramped her stomach. She pulled up her knees to ease the pain. She had no idea what time it was. She was falling back to sleep when her heart leaped in shock at the sound of a dog, barking very close to her head. She cowered away and the dog barked even more fiercely, scrabbling at the bottom of the door. Helen sat upright, terrified, her back against the side wall of the shed, as the door rattled in its frame.

She didn't hear the angry shout of the dog's owner but saw the flash of a torch. The barking reached a crescendo and then suddenly it was gone. Helen waited, her heart thumping, and felt her chest begin to tighten. She pulled in her breath, dirt and dust from the shed invading her nose and mouth. She found her bag and felt in it for the inhaler. It would make her sick but she didn't want to die, not here.

The medication sprayed into the back of her mouth and down her throat, forcing its way through tight bronchial tubes and into her lungs. She drew it in, gulped and pulled again. A moment later her empty stomach heaved and the remains of the chocolate bar slipped from her mouth and out onto the concrete floor of the shed. And a moment after that Helen slid to the floor herself, unconscious.

And there she stayed all the following day. She didn't see the police car that stopped at the petrol station early on Tuesday morning to ask about the CCTV near the pumps, which wasn't working. She didn't hear the conversation that revealed none of the staff had reported anything unusual during the previous day. The man who been on duty the previous evening was a grumpy sod, they were told. It was his day off and he didn't answer his phone. As the police car pulled away its occupants paid no attention to the little shed across the garden. Why would they?

Helen lay still until light from the window woke her. She could smell her own vomit and badly wanted the toilet. Almost by instinct she shuffled across the deserted garden, relieved herself, washed in the cold tap water and went back to the shed. The effort exhausted her. The smell of half-digested chocolate lingered in the small space. She would walk the rest of the way home, she told herself, but not yet. All she wanted to do now was lie down and sleep for a little longer. Her breathing was shallow, her body cold. She needed to wake soon, or she might never wake again.

Chapter 16

Rose woke early on Tuesday morning feeling cold and anxious, and pulled the blanket off the floor to wrap it round herself, hearing the splash of water into the kettle and the familiar sound as it was set on the Aga. She held the blanket round her as she shuffled into the kitchen like an old woman. Eric was standing by the stove, his head bowed.

'I couldn't sleep last night,' she said. 'Didn't want to wake you.'

Her husband said nothing, silently going through the motions of making tea.

'Steve Vincent rang late,' she said. 'He's coming this morning.'

Eric jerked his head. He'd heard her.

Rose went on. 'He'll check the herd again, before…'

'Before they shoot them all?' said Eric, bitterly. 'He's wasting his time.'

'Well, he's coming anyway. We should be grateful.' She watched her husband fumbling with the tea caddy. 'Leave that,' she said. 'I'm here now, I'll do it.'

He turned away and sat at the table, head in his hands.

'Don't you want him to help us?' Rose asked. She'd thought Eric would be pleased, or relieved, but he just shrugged. Headlights bounced through the window nearest the lane. Rose turned to go upstairs. 'Give them tea, whoever it is,' she said to her husband. 'I have to get dressed. Slow things down until Steve gets here.'

When Rose returned to the kitchen Matias was standing by the stove, sipping tea. He raised the mug to her. 'Getting used to this,' he said, smiling.

She looked around. 'Where's my husband?'

Matias pointed towards the back door. 'Out in the yard. Said he had to do something.'

Rose ran to the door and opened it. She could see the light in the cowshed. For a moment she held her breath before she saw Eric's dark shadow moving around and turned with relief back into the relative warmth of the kitchen.

'Steve Vincent is coming,' she said.

Matias raised his eyebrows. 'Who called him?'

'I did,' said Rose. 'He's been our vet for years and I wanted him to be here. He knows the herd.'

'You think I got it wrong?' asked the Spanish vet.

'No, I'm sure you did the proper checks,' she said. 'But...'

'You think I got it wrong,' he repeated. 'That's OK. If they were my cows, I'd do the same. I'm just surprised he's coming. I know how busy he is.'

'He's a friend,' said Rose.

Aidan came downstairs, drawn by voices and the prospect of tea. 'I was going to bring you some,' said his mother.

'I'm here now,' he said, rubbing red eyes. 'Morning,' he said to Matias, who raised his mug. 'Ready for the big day, are we?'

Rose interrupted before the boy's bitterness spilled over any further.

'Steve Vincent is coming.'

'Good for him,' Aidan replied. He picked up his tea and went back upstairs.

Rose smiled weakly. 'He's only young,' she said. 'And he cares about the farm. More than I do,' she added. 'Did you know we lost our sheep?'

Matias nodded. 'Many farmers let their sheep go to save the cows.'

'That was hard,' said Rose. 'And today will be hell for Aidan and my husband. The farm's their life.'

'I know.'

The phone rang. It was Steve, saying he would be late, stuck behind a quarry truck that had shed its load. 'If the gang comes, stall them,' he said. The line was crackling, some of the words indecipherable.

'What shall I say?' Rose asked.

'Think of...' was all she heard before the line went dead.

Rose turned to Matias. 'Steve's stuck. He says we have to stall them till he gets here.'

'How?' said Matias.

She shrugged and closed her eyes, thinking furiously about what to do. A few minutes later the knock on the back door was loud and insistent. They looked at each other before Matias stepped across to open up. A large man in a white suit stood there, like something out of a science-fiction film.

'My team's ready to go,' he said, looking at a clipboard in his gloved hand. 'Cows in the yard?'

Matias turned to Rose. 'My English not good,' he said, making his accent much thicker than normal. 'The farmer, he not good.'

'Tell me about it,' said the man. 'Better get the job done, right? No point hanging around. We've got four more on today.' He turned away.

'Wait!' Rose cried. 'My husband's out there. He's got a gun... says he'll shoot the first bastard who steps into his barn.'

The man turned back and rolled his eyes. 'Oh, Christ,' he said. 'One of those, that's all we need. He's breaking the law, love, does he know that? We can get the police in.'

'Police?' said Matias. 'Yes, police. This man, he crazy.'

'And who the hell are you?' said the man, venting his irritation on the foreigner.

'He's a new vet,' said Rose quickly. 'Learning the job. The real vet's on his way. We'll have to wait. We don't need the police, not yet.'

'Bloody madness,' grumbled the man. 'I'll have to make a call.'

He pulled the door shut with a bang.

Rose and Matias looked at each other. In an accent that was even more of a caricature than before, Matias said, 'This man, he crazy,' and the two of them laughed at the lunacy of it all. From upstairs Rose heard Brian's voice. 'Mam,' he was calling. 'Who's here?'

'I have to go to him,' she said.

Upstairs she said to Aidan, 'Go in the barn and find your dad. Tell him not to come out until we call you, OK?'

'What's going on?'

'Just do it,' said Rose. 'If any of the blokes try to talk to you, ignore them. I think they're still at the end of the lane. We have to stall till Steve Vincent gets here. Just do it, Aidan. Now!'

The standoff lasted no more than half an hour but it felt like half a day. The killing gang stood at the end of the lane, kitted up and stamping their feet against the cold while the leader tried unsuccessfully to get a signal good enough for his phone to work. Aidan and Eric stayed in the barn, Matias and Rose in the house, talking with Brian and keeping him well away from the window that overlooked the lane. The boy could sense the tension and clung to his mother, clutching his toy lamb under his arm.

They heard voices at the gate, then a car pulled into the yard and Steve pushed open the back door.

'Thank God,' said Rose.

'Where is he?' Steve asked. 'Eric… where is he?'

'In the barn, Aidan's with him. He's OK.'

'Bloke out there said he was threatening to shoot them,' Steve said.

Matias held up his hands. 'We made that up, just to keep them out till you got here.'

Steve shook his head. 'Was that the best you could think of?'

'Well, it worked, didn't it?' Rose intervened. 'I told them Matias was a trainee, and we had to wait for you.'

'Lies on lies,' sighed Steve. 'I'll have some explaining to do.' He turned to Matias. 'Show me the suspect cow, quick. I need to tell these blokes something before they complain even more.'

Matias went out with him. Dawn had broken and the sky was getting brighter every minute. Matias looked for the cow that he'd marked and separated from the others and ushered it out into the yard. There were no signs of lameness. As they watched, the cow began to walk towards the quad bike, sniffing round the exhaust. Then she licked the sides of the wheel rims, and kept licking.

'It's the salt,' said Steve. 'They've been salting the roads.'

He pulled the cow towards him and used gloved hands to open her mouth. 'Shine your torch in here, will you?' he said to Matias, who was standing close to watch his boss at work. They both peered into the cow's mouth. Steve stood back, wiping his hands on the overalls that he would bag up for burning when he left the farm. Then he walked across to the cowshed and called to Eric, who appeared. They shook hands.

'Who uses the quad?' Steve asked.

Eric looked puzzled. 'Me and Aidan,' he said.

'Do you take it on the road?'

Eric shook his head. 'Nay. Never go off the farm.'

'What about Aidan? Is he around?'

'I'm here,' said a voice from the dark end of the barn. 'Mam told the men Dad was going to shoot them. We've been keeping out of sight.'

'Lucky I haven't got the police with me,' said Steve. 'Look, I need to check something with you. You're not in trouble, you just need to tell me the truth.'

Aidan looked at the vet, embarrassed. It didn't help that he'd known him since childhood. Steve said gently, 'I need to know if you've taken the quad off the farm, on the road?'

Aidan said nothing for a few moments. 'What if I have?' he said eventually. 'I have to get out sometimes or I'd go mad.'

Eric shook his head.

'I understand that,' said Steve. 'I'd feel the same myself. I'm asking because they've been salting the roads and there's salt on the bike. The cow's been licking the hot exhaust for the salt and it's burned her mouth.'

Aidan looked at him. 'Is that what's the matter with her? Not…'

'Could be,' said Steve. 'I'll have to check her again. Ministry policy would be to shoot the lot right now as a precaution, but I can't bear to see another herd of cows killed that aren't sick. If I knew there was a chance that this one is OK it would make it easier to explain why I'm sending the killing gang away.' He hesitated. 'And you know what else matters here.'

Aidan looked down at his feet. Eric put a hand on his shoulder.

Steve went on, 'Going off the farm puts the herd at risk. I know you're careful but there's always a chance of bringing it back on a vehicle. You've seen those damn' trucks carrying carcasses down the roads, leaking filthy fluids. That's what spreads this bloody thing around.'

The boy looked up, close to tears. 'And the ash from the fires,' he said bitterly, 'and rats and foxes, and people like you coming and going. If our herd goes you can't blame it on me.'

Steve kept his voice low. 'I wouldn't do that. And I'll keep all this to myself. You will too, right?'

Aidan nodded. 'Going back to bed,' he muttered, and turned away before swiping his sleeve across his eyes.

'Tell your mam we might need more tea,' called Steve. 'This'll take a while.' To Matias he said, 'I have to check the whole herd. Stay here for now. I'll tell the gang it looks like a false positive and they'll have to come back later, if we need them. Right?'

When Steve got back to the shed, Eric was standing out of sight, cigarette in hand. A lit cigarettes in a barn was a bad idea, but this was not the time for a lecture about fire safety. 'Come with me,' said Steve. 'I reckon we know why that cow is drooling, but now I need to check all the others. OK?'

One by one, he began to check the cows. For a while Eric stood by the door, watching. There was no sound save for the chewing and shuffling of the animals and Steve's soft murmuring as he spoke to them. Suddenly the vet was aware of Eric standing behind him, leaning in close. 'Find it,' the farmer whispered. Steve didn't turn round. 'Find it,' said Eric again. 'We need the money. I can't go on with this. The compo… We could start again. Anywhere, away from this damned place.'

Steve stood still. He was shocked but he understood. Many of the farmers he saw would do anything to save their animals, but some of them were close to breaking point. And some of them were already dead, hanged in the barn that had once sheltered their beasts, or despatched with their own gun.

'Go inside, Eric,' said the vet, without turning his head. 'I won't be long.'

Behind him he heard the wretched man turn and shuffle away towards the farmhouse.

Rose watched her husband cross the yard. She'd been back at the farm a matter of hours, but knew already that she couldn't stay. Alex was still out there, but after what had happened to Helen she couldn't trust him any more, and without the phone she was powerless. She could leave, but where would she go? Then there was Eric. She could see now why Aidan was worried. What if he told his dad about the phone and what he'd seen on it? What then?

Eric slumped into a chair at the table, and Rose tried to smile as she turned to him.

'What does Steve say?'

Eric didn't look up. 'I don't care any more,' he said.

It was another hour before Steve Vincent came in. He scrubbed his hands at the kitchen sink. Eric said nothing, but Rose watched the vet carefully when he spoke to them. 'I think the herd's clear,' he said, 'but after that first report, I'll have to send samples for testing. It'll take a day or two, they're backed up at the labs.'

'We just have to wait?' said Rose.

He nodded. 'Sorry. I've sent the killing team away for now. They grumbled, but so what? Plenty more work for them to do today.'

He looked at Eric, still slumped in his chair. 'I've asked the lab to ring me, not here. Hope that's OK?' He caught Rose's eye and jerked his head towards Eric. 'We'll have to look out for each other for the next day or two,' he said. 'Where's Aidan?'

'Upstairs,' said Rose. 'He's doing a lot of the work now, learning fast. Staying off school was good for him, in a way. He was constantly in trouble when he was there.'

'Any news of Helen?'

Rose shook her head. 'I'm sure they'll find her soon. There are notices in all the papers, and on the radio. A child can't just disappear.'

Steve put his hand on her shoulder. 'Can't imagine what all this is doing to you,' he said. 'How do you stay so strong?'

Rose said nothing. A wave of guilt flooded her.

'We all need strength,' he said, turning away. 'This could go on for weeks, months even. I'm exhausted.'

'We all are,' Rose agreed.

Eric made a strange sound, got up and went out of the room.

'Keep an eye on him,' said Steve. 'Try and get him to talk, to some of his farmer friends if he won't talk to you.'

'They're all as bad as each other,' said Rose. 'They think talking's for the women.'

'And that's why the women are coping better,' said the vet, picking up his coat.

Chapter 17

In Carlisle, at about the same time on that Tuesday morning, Margaret Wetherall woke to find her son standing by her bed. She could smell his muddy clothes and hair, tobacco and the sweet tang of cannabis. She recognised the state he was in and shrank back into her bed.

'What do you want?' she said.

'I want food and a bath, and some clean clothes,' he began. 'And I want no one to know that I'm here, no one to know anything about me. You clear about that?'

She nodded. 'Maybe someone saw you come in.'

'Think I'm stupid? No one saw me. Come on, get up. I haven't got all day.'

'Where have you been?'

'None of your business,' he hissed at her. 'Just do it. Hurry up!'

Alex went back downstairs, making sure that all the curtains were drawn tight. His mother followed him. She could see he was in no mood to be challenged, by her or anyone. She'd seen him like this before and didn't want him around. With any luck he would take what he'd come for and go. The police were looking for him. Surely they'd be checking this house. They could be out there now, watching.

Margaret began to gather food from the larder to make him something. He might be easier to handle when he wasn't hungry. 'The police were here,' she said.

He took a slice of bread from the packet and stuffed it into his mouth. 'When?'

'Sunday. They know it was you who took the girl.'

Alex laughed, but without humour. 'They've known that since the start.'

'But they might come back.'

'Really? And if they do, you'll tell them I'm not here, I haven't been here, and you don't know where I am. Won't you, Mother dear?'

She hated his sarcasm and said no more.

He ate everything she put in front of him, and then demanded more. Filthy clothes piled up in front of the washing machine after he'd had a bath and changed into some of the fresh clothes she still kept upstairs. He'd shaved off his beard, cut his hair and was wearing a pair of glasses that she hadn't seen for years. He looked different, which was probably the idea.

'What are you going to do?' she asked.

'Have a kip,' was his only reply.

'I might have to go out. There's no food left.'

'Fine. Everything normal,' he said. 'And if you say a word to anyone, I'll kill you, even if I have to wait. You know that, don't you?'

She nodded.

When Margaret left the house a little while later she checked up and down the street, but there was nothing out of the ordinary. No strange cars or people loitering, trying to look inconspicuous. But as she turned the corner on her way back from the shops she saw the car parked outside the house and stopped. She couldn't see inside but she knew it was them.

They were looking for him, of course they would come here. She kept walking, and as she reached her house the car door opened beside her and the Pritchard woman got out. Margaret hesitated. If Alex was upstairs in his old room at the front he might hear whatever was said. Or maybe he was watching, though that would have been more risky.

The woman smiled and held out her ID card, even though Margaret knew full well who she was.

'DC Pritchard,' she said, smiling.

'I know who you are,' said Margaret. She was keeping her voice low and prayed that Pritchard would do the same. 'Who's that in the car with you?' she asked, peering in through the window.

'My sergeant,' said the policewoman. 'You've met her, I think.'

'What do you want?'

'I think you know why we're here, Margaret.'

'Alex,' she said. There was no point in playing games. If they were going to search the house they would have brought more people.

'Have you seen him recently? Heard from him?'

'What's he done now?'

'Oh, Margaret, you can do better than that,' said Pritchard. 'He abducted a young girl and held her against her will. She was lucky to escape.'

Margaret put down her shopping on the doorstep and stood with her back to the door. 'But you didn't get him, did you, or you wouldn't be here?' The bold words came easily, drawn from a deep well of defiance. She spoke them loudly, hoping he would hear.

The policewoman stared back at her. On the far side of the car the other woman got out and stood looking at them.

Margaret made a decision. She nodded her head slightly, once, then again. She put a finger to her mouth and frowned.

The younger policewoman, the sergeant, seemed to understand. 'So you've not seen him then?' she said, more loudly than was necessary.

'Not for a while,' said Margaret.

'We need to find him, and you'll be in trouble if you don't help us. You know that, don't you? Accessory to a crime, Margaret, it's a serious matter.'

'You can't bully me,' she said. 'And you're not getting in without a warrant,' she shouted. The neighbour's front door opened and a woman's head peered out. 'And you can mind your own sodding business and all!' The head withdrew.

The two policewomen looked at each other briefly, got back in the car and drove away.

Margaret picked up the bag of shopping and unlocked the door. He was standing in the dark hallway and grabbed her by the neck as she stepped forward. The shopping scattered across the floor.

'What did you say to them?' His voice was hard.

'Nowt,' she tried to say, but the word dried in her throat as he held her coat collar in a tight grip.

'I saw you, you were talking to them.'

She wriggled free. 'But they've gone, and you should too,' she said. 'You can't stay here. They'll be back.'

'That money,' he said. 'Is it still in the house?'

'You said I couldn't put it in the bank,' she said. 'It's in the spare room.'

'It's mine,' he said. 'I'm taking it.'

'But what about me?'

'Too bad. I'm taking it.'

He began to walk away and she stooped to pick up the shopping from the floor. Suddenly he rounded on her.

'You told them something,' he shouted. 'I know you did.'

'No!' she cried. 'I said nowt.' She flinched away from him.

He snatched a tin of soup from her hand and hit her with it, hard, across the side of the head. She fell back against the door, then slid to the floor. He stood in the narrow hallway, blocking her way, staring down at her.

'How come you're so pally with that older one? How come she calls you "Margaret" like you're old mates?'

She sat on the floor, feeling the side of her head where the blood was warm on her fingers.

'I know 'er dad,' she said. 'Everybody knows him. She used to work with him, at the hairdresser's. Lives Workington way.'

'A cop who's a hairdresser?' he said. 'That's rich.'

'Anyway, it wasn't her,' said Margaret, thoughtlessly.

'Wasn't her what?' Alex said. Margaret knew she'd made a mistake, but it was too late. 'She wasn't the one who asked where you were. It was the other one, the one who was in the army.'

'What are you on about?' He kicked at her legs and she slumped back against the door. 'Hurry up.'

Margaret was properly afraid now, hurting, babbling. 'She went on and on about where you might be. Threatened me. Said she'd take me in… I had to tell her something, so I just said you used to go fishing.'

'Did you tell them where?'

'No,' she lied again.

'Army, eh? Probably a Red Cap bastard. Another bloody woman. What's 'er name?'

'Penrose… DS Penrose.' Margaret hesitated. While she was talking he didn't hit her, so she kept on. 'She told me where she lives, up Whinlatter.'

'Whinlatter? She's lying. There's nowt up there except trees.'

'Well, that's what she said. A cottage behind some big place, she told me.'

Margaret looked up at her son, trying to work out whether he'd calmed down. She wanted to get up off the cold floor, but she was afraid he would kick off again. He was standing quite still, holding the tin of soup in his hand. How did this happen, she wondered. His dad had had a temper, but nothing like this. Alex stared down at her again, as if looking at a dog that wanted to go out.

'That sergeant… Penrose,' he said. 'Is she on her own?'

Margaret didn't know, but was afraid to say so. 'Yes,' she said. She held her breath, thinking he was going to hit her again. Without a word he turned away and she began to struggle to her feet.

Suddenly, Alex twisted round and kicked her. She felt his boot hit her stomach. As her knees buckled there was another blow to her head.

'That's for never coming to see me,' he said.

Beyond the rushing in her ears Margaret heard the steady thump of her son's boots going back up the stairs, and then everything went dark.

'Are you sure?' DI Bell asked. He was thinking about the manpower he would need to take down an armed and desperate man in the middle of the city. They already had another big search on their hands, but that had proved fruitless so far. There were notices in all the local newspapers and on Radio Cumbria, even Border TV, but the girl seemed to have disappeared without trace. Bell was already under pressure from his superiors. And now this.

'He's there,' Maureen insisted. 'Margaret was trying to warn us without him hearing, I'd swear to it. We know he threatens her, has done for years.'

Bob Carruthers stood up at his desk in the corner, waving a piece of paper. 'Got his record from Durham jail,' he said. 'They thought he was dangerous: mood swings, bursts of temper. But the psychs wouldn't swear to it so they couldn't hold him.' He glanced again at the paper. 'I got his visitor record too. No visits from his mam the whole time he was inside.'

'What about the army?' said Dinger. 'What did they say?'

'Much the same,' said Bob, shuffling papers on his desk. 'Temper. Paranoid. Obsessive.'

Anna said, 'Sounds like he's been obsessed with Rose Heslop for years.'

'She's used him,' said Maureen.

Anna pushed herself away from the wall where she'd been leaning. 'Well, Rose must be desperate too, in that case, to pin her hopes on a loser like Alex Wetherall. Why would she? Doesn't make sense.'

Maureen threw up her hands. 'Sense doesn't come into it, Sarge. Rose is desperate to get off the farm, away from that dismal husband of hers. Wetherall's got money, and she can get what she wants out of him. Women go for that when they have to.'

Anna raised her voice. 'We're too weak to help ourselves, is that what you're saying?'

Bell held up his hands. 'Girls, girls. We're talking real people here, not feminist theories. Fact is we're still guessing about Rose, and now we've got this lunatic with a gun and a temper, basically holding his mother hostage in her own home. That's what you think, right?'

'Right,' both women said simultaneously.

Bell went on, talking slowly, to impose his authority. 'We can't take both of them down at once. Rose is at the farm, and won't be going anywhere unless Alex is there to help, according to what we're thinking now. We're sure she has a phone but so far we haven't found it.'

'And there's no signal at the farm anyway,' said Anna.

Maureen turned to face her. 'But maybe there is behind that barn, where we found the earring.'

'Enough!' Bell shouted. Carruthers ducked down out of sight. 'Priorities,' Bell went on. 'Rose can wait. Wetherall and his mam can't. Penrose, tell Carlisle we need back-up from them, and a squad to storm the house. Might be a bit OTT but we have to risk it. We've lost him once, don't want to lose him again.'

An hour later, men were posted at both ends of the alley behind Margaret Wetherall's house while Bell and Penrose, wearing Kevlar vests, stood behind the heavily protected team who were preparing to storm in. Maureen waited with another group of uniformed men a little further down the street.

'Going in,' Anna whispered into her phone.

'Police!' Bell shouted. 'The house is surrounded, Alex. We're armed. Put down the weapon and open the door.'

There was no response. Bell raised his hand to get the door rammed, but Anna raised hers too. 'Wait!' she cried. 'Listen.'

All of them stopped and listened. 'Hear it?' said Anna. Bell shook his head. 'Someone moaning, just behind the door.'

'Go for the lock,' he said to the man with the sledgehammer. 'Keep it high. Careful now.'

One hefty blow caved in the lock and the officer put his hand through to undo the door from the inside. He pushed, but the door stuck. He pushed again, to no avail.

'Any movement at the back?' Bell said to Anna. She spoke into her phone, then shook her head.

'We could ram this door, or the window,' the man with the sledgehammer said.

Bell made a decision. 'Round the back,' he said. 'Ram the back door instead. We need to get in fast, window might be too slow.'

The officers ran down the alley, with Bell in pursuit. Anna stepped up to the door. 'Margaret?' she said, putting her ear to the letterbox. A muffled groan came back.

'It's her,' Anna called to Maureen, who was waiting by the car a few yards down the street. 'She must be hurt. Call an ambulance *now*.'

She turned back to the door. 'We can help you, Margaret. We'll be there soon. Hang on.'

There were shouts and crashing noises from inside the house and the front door was pulled inwards a few inches. A man's head appeared in the space. 'Woman here, Sarge, jammed against the door. Don't want to move her.'

'Any sign of him?' Anna asked.

'Gone,' said the officer. 'House is empty.'

'Damn!'

At the end of the street Maureen directed the ambulance towards the house, having guided it through the cordon that she'd organised to keep out traffic during the raid. 'The lady's stuck behind the front door,' said Anna. 'We don't want to move her to get it open, so you'd best go in the back, just down the alley and round to the right.'

The paramedics picked up their gear and set off. Shortly there were voices on the other side of the door, and a few minutes later the paramedics appeared again, this time carrying a stretcher between them. Maureen said, 'Can I go with her, Sarge? She might have an idea where he's gone this time.'

Anna nodded. 'He's making fools of us, that's for sure. We need to find that gun.'

The ambulance drove off, siren wailing, and Anna and DI Bell organised a meticulous search of the house for any clues about Alex's plans or possible next steps. Anna checked the calls made from the landline, just in case he'd used it. The last call was to a mobile number. Who would Margaret know who had a mobile phone? Anna tried the number, but there was no response. It was either turned off or on silent. Maybe Maureen was right about Rose having a phone, although she could have ditched it by now. She must know that she was under suspicion, and a mobile could be damning if anyone found it.

They'd lost him again. They were being humiliated by Alex Wetherall and Anna was furious. Later, looking back, she wished she'd saved her energy for what was to come.

Chapter 18

Anna found Bell in Margaret's kitchen, helping himself to a biscuit out of a tin. Strictly against the rules, but he was past caring.

'This business'll be the death of me,' he grumbled. 'The bastard's making us look complete idiots and I'm fed up of reporting to the Super that we're no nearer finding him. No clues, he could be anywhere.'

'Maybe Margaret will know something when she comes round,' Anna suggested, although she knew it was unlikely. Anyone who could attack his own mother so viciously was unlikely to have confided his plans to her.

'Paramedics weren't sure she'd pull through,' said Bell. 'She's not well to start with and a few kicks in the stomach won't help.'

'He seems to be getting worse,' said Anna. 'It could be PTSD, untreated and going downhill fast now.'

'You sound like a defence lawyer, Penrose,' said Dinger. 'OK, he was in the army and could have had a bad time, but that's no excuse for kicking the shit out of his own mam.'

'I'm not making excuses for him,' said Anna, 'but the violence seems to be escalating. Mrs Wetherall said he could have funny turns, but nothing as bad as this. Something must have set him off.'

'And now he's out there again,' said Bell. 'I've got Bob checking reports of stolen vehicles.' He pulled the phone from his pocket and hit the speed dial.

'Anything?' he said, and listened for a while. 'OK, Bob, put out an alert for the car and the pushbike. He wouldn't get far on a bike, but probably thinks we'd never check those. We're coming back when we've finished here. Pass that car registration on to the army guys, OK?'

Anna passed on the information about the last call on Margaret's phone. 'If it is Rose's number, he must assume she's still wanting to talk to him.'

'He's daft enough not to get the message if she's dumped him,' said Bell. 'Has she ever admitted to being in touch with him?'

Anna shook her head. 'Not so far as I know. She's clever enough to know how to stick to a story.'

'So you buy Pritchard's theory about them being in this together?'

'Maybe, but it's all conjecture. Without the phone, we've got nothing.'

Bell took another biscuit. 'No point in hanging around here. He could be anywhere again. Tognarelli's taking over the search for Helen. Looks like it's perked him up. He was a good copper in his day. I'd better go and check on developments. When I called him earlier on, he said there'd been a few calls after the report on Radio Cumbria. Half of them will be dead ends, but you never know. She can't have got far.'

They looked at each other, both thinking the worst. 'There's some sick sods out there, I know,' said Bell. 'Someone else could've picked 'er up.'

'What I can't work out is why she didn't just head for the nearest people, tell them who she is and ask them to get help.' Anna thought for a few moments. 'Unless...' she began.

'Unless what?'

'Unless the asthma kicked in, and the wrong inhaler. That could put her out cold for a while. Or worse.'

'Can't do much about that,' said Bell, 'but I'll mention it to Tognarelli.' He hesitated. 'Just remember who your boss is, right? It's not him, it's me.'

Anna didn't respond. Whatever she said, Bell would hold it against her. She changed the subject. 'By the way, I did a quick check on Barry Blake, Rose's boss, the man who brought her down to Workington. Clean as a whistle.'

'Still doesn't stop Rose pulling him into something though, does it? What do these blokes see in her? Can't make it out meself.'

Anna smiled. She could see it. Rose had perfected the art of making certain men think she needed them. And they fell for it every time.

Once Bell had gone, Anna tried to make some sensible decisions about how to make best use of the rest of the day. They were still waiting for Wetherall to make a mistake, to be sighted, for some clue as to his whereabouts, without which the search area was just too wide. All they could do was wait, and she hated waiting. If the man was as mad as he seemed to be, the farm was the most obvious place for him to go, having presumably failed to contact Rose in any other way. And that was assuming the theory about him and Rose was correct. It was slender, but it was the only lead they had so far, and Anna couldn't bear to do nothing. She checked with Maureen, but Mrs Wetherall was still too ill to speak. Dinger was on his way back to Workington. Going to the farm had the advantage that she would be near home, and she was still dog-tired from the exertions of the weekend.

Driving towards the farm, on a straight stretch of road, her eyelids felt heavy. She blinked and shook her head, but almost at once the drowsiness hit her again. This time she jerked awake suddenly as the car veered across the road and hit the hedge on the other side. It could have been a wall, she realised, shocked and shaking. And if there had been more traffic around she could be dead. Slowly, her mind cleared by the shock, Anna managed to manoeuvre the car back on the road. It was muddy and scraped by the hawthorn branches of the hedge, but driveable. She set off very slowly, breathing hard.

At the next junction, she pulled to the side of the road and stopped. This was madness. She was in no fit state to drive any further. Instead of turning right towards the farm, Anna turned left towards the forest and her cottage. Too much adrenaline had exhausted her: she needed food and sleep urgently.

The afternoon was overcast, fell tops blotted out behind banks of racing cloud. By the time she reached the entry that ran behind the big house towards her cottage, wind was thrashing the tree tops in the forest around the houses and it was almost dark. The big house that stood by the road in front of her cottage was in darkness as it had been since the FMD outbreak started. The owners, who did bed and breakfast there during the tourist season, had obviously decided to take a holiday while they had the chance. Occasionally someone came to check on the place but there'd been no sign of that for a while.

Anna parked the car by the side of the cottage as usual and slumped in her seat for a moment, summoning the energy to get out. Overhead the wind was roaring in the trees like a train. Once inside, she leaned against the door and breathed steadily in and out, aware of a thumping headache and the sharp pricking of her eyes. She checked her phone. Nothing from Maureen. Then she rang the office but no one picked up. When the message machine clicked on she said, 'On my way to Heslops' farm, out of mobile contact for a while.'

No need to tell them she'd taken a couple of hours off. She didn't want to give Bell any reason to complain that she wasn't up to the pace.

Anna turned up the thermostat and heard the comforting thrump of the boiler as it kicked in. The water would be hot enough for a shower in a little while, but before that she needed a drink and some food. She'd found a good baker's in Cockermouth, a butcher where they roasted their own ham, and a really good cheese shop. When she opened the fridge there were all the makings of a gourmet sandwich, better than the rubbish she could get at work. One of the joys of living alone was that things were always in the same place when you got home, and satisfaction at this made her smile as she made the sandwich she'd been thinking about for a while.

When it was eaten she put her head back for a moment as tiredness overcame her once again. She jerked awake and checked her watch. Outside the noise of the wind continued unabated. Nothing would happen tonight, surely. As she stood under the hot shower, Anna convinced herself that a short sleep was essential to her efficiency. If she set her alarm she could check in mid-evening, go up to the farm if it still looked to be useful to do so, and then at least she'd be alert and functioning, not the zombie she'd felt like for the past few hours.

Maureen stayed at the hospital with Margaret while the medics decided whether or not her internal injuries needed surgery. Margaret was half-conscious most of the time and Maureen was finding it hard to keep awake herself. She checked with DI Bell and was told to stay put until they were sure that Margaret had told them anything she might know about her son's whereabouts.

Maureen looked at the woman's bruised face and then gently nudged her awake.

'Can you hear me, Margaret?' she said, bending low to whisper against her ear. 'You're safe now, in the hospital. It's Maureen here. I came with you in the ambulance. Can you hear me?'

Margaret turned her head slightly towards the voice and her eyes flickered open. 'Alex,' she said, her voice a croak.

'He's gone,' said Maureen. 'He won't hurt you again.'

'He kicked me,' said Margaret.

'I know, and the doctors have had a good look at you. You'll be fine, don't worry.'

Margaret's eyes were wide open now. 'Where is he?' she said in alarm.

Maureen said quietly, 'He'd left the house when we found you. Did he say where he was going?'

Margaret shook her head, a slight movement against the pillow. 'I don't know why he did this,' she said. A tear ran down the side of her face. 'His dad beat him,' she went on, 'but I never did.'

'Do you know where he might have gone?'

'I told you about the fishing place,' said Margaret. 'That's what made him angry.'

'And he got away from us there by walking across the Solway, in the middle of the night. That was a daring thing to do.'

Margaret smiled. 'He was a soldier,' she said. 'Fought for his country.'

'Yes,' said Maureen. And now he's completely mad, she could have added, but stopped herself. There was something else she needed to check.

'Margaret, did Alex ever mention someone called Rose? He knew her when they were kids. Rose Haile, or Rose Heslop. Do those names ring any bells?'

Margaret closed her eyes for a moment and Maureen wondered if the chance for talking was already over.

'Dark hair, pretty,' Margaret murmured.

Maureen leaned in closer. 'Go on,' she said.

'He kept a photo in his wallet. I saw it once.'

'When was this, do you remember?'

'Pretty girl,' the woman repeated, but then she turned her head away and Maureen heard the steady breathing as she slipped into sleep.

Anna woke with a start. The radio alarm hadn't come on, but something had woken her. Could have been the noise from outside. She lay still and listened. Beyond the overhead roaring of the wind was another sound, more regular, something banging. Maybe it was one of the shutters of the big house next door. They gave the place an attractive Swiss look, but they were a nuisance at times when they weren't securely fastened. The explanation satisfied her and she lay still for a moment before glancing at the illuminated dial of the clock by her bed. Just after eight. She'd been asleep for an hour or so, and felt much better for it. The banging had stopped.

She clicked on the bedside light, pushed back the duvet and put her bare legs to the floor. It was cold in the bedroom, and she found a pair of warm tights and lined trousers that would be more suitable for the trip up to the farm that she still planned to make. Might be better to arrive at an unsocial time, and catch them all off guard. She found a thermal top in the drawer, slipped it on, and pulled on her fleece jacket over it. Not exactly elegant, but it would suffice for an evening visit to a rundown hill farm.

The wind seemed to be even louder than before, and then the lights began to flicker, on, then off, then on again. Anna stood quite still, almost willing the wind to die down, to let electricity flow along the lines that were jumping and twisting in the storm. She realised she was not breathing and exhaled slowly as the light stayed on, for the time being at least. She'd been warned about weather like this and she was ready. On a shelf under the sink downstairs was everything she needed: the battery-powered radio, the little Primus stove and kettle, candles, matches, the wind-up torch. And if the power was off for long, she could always escape in the car to the warmth and light of the town and the office.

Downstairs she lit a candle to avoid being plunged into total disorientating darkness if the power went off again. The flame flickered and flared and the kitchen seemed cooler than it had been before. She wondered if she'd left a window somewhere not quite closed. And what about the door? She'd run into the house so hurriedly that she couldn't remember having locked it behind her, and did so now. Anna Penrose, she told herself, you should be more careful.

The delicious bread was still sitting invitingly on the bread board. She cut another slice, buttered it, and stood by the window while she ate it, looking out at the night. The forecast for the following day was pretty awful: high winds, rain, even some sleet or snow on higher ground. Someone had told her that the worst of the winter in Cumbria often arrived in March.

There was a sudden movement behind her. Something hard and metallic pressed against her cheek, while an arm slammed across her throat, choking her. Instinct made her kick back with one leg, but the metal pressed harder into her cheek.

'Don't bother trying to move,' said a voice. 'The gun's loaded. I could shoot you like a sick sheep and no one would hear.' Alex Wetherall laughed. 'Leave you by the gate and they'd pick you up in a white truck and take you for burning with all the others.'

As she struggled to breathe, the lights went out.

Chapter 19

Anna stood quite still, feeling the gun barrel against her cheek, seeing the layout of the kitchen in her mind's eye. Behind her, a step away, was the worktop where she'd been cutting bread. The knife was still there, but could she reach it? For a moment she thought about how she might use it, how to stop his finger pressing on the trigger and blowing off the side of her face before she died. Would he do it? Was he crazy enough? Questions buzzed in her mind. Clear your head, she told herself. Focus. He was breathing heavily behind her, and she felt the tension in his arm.

'You don't want to do this, Alex. Harming me will be the end for you.'

'Shut up,' he hissed at her. 'Shut the fuck up!'

The lights flickered on again, but only for a second. The candle had already died. Outside, wind thrashed the trees and something fell against the back door with a thump.

'Move,' he said, pushing her in front of him, the gun still jammed against her cheek. With his other hand he felt along the side of the table, found the chair and on it the woollen scarf Anna had discarded when she came into the house. He held it in front of her face and she felt its thick coarseness against her mouth. 'Open your mouth,' he said. 'Do it, now.'

The scarf was forced between her teeth, tightening as he pulled it round her head. The gun had left her cheek while he did this and she struggled, but he pulled the scarf tighter still and held it, tucking it under at the back, pulling her hair until she cried out. The gun barrel bit once more into the side of her forehead, but the scarf was almost covering her eyes. He forced her head down and bashed it on the table, then flung her, stunned, to the floor.

She heard him pace up and down the small kitchen, while he lit a cigarette, the old floorboards moving under the weight of his boots.

'Stuck-up bitch,' he muttered to himself. 'You were never in the proper army. And now you're in the fucking police. Bitch!' He kneeled down beside her. 'Before I kill you, you'll do what I want, right?' She nodded and tried to speak but only a grunt emerged. Face even closer to hers, he hissed, 'I don't care about anything else – I want my Rose. And she wants me, but she's stuck with that loser. Needs me to get her out. Right?' Anna nodded again.

He stood up. 'Where's the phone? Mine's not working.'

Anna raised her head, wincing with the pain. He was standing over her, the gun pointing down. She shuffled back, then slowly lifted her arm and pointed towards the windowsill where the cordless phone sat in its cradle. It wouldn't be working because the power was out, but he clearly didn't realise that. He side-stepped towards the window, keeping his eyes and the gun on her, picked up the phone and put it on the table. Then he began opening cupboards and drawers, feeling inside for anything he could use to bind her tight. With an old plastic bag he tied her wrists to the table leg, then undid the scarf and used it to tie her legs together at the ankles. She put her free hand to her mouth but he slapped it away before he pulled her up to lean against the table leg. Her head was spinning but she forced herself to think.

There was a click and a beam of light glared into her face. He'd found an old torch in a drawer, not the flash new wind-up one that was sitting on the shelf under the sink. Now he held the torch in one hand and the gun in the other. When would he realise that the line was dead? She watched carefully as his fingers pressed the keys. It was a mobile number, not a landline. Rose's phone, the one she'd denied having.

Alex put the phone to his ear. 'Rose?'

Anna watched his face.

'Rose!' he repeated, looking at the handset as if it were a threat. 'It's dead,' he said angrily. 'Useless.'

'It's the storm,' Anna whispered, fearing his anger. She flinched as he threw it hard against the back door and it fell to the floor in pieces. 'What are you going to do?' she ventured, wanting to keep him talking but not knowing what to say.

'She's mine,' he said. 'Mine. I'll go and find her. She'll be waiting.'

'You want to be with her,' said Anna, 'I know.'

'You know nothing,' he roared at her, raising his fist.

He leaned forward again. Cigarette smoke curled from his nostrils. 'All my life,' he said, 'I've been waiting. In the army, in jail, waiting. For her. She made a choice, but she knows it was the wrong one. She knows it has to be me for her. I'm the only one. And now we have Helen. We're a family.'

'When did you know?' Anna whispered, careful not to challenge him. 'About Helen?'

He found a chair behind him and sat down. 'I always knew she was mine. Rose told me, but I knew already.'

'You know we haven't found her yet? She's out there somewhere, alone, in danger. That's down to you.'

He shrugged. 'It was an accident. Accidents happen. Not my fault. Anyway, she'll be all right. Young girl, pretty, everyone'll care about her, won't they?'

He can't think of anything except himself, Anna realised. Nothing else mattered. If Rose rejected him, he'd turn on her as well.

He seemed calmer, and Anna thought she might push a little harder. 'How can you be sure that Helen's your child?'

He glared at her. 'My Rose would never lie.'

'But she has lied to her husband, hasn't she?'

He got up abruptly. 'You don't get it, do you? Dried-up old bitch like you, you'd never understand. Rose has to lie to him, to keep us together.'

He crouched down by her again, his expression defiant. 'But she could never lie to me.'

Anna gulped. She had to push him. 'Why did Rose not come to you when you took Helen? She's betrayed you, Alex.'

Anna turned her head, expecting a blow, but none came. Instead he got up and scratched his head with the barrel of the gun.

She pressed on. 'You'll never get close to the farm, not now. My boss hates you, and he's missed you twice. This time he'll be waiting.'

Alex smiled. 'Thick coppers,' he said. 'I hate them too. Getting across the river, that fooled them. Stupid fuckers, crashing around with dogs. I could hear them, when I was out there. I could see the lights of their cars.' He laughed out loud. 'Piece of cake.'

She studied his face. He thought he was invincible. 'We knew you were at your mother's house,' she said, trying to prick his bubble. 'And you beat her up, your own mother, an old woman. Make you feel like a big man, did it?'

'She's a cow. Wish I'd hit her harder. Her fault things went wrong for me, and when they did, she kept away. Never came to see me in the nick, not once. Miserable old bitch.'

'They'll get you, you know. For Helen, for your mam, for giving us the run around. You won't get away with any of it.'

Alex spat. 'Watch me. I'm not stupid. I know what I'm doing. Where's the booze? I want a drink.'

'Cupboard by the cooker,' said Anna. Maybe drink would distract him, make him sleepy. She'd done her best to brace her wrists when he tied them and now needed time to test whether she could loosen the ties a bit more.

Alex peered into the cupboard and found the bottle of cooking brandy. He sat down at the far side of the kitchen table, put the gun down, stood the torch on its end so that the light pooled on the low ceiling and twisted the cork out of the bottle. It was nearly full. He put it to his mouth and took a long gulp, choking as the liquid spilled over and down his chin. The smell of brandy filled the room. Anna kept as still as she could, waiting. Alex took off his hat and put it on the table in front of him, took another long pull on the bottle and then leaned forward and put his head down on the hat, as if a weight had been lifted and exhaustion had suddenly overtaken him.

Anna lowered her head and tested the plastic round her wrist with her teeth. She found a loose end and worried at it for a minute or two. Nothing. The knot stayed tight. She craned her neck to try again. Unless she could loosen her wrists, the bread-knife would be out of reach. She couldn't see it, but knew it was there. He hadn't spotted it. Alex remained quite still, she could hear him breathing and muttering to himself. She found the loose end again and teased at it, gently working it to and fro. It began to ease just a fraction, enough to keep her going. Saliva dribbled down onto her hands.

Above her head, Alex suddenly spat brandy onto the floor. 'Where's the proper stuff?' he said. 'This is shite.' She licked her lips and answered, keeping her voice even. 'Whisky, by the fireplace in the other room. Single malt.'

The table moved as he pushed himself back and trod heavily into the next room, returning a minute later to resume his silent drinking. She waited a moment before she too resumed what she was doing, revelling in the sensation as one of the plastic strands gripped in her teeth slid slowly out of its knot. She waited, listening. His breathing above her was slower now, more regular. Whatever she had to do, this was the best chance.

Her hands were free, wrists sore from the plastic, but she kept them clasped together while she thought. The torch's beam was fading slowly, from yellow to amber, and she knew the light would fail soon. As if to compensate, another flickered outside. Lightning, she guessed, and waited for the rumble that might follow. There was no thunder but suddenly car headlights curved around the small room. Her heart bumped. Someone was out there, but the lights disappeared as quickly as they'd come and the hope died. Alex moved slightly and the bottle on the table wobbled, but stayed upright. The movement stopped. It had to be now.

She pushed herself up slowly. The table must not move. Just a few inches higher, her thighs burning under the strain. Then slowly onto her knees and extending her arm out towards the worktop, the tips of her fingers straining towards it. The knife was there, she could feel the end of the handle. She placed her two longest fingers to either side and closed them together but couldn't grip it properly. Don't give up, she told herself. Again, the same manoeuvre. Hardly daring to breathe, she stretched until elbow and wrist would stretch no more. This time as her fingers closed together the end of the handle stayed between them and she pulled, gently, concentrating on the movement. At the point when she could control her arm no longer, she folded her thumb round the end of the handle and slid it silently towards her, then lifted the knife down and onto the floor.

The roaring of the wind was even louder now. Alex stirred and the chair scraped back again on the slate flags. He was on his feet, holding the torch and the gun. Anna crouched, sliding the knife further under her body and then sat back on it, feeling the serrated edge and the curve of the handle. Alex walked towards the back door and put his ear to it, then moved across to the tiny window, keeping his eyes on her as he did so. 'Who lives in the house by the road?' he asked, gesturing in that direction with his head.

'No one. It's empty. In the summer it's a guesthouse, but not now.'

Almost as she finished speaking, as if to expose a lie, car headlights flashed through the window onto the far wall. Alex bent low, cursing, and the lights disappeared. He went to the front window and peered out into the storm.

'Your car keys,' he said. 'Where are they?'

Anna closed her eyes. She needed to slow things down. 'I'm not sure,' she said, praying that the fading torch beam wouldn't pick up the keys lying on the worktop where she'd left them. She needed time. 'They may still be in the car. Sometimes I leave them there. It's not locked.'

He shook his head. 'You're coming with me,' he said.

Her heart sank. 'Where?'

'When I go to fetch Rose. You're my free pass, if that stupid husband of hers calls the police. I can trade you for her.'

So he needs me alive, she thought. 'Let me find the keys,' she said, knowing he wouldn't agree.

'No!' he shouted. 'You stay right there, on the floor, where you belong, bitch.'

'But I could have dropped them,' she persisted. 'I don't know.'

'Shut up,' he bellowed, and she shrank away from him, reaching under her legs to find the handle of the knife. The urge to attack him was strong, but it was too risky while she was still tethered. He could kill her in a moment of fury, despite his lunatic plan to use her as a hostage.

The car was parked a few yards from the back door and that would be all the time she would have to free herself. The torch battery was almost dead but he picked it up, pushed the whisky bottle into the pocket of his jacket and walked towards the back door, gun still in hand. The door was unlocked and he pulled it open. Wind and rain swept inside and Anna saw that a branch had fallen just outside. Alex tried to lift his leg over it but he was unsteady and had to step back, bending to move the branch away.

This was her chance, her only chance. Her fingers were stiff and numb and she might have to use the knife to cut the scarf away from her ankles. The knot was tight and the fabric of the scarf had been stretched, making it tighter still. She heard the door of the car open and pictured him looking for the keys, cursing. Keep looking, she urged him silently, as the knot refused to budge. She wriggled her ankles, cursing the boots that she was wearing. Unless she could get them off, there was no chance of slipping her feet out of their confinement.

Too late. He came back into the room and threw the dead torch onto the table. 'Can't see a thing out there. Batteries?'

'Candles. Upstairs, in the drawer beside the bed. And matches there too. I can find them.'

'No. You stay here.'

'The stairs are right behind you,' she said. Anna felt that she was gradually regaining some control. The space was familiar to her, but not to him. He was disorientated by the darkness and unsure what to do with her, while her next steps were all too clear. When he clumped up the narrow stairs she freed her hand and turned the knife towards her ankles, cutting the scarf carefully, wishing the blade was sharper.

As the boots returned down the stairs a wavering glow came too, from a candle held in Alex's hand. The last threads gave way. Anna left the scarf in position and pushed the knife back under her ankles, gripping the table leg as she had done before and praying that he wouldn't see the plastic ties had moved.

'Now you can look for the keys,' she said. 'If I brought them into the house, they'll be on the worktop behind me.' He came nearer and she huddled down, praying that his focus on the keys would distract his attention from the tiny shreds of wool littering the floor. She heard the rattle of the keys as he picked them up.

'Let's go,' he said.

It wouldn't do, not yet. She needed him off balance. 'Your hat,' she said.

As he stretched across the table she jumped up with all her strength, pushing the table up and into him. He fell sideways, and she jammed the knife into his knee, pulling it out before she leaped over his legs and ran towards the back door, leaving him roaring in pain and fury behind her. She had the knife, already sticky with blood, and she knew how to use it, if she ever got the chance again. For now, all she could was open the door with one movement and run, not daring to look back.

She heard his voice. 'Bitch!' he screamed. 'I'll kill you.' But it wasn't close. After only a few desperate strides into the trees she slipped and fell headlong, feeling the brambles tearing her face, catching her hair. She lay for a moment, winded, and smeared mud on her stinging cheeks to disguise the white oval of her face if lightning or headlights illuminated the darkness around them.

Should she get up? If he was close behind he might see her once their eyes had adjusted to the darkness. Branches still waved and creaked above her head. Then she heard him crashing through the undergrowth, shouting, cursing, but he was off to her right and she began to crawl away from him, knees scraping on the forest floor and the litter of pinecones.

The first shot rang out. He was firing blind, in rage, but Anna dropped flat and lay still. He'd lost her, unless she was foolish enough to give herself away. He was tough, but she knew she had hurt him badly. Surely he would give up, turn back and take the car before blood loss weakened him. Another shot. She had recognised the gun he was carrying and the clip held fifteen rounds. If it had been full, it would have thirteen shots left. She raised herself slowly to a crouch, picked up a rock from the ground and lobbed it high to her right. As it crashed down through the trees another shot rang out. Twelve. She stopped and listened again. No sound except the wind in the trees and the thumping of her own heart. Then she heard him, grunting at first, before the grunt rose into a wail of pain and rage. He was not far away, but he had stopped moving.

She had been trying to circle back towards the road, and crawled through the thinning trees until she could see the outline of her cottage about fifty metres away. Then she saw him, limping out of the forest towards her car, one hand holding his damaged knee and the other still clutching the gun. As she crouched back into the shelter of the trees the rear lights of the car pierced the darkness ahead of her and the engine sprang to life. Then headlights lit up the forest on the far side of the clearing and Anna saw the outline of the car moving slowly at first, then picking up speed as it turned the corner towards the road. She sank to her knees on the sodden pine needles and sobbed with relief. Blood from the scratches on her face mingled with tears and the rain that had begun to spatter through the dark trees as the clouds burst overhead.

The sound of the engine died away but for a few minutes Anna stayed quite still, afraid that he would trick her by turning back. But there was no sound now save for the creaking of branches over her head and slowly she got to her feet, soaked and shivering with cold. Suddenly overcome with an urge to find the warmth and safety of her home, she pushed herself forward to run through the last line of trees. She didn't see the branch that lay across her path, and tripped, feeling the burning tear in her ankle as she crashed to the ground. When she tried to get up, her right foot was too painful. The wind found her and bit into her skin. There was no shelter. The cold was unbearable and no one would hear her calling for help.

Chapter 20

Alex cursed as he pressed down on his left leg to put the car into gear. The bitch had hurt him. He could feel blood running down his leg and the pain in the knee was bad, too bad for him to try and find her in the forest, wasting too much time there. He knew she would probably see which way he drove away, but he'd got this far by leading those stupid coppers all over the place, tying them up in knots. He could do the same now, doubling back in Keswick while they were still trying to figure out where he was heading. The bitch's phone was in pieces, she was out of mobile range and stuck with no car, miles from anywhere. The one he'd stolen in Carlisle was no use to her, in a ditch down the hill with no petrol. With any luck he'd winged her, or she'd be too scared to get help. It was a detail. He was so close now nothing would hold him back for long. Finding Rose was all that mattered.

The roads were deserted and he was able to drive for long stretches without changing gear. The pain in his knee was bearable. Once Rose was with him, she could drive and they would be away, together. Helen might be out of reach for now, but they would find a way. She would come to them, once she knew the truth.

The map he held in his head served him well. Approaching the farm directly wouldn't work, but there was another way, from a narrow lane that ran on the far side of their deserted fields. He could leave the car there and walk across to the farmhouse.

When he found the place, he cut the engine. It was windy but the rain had stopped. Clouds were threatening, scudding in front of the moon, but he had plenty of clothes from his room at his mother's, and in his bag he had some good cannabis, the gun and a hefty roll of banknotes. He swallowed a handful of painkillers washed down with the dregs of Anna's whisky and waited, eyes closed, for them to take effect.

As he sat in the car, a single headlight bounced across the field that lay between him and the farm. He slumped down, but kept an eye on the quad bike as it slowed on the far side of a gap in the wall, nosed through the gap and turned down the hill. No point in keeping gates closed when the stock were dead or barricaded in their sheds.

So far, so good. The pain in his knee was tolerable. Alex eased out of the car, slung the bag over his back and set off across the field. It wasn't far. Rose had talked to him about the layout of the farm and he knew that the first building he could see was the hay barn, with the milking parlour next to it, and the cowshed beyond that. The lambing shed for Rose's precious sheep was at the far end of the yard. On the right was the farmhouse. No lights anywhere, but he guessed that the power was out here too. The valley below the farm was in total darkness, but there was enough light from the moon's periodic appearance for him to make his way across the field, staying close to the wall. Another gate was left open, and old tyre marks from the quad bike were clearly visible as he picked his way across.

As he neared the buildings a faint glow told him that someone was in the farmhouse with a lamp or candles. He was limping now, holding on to the wall where he could to take the weight from his knee. At the end of the wall, by the gap that led into the farmyard, he stopped and listened. Nothing except the wind whining in the dead power lines. He crossed the yard with his back to the farmhouse wall and inched his way towards the window where he could see the light. When he reached it, he peered inside and his heart jumped in his chest. She was there, right there, sitting at the table with the lamp next to her, looking at a newspaper. Beside her was a mug, a wisp of steam curling up from it. He looked at the bowed head, the dark hair, the hand resting on the table. He'd sent her a text before he left Carlisle: *I'm coming. Be ready*. She must know that he would come for her. She would be waiting.

He craned his head to look further into the room. No one else sat at the table, or in the big chair that faced the near wall. It was late. Maybe the useless husband was asleep already, or drunk and insensible. She'd told Alex about his drinking. No wonder she wanted to get away. He raised his hand and tapped on the window, gently, very gently, and watched. She raised her head and saw him, putting her hand to her mouth, eyes bright in the lamplight. She shook her head and got up slowly, holding the lamp as she walked towards the door. He took a few painful steps towards it, his heart racing. The door opened a fraction and he heard her voice. 'Not here,' she whispered. 'In the hay barn. Go!'

The door closed again and he turned, the bag still on his shoulder, and limped across the yard. There was a small door set within the bigger one of the barn and it creaked as he opened it. Inside it felt warm away from the wind. Huge round bales of hay were stacked up against the walls but there was enough floor space remaining for him to find a spot to sit down on a smaller pile of hay and lean back, watching the door. As it opened a minute later he smiled. She was here. At last.

Rose was not smiling when she stepped into the barn, holding a lamp in her hand that swung gently, casting moving shadows.

The door behind her creaked shut and was still. They were alone. Rose put down the lamp on one of the hay bales. Alex tried to get up but couldn't move his leg. He stretched out his arms towards her but she stepped away from him.

'Did you get the message?' he asked. 'Are you ready?'

She stared at him. 'What message?'

'I texted you. I left messages. That's why I gave you the phone. You said you had a signal. I told you I'd be here.'

Rose turned to check the barn door was properly shut and sat down on the bale beside the lamp. She put her hand to her face, struggling to know what to say. 'Aidan has my phone. He knows, Alex. He knows about us. You can't stay here. Eric's asleep, and Aidan is out, but you can't stay. Brian's in bed. I have to be here.'

He looked at her, puzzled. 'But you said…' he began.

'I know what I said. But I can't leave.'

He began to speak, but she held up her hand. 'Why did you take Helen? Where is she?'

'I wanted to see her, and then I thought that if she was with me, you would come too. You would bring the boy, and we could all go away, together.'

Rose closed her eyes. This was what she'd feared, from the start of this whole mad business. All she'd wanted was a fling, someone to help her get away from the farm when she was ready, when the time was right.

She looked at him reproachfully. 'Helen's just a child, and now she's lost.'

He shook his head, denying any blame for that. 'She was fine when I saw her last. I got her a puffer. When the van crashed, she just ran away. I had to go, couldn't stop to find her. They were after me, Rose, I can't go back to jail. I'd rather die.'

She held up her hand again. 'Keep your voice down, for God's sake. What if he finds you here?'

'Who? Eric?' Alex smiled. 'You don't care about him.'

'The police will come. They'll come here soon, I know it.'

He frowned. 'What did you tell them?'

'Nothing, I told them nothing, but they could see... you can't stay here, Alex. Go to your mother's. I could come to you there when... things calm down.'

Rose put out her hand and he took it, put it to his lips, smiling.

'I fixed her,' he said, 'and that other stuck-up bitch.'

'Fixed who?' Rose pulled her hand away. 'What do you mean? 'The army bitch. She had it coming,' he said. In his mind Anna had been dealt with. First his mother, then the bitch. Now he would claim his prize after all these years. He reached for Rose again and tried to get up, but faltered and lay back again, feeling the pain.

Rose got to her feet and backed away, looking down at him. 'What have you done, Alex?' she whispered. The lamp swung gently in her hand, light glancing round the barn and the stacks of hay bales.

He shook his head. 'Doesn't matter,' he said. 'I'm here now. We can go away, like we planned. The car's close by. Just bring a few things, and Brian. You've told him, haven't you?'

She turned away, took a step towards the door and then turned back to look at him. She put down the lamp and stood with her head down, taking a deep breath before she answered. 'Not yet,' she said. 'We can't go yet, Alex. You'll have to go away and wait for me. I'm not ready.'

'But I can't wait any more,' he said. 'Look... look.' He reached for his bag and pulled it towards him, feeling for something inside. He pulled out the roll of banknotes.

'Here,' he said. 'We have all the money we could need, enough for us both and the boy. And Helen too. She'll be home soon.'

Rose picked up the money and stared at it before handing it back to him. 'What about Eric?'

Alex put the bankroll back in his bag. 'I can deal with him. Just get him out here.' He pulled out the gun and smiled at her. 'Easy,' he said.

Rose stood quite still for a few moments, her eyes closed. The lamp hissed. Outside the wind whined around the old buildings. She sat down next to him and reached her hand towards his face. 'You would do that for me, Alex?'

He turned and kissed her hand. 'I'd do anything for you, Rose. You know that. I love you.'

A tear crept down Rose's cheek and she wiped it away. 'I know you do,' she said. 'Now let me help you,' she said. 'Show me what you've done to your leg. You need to be able to walk, don't you, so we can be together?' He kissed her hand again, then lay back while she kneeled down beside him, looking at the wound in his knee.

'She did this,' he said. 'The army bitch. She cut me.'

Rose got to her feet. 'I'll go and get some things,' she said. 'I'll take the lamp, OK, and bring something to bind your leg, and some food. And whisky. I know where Eric keeps his spare bottle.'

Rose disappeared, pulling the barn door closed behind her. When she came back a few minutes later she was carrying a bag, and took out the contents one at a time while he watched. 'Some whisky,' she said, 'and some pills for the pain, and a bandage too. Lie back, pet, let me fix your leg. And have some whisky, it'll dull the pain.' Rose cut the bloody trouser leg back and winced when she saw the damage. Talking softly to him as if to a fretful child, she dabbed at the wound with antiseptic and then bound it up with a bandage. Alex watched, relishing the whisky and her closeness, murmuring her name. After a while he lay back.

Then the barn door creaked open.

A few minutes later, in his bedroom in the farmhouse, Brian Heslop heard a noise and was suddenly wide awake. He got out of bed and stood for a moment on the cold floor, wondering what to do. No one was where they should be, and nobody took any notice of him. He wanted his mother, but he couldn't find her. She wasn't in her own bedroom, and she wasn't in his. Maybe she was downstairs.

He walked across his bedroom and out of the door, turning towards the stairs. At the top he stopped and listened. He often stood there and listened to voices downstairs. Sometimes he sat very still just at the top of the stairs, where he could see down into the kitchen but no one could see him unless they looked really hard. He liked doing that, being invisible. Brian shrank back as someone lit a candle in the kitchen and glow seeped up the stairs towards him. He could hear voices now, Aidan and Dad speaking, but not Mum. Where was she?

Brian wanted his mother but he dared not go downstairs. Instead he went back to bed and waited for the next thing to happen. He didn't have to wait for long.

Chapter 21

DI Stanley Bell woke suddenly when both the light and the radio beside his bed flashed into life simultaneously at just after six on Wednesday morning as the power was restored in Workington. He turned off the light so as not to disturb his wife, snoring gently at his side, and turned down the volume to listen for a while. Radio Cumbria was reporting widespread power cuts across the county, along with felled trees and flooded roads as a result of the overnight storm. He was glad he'd sent everyone home before ten the previous evening. They were all exhausted and demoralised after the fruitless searches for Wetherall and the girl, and he'd reckoned that the investigation would be so hampered by the weather conditions that they might as well take advantage of the chance for a rest. Penrose had left the office before that decision was made, but they'd heard nothing from her since then.

All Bell's suspicions were confirmed by his sergeant's behaviour: women were just not ready for senior responsibility, and this woman in particular had a lot to learn about being part of a team, no matter what glowing references had come from the army. Too bloody clever by half, that was his verdict, and he would tell Tognarelli so if he ever got the chance.

Bell swung his legs out of the warm bed and checked his watch. Landlines down, but anyone in his team should be reachable if their mobiles were charged up and the transmitters still functioning. Carruthers and Pritchard both responded to the summons into the office for an urgent review at eight o'clock. Penrose's phone went straight to voicemail. Just for good measure, Bell called Wong's mobile number too. They were short-handed and he was obviously keen to learn. When Wong replied that he was in Carlisle and hoped he could get down to Workington in time given the mess on the roads, Bell had a sudden thought.

'If you're coming from there, can you divert and see what's happened to Penrose? God knows why she wants to live out in the wilderness and the power's probably still off out there, but we've heard nowt since end of yesterday afternoon. Maybe car trouble or summat. Do you know where she lives?'

'Yes,' said Wong.

Oh, you do, do you? thought Bell to himself as he put down the phone and pulled on his clothes.

Anna knew that wet clothes were worse than no clothes at all and she'd stripped down to her underwear when she finally reached the cottage, and taken off the boots to ease her throbbing ankle. She kept on the red thermal tights that dried fast and would help retain some body heat. Getting up the stairs with a right foot that wasn't functioning proved too difficult. She wrapped herself in the blanket off the back of the couch in the living room, and lay down, exhausted by fear and pain. With no light and no hot water it wasn't worth trying to clean up the scratches on her face and hands. The sickening smell of the spilled cooking brandy hung in the air. She slipped into sleep.

When light flashed through the uncurtained window and lit up the small room in a moving arc, Anna woke suddenly. A car. What if it was Alex coming back? What if he still wanted to use her as a hostage? The knife, where was the knife? The headlights went off suddenly, plunging the room into darkness again. Anna pushed away the tangled blanket, put her left foot to the cold floor and then swung round to test the right one as well. Too painful to stand on, but she could wiggle her toes, so probably not broken. She listened, but the car engine was silent and there was no sound of movement. Feeling her way as her eyes adjusted to the darkness, and keeping the pressure off her foot by hanging on to whatever furniture she could reach, Anna struggled back into the kitchen and round the edge of the upturned table towards the worktop under the window where she'd left the bloody knife the night before. The back door was still open. Why hadn't she locked it after she'd crawled back into the house? She could hear footsteps coming towards the door and positioned herself behind it as best she could, weight on her good leg, knife ready in her hand. She took a deep breath.

The knock on the door surprised her. Before she had time to decide what it meant the door began to open, torchlight penetrated the darkness and a familiar voice said, 'Hello? Sarge?' She fell back against the sink as the door opened further. Tony Wong looked down at her as she crouched on the floor, still holding the knife. Anna felt herself flush, suddenly aware that she was wearing a bra and leggings, and not much else. He gasped and looked away. The vision in front of him, revealed fleetingly in the edge of the torchlight, was of a woman with wild hair, a blood-streaked face and red legs to match, pale chest and arms and a turquoise bra. He admitted later that he'd never seen anything like it before, ever.

Torchlight veered drunkenly round the room as he stepped round the door, took the knife from her grasp and placed it in the sink, then used both hands to pull her gently up. She winced as he picked up a chair and lowered her into it. For a moment she was overwhelmed. Relieved of the fear that had pressed heavily on her through the night, she could hear herself whimpering.

Torchlight flashed round the room as he looked for something to stop her shivering, found the blanket and wrapped it round her shoulders. He stepped back and surveyed the room where the smell of brandy still lingered in the cold air. He flicked the light switch, with no response, before kneeling down to study her scratched face. A solitary tear ran down her cheek.

'What happened?' he asked.

'Alex Wetherall,' she said. 'Took my car. Hours ago.'

Tony nodded.

'On the shelf below the sink,' she said, finding her voice with some difficulty. 'I had things ready for a power cut. He didn't find them.'

Tony stepped round her and found the shelf, lifting up the lamp and the Primus stove. 'An emergency stash,' he said, smiling. He filled the tiny kettle at the sink, set up the stove and lit it. 'Reminds me of camping,' he said, 'that sound, and the blue flame and the smell.' She leaned back in the chair, relaxing into safety, and smiled back at him.

'Can I get you some clothes?' he asked. 'You need warming up.'

'I can't get upstairs,' she said. 'You'll find stuff in my bedroom, on the left. And in the bathroom cupboard.'

'I'll sort it out. Do you have antiseptic? Any bandages?'

She nodded.

'OK, you watch the kettle, I'll be back.'

After he'd helped her into the clothes that he found upstairs, Tony kneeled in front of her, dipped cotton wool into warm water laced with antiseptic, and gently wiped the dried blood from her face and hands. When he brought the hissing lamp close to her cheek and touched the purpling bruise gingerly with his fingertips, she sat still and let him do it. No one had shown her any tenderness for so long, and she struggled with her reaction, trying not to look into the face so close to hers. It was easier when he sat on another chair and took her painful foot onto his knee. He moved it carefully one way, then the other. 'Not broken, I think,' he said. 'Swollen, probably sprained. I'll bind it up tight and you can sit in the back of the car with your foot up while we drive in.'

'Where are we going?'

'To the station first, so you can make a statement about what happened here, and then to the health centre when they open up.'

'Shall I tell you what happened?'

'If you want to, but you should save your strength. You've had a bad time, but you'll be fine now.'

After a hot drink and a final check around the house, Tony put the bloody knife into a plastic bag to take with them, and brought his car round close to the back door. Anna stood unsteadily on her good leg and put her arm round his neck as they manoeuvred out of the door and into the back seat of the car. Ice cubes from the freezer were still solid enough to ease the swelling. They drove in silence down the hill towards Workington and the lights of civilisation. Then Anna began to talk, as if she were rehearsing the key points of what had happened, and Tony listened carefully while he drove.

In the Workington CID office, Dinger, Maureen, and Bob were sitting round the big table. It was well past eight and Dinger was impatient. DCI Tognarelli was on his way down and nothing was going to plan. They all turned as the door opened and Anna limped in, holding onto Tony's arm. Dinger's pre-rehearsed reprimand froze on his lips. Maureen was the first to her feet, taking Anna's hand and guiding her into a chair as Bob Carruthers gaped.

'Bloody hell,' said Dinger. 'What happened to you?'

Wong was all business. 'Wetherall was at her place, beat her up, took her car. She escaped, got very cold and wet, and sprained her ankle. She's OK, but someone needs to check that ankle. I'll take her when the health centre opens up.' He checked his watch. 'Won't be long. She'll be fine till then.'

Anna looked at them all. 'I'm OK,' she said. 'I managed to stick a knife in his leg. Tony has it bagged up. Wetherall took my car. Said he was going to the farm to find Rose but he drove away up the hill, towards Keswick.' No one spoke. 'I should make a proper statement shouldn't I, while we have the chance?' she went on. 'Add to the list of charges for when we pick him up.'

'Are you up to it?' said Bell. Maureen placed a cup of coffee and several biscuits on the table in front of Anna, who looked up and nodded her thanks. 'Of course,' she said. 'I feel much better already. Tony got me warmed up before we left the house.'

Maureen glanced at Bob Carruthers and put a finger to her lips, knowing full well what he was about to say.

While Anna made her formal statement to the desk sergeant in another room, the rest of the team checked and reviewed what they knew and needed to do next. Wong didn't take a seat at the table but sat to one side.

'Rose is the key to all this,' said Maureen, gratified that her instincts were clearly being confirmed. 'Everything he's doing is driven by that. Look at the number of times he could have got away, right away, and he keeps circling back.'

'And he still has that gun,' said Bell. 'Get Anna back in here as soon as she's finished her statement, Maureen. She must have seen the gun if he had it with him.'

'He did,' said Wong, from his perch near the door. 'She told me that.'

Bell turned to him. 'You still here? So where did that bruise on her face come from, did she tell you too?'

'That's where he slammed her head down onto the table. The scratches and the ankle injury happened outside, when she got way from him, into the woods.'

'Christ, she was lucky,' said Bob.

'Not just luck,' said Wong. 'She could just have given up, let him take her.'

'Is that what he tried?'

'Wanted to use her as a hostage.'

Bell blew out, shaking his head. 'Nasty.'

The desk sergeant had found a crutch in the lost property cupboard and Anna was using it when she came back into the room. This time Bell got up and helped her into a chair next to his. 'Are you OK?' he asked. 'Are you sure? Can you tell us about the gun?'

'A SIG Sauer P226,' said Anna immediately. Bob started to scribble. 'Fifteen shots in the clip. He fired off three while he was with me. No sign of another clip, so his firepower may be limited. And his left knee is quite badly damaged, but I don't think he's bothered about the pain. The man's flipped, he's way past any rational plan. He wants to be with Rose, convinced that she wants to be with him. And he thinks Helen is his kid too.'

Maureen smiled, and said, 'Rose is at the farm, so that's where he's heading, I'll bet on it.'

'And he's armed and crazy,' said Bell. 'Picking him up there will be a huge operation.'

'Tethered goat,' said Wong, and again they turned towards him.

'Is that some Chinese thing?' asked Bell. 'Like eating dogs or summat?'

Anna raised her voice. 'Come on, sir, work it out. Alex wants Rose, so we use her as bait. Bring her down here, and wait. It's a trap and he'll walk right in because he's lost the plot and she's all he cares about.' She paused. 'Tony's right. If you want to catch a tiger, you tether a goat to a stake and wait for the tiger to show up. That's what we need to do.'

'But what if he's already at the farm?' Bell asked, looking at his watch. 'It's nearly nine. We could be too late. Then what?'

Chapter 22

'We can't afford to screw this up,' DI Bell announced to whoever was listening, which now included DCI Tognarelli who'd arrived to report on the plethora of unsubstantiated sightings of Helen.

Bell felt the need to be circumspect in front of his boss. 'Two raids so far, no result, expensive and embarrassing,' he said. 'Can't happen again, right? This time we wait until we're sure.' He sat up straighter in the battered chair and raised his chin with Churchillian determination. 'Every possible lead needs to be checked until we know exactly where he is. All escape routes covered and tight. We'll need armed officers. He could have more than one gun, for all we know, or more ammo than we can guess at.' He looked across at Anna. 'He's desperate and probably beyond caring about his own safety. Right?'

She nodded. 'From what I saw, yes,' she replied. 'I'm going to see the doc, won't be long.' She thumped on her crutches towards the door. 'Don't go anywhere without me. I deserve to be in on this, wherever it takes us.'

Maureen nodded, but Bell wasn't so sure. 'See what the doc says. Let me know.'

'What are you going to do?' Anna asked.

Tognarelli responded. 'DI Bell can supervise here and I'll report to the Super and the army liaison guys.' He turned to

Bob Carruthers. 'Circulate the details of Penrose's car for possible sightings and get someone to have a look at the farm from a safe distance.'

For a while the office hummed with phone calls. 'Power's back up in Lorton,' Bob Carruthers called from his desk. A few minutes later Maureen chipped in. 'Report from a taxi driver in Braithwaite. Says he was cut up by a car late last night. He thought the driver was drunk and took the number, reported it to the local nick. It's Penrose's.'

Wong had taken up duties at the big whiteboard to gather information into one place. 'What time?' he asked, pen in hand.

'Around ten. Car came out of the Whinlatter junction without stopping and nearly took him out. Clipped the hedge on the wrong side and swerved but kept going.'

'Binoculars, a telescope, whatever you've got,' Bell roared into the phone. 'Get as close as you can, keep out of sight and see what's happening. If you need to move around, do it. Use your initiative, for fuck's sake. We need to know what's happening without getting too close... What? Yes, the man we're after is armed and crazy... OK, take someone with you if you want, and a working phone if you can find a signal up there. And step on it!'

He slammed down the handset, shaking his head. 'Muppets, all of them.'

The phone rang again. 'Yes, sir,' said Bell. Two minutes later he ended the call with an uncharacteristic smile on his face, just as the door opened and Anna hobbled back in.

'Result!' Bell cried. 'At last, someone who knows what we need right now. God bless the army.'

'Sending in the tanks, are they?' said Anna. Maureen and Bob had looked up to see what the fuss was about.

'Better,' said Bell. 'Brigadier Bertie has a helicopter coming in to pick up some bigwigs for a trip back to London and says he can spare it for half an hour for a spin over the farm. They can check who's there, movement, cars, anything we want that they can see from the air, well out of range of matey's gun if he's there, and give us an instant report back. Brilliant! We just sit tight for a little while, see what they tell us. OK?'

It didn't take long. Only fifteen minutes later, the phone rang again. The report was brief. Bell groaned. 'Have you called it in? OK. We're on it.'

He pushed back his chair and picked up his jacket. 'Bob, tell the firearms team to get moving. We're off to the farm. The bloody place is on fire! You're with me. Maureen, take Wong with you.'

'What about me?' yelled Anna to Bell's retreating figure. Wong turned back for her. 'Come on, you can't miss this,' he said. 'I'll carry you if I have to.'

The route up to the farm was more difficult for the police cars than it was for the fire engine ahead of them. They saw its blue lights flashing and heard the siren, but didn't see the depth of water on the flooded road until it was almost too late. The flood was washing up on the sides of the road when Bob in the leading car slammed on his brakes, realising just in time that they might drive into it but were unlikely to get through. Precious minutes were wasted while they turned the cars to find another way across the valley. The minibus carrying the rest of the firearms unit was high enough to drive through. 'Wait at the gate,' Bell yelled to the driver. 'Don't go in until we get there.'

Anna held on tight in the back seat as Maureen pushed the car as fast as was possible along the narrow lanes. They could already see the plume of black smoke rising over the crest of the hill ahead of them before it shredded and blew sideways on the wind that had calmed since the fury of the night before, but was still strong enough to encourage a burning building.

Wong in the passenger seat had his bag on his knee and was checking his camera and the handheld video that he loved to use at a crime scene.

'Do we know if the chopper reported anything else?' Anna asked.

'It's still there,' said Wong. 'Look.'

The helicopter came over the brow of the hill, circled round in an arc right above them and went back towards the farm. As they drew closer, higher up the hill, they could see it hovering almost motionless just out the smoke, until it turned and clattered off towards the north and its prestigious passengers.

Round the final bend in the road at the end of the farm lane the firearms unit minibus was parked askew on the muddy verge. The farm gate was open and the blue light of the fire engine was just visible at the very end of the lane. One of the firemen was standing by the wall when Maureen pulled up behind the minibus where the armed officers were still sitting awaiting orders. 'Stay here,' Wong said to Anna. 'I'll see what's happening.'

They all pulled on their overalls and boots. The risk of Foot and Mouth contamination was still ever-present, even in a different kind of crisis. 'I'm off to check with the fire boys,' Bell said. 'Maureen, stay here with the radio. No mobile signal. The rest of you, wait here.' He set off walking down the lane, a solitary squat figure picking his way through the mud towards the farmyard.

As Bell rounded the corner into the yard the scene was quieter than he'd expected. At the far end, beyond a closed gate, a herd of black and white cows was scattered across the field, enjoying a freedom they hadn't had for weeks. Two men in overalls and dirty yellow waterproof jackets were standing leaning on the gate. Hoses ran from the back of the fire truck, each held by two firemen as one jet of water played onto the steaming roof of the barn and the other through the open doors onto the far wall.

Grey smoke swirled round a yard that was awash with water mixed with dung and hay. Bell was grateful for the big boots.

A large man in full fireman's rig walked towards him. Bell produced his ID and shook the man's hand. 'You were quick off the mark,' said the fireman. 'We were expecting a couple of coppers and you arrived with a squadron.' Bell was about to explain when the fire chief went on. 'Well, you'll need a full team on this one. When our men went in to pull out the burning bales they found more than they bargained for.'

'Is there something in there?' asked Bell, peering through the smoke into the barn.

'Someone,' said the fireman. 'A bloke, and he's dead. So it's over to you, Inspector. Fire's almost out. We've left him in situ for you guys.'

'Any ID?'

'Not that we've found.' The fireman gestured towards two figures standing by the gate at the end of the yard. 'But I reckon those two know who it is.'

'What have they said?' Bell asked, looking across.

'To us, not a word, but they've been talking to each other. Arguing, by the look of it. When we got here they were more bothered about getting the cows into the field than what was going on in the barn.'

Bell looked back towards the smoking building.

'Do we know what happened in there?'

The fireman shrugged. 'That'll be for your blokes to work out. But one thing's pretty clear. The man's got a hole in the side of his head and a gun in his hand. That should give you something to go on.'

He walked away towards the barn, peered inside and had a brief conversation with his men before coming back.

The fireman took off his helmet and scratched an impressive mane of grey hair. 'We reckon it's probably safe to go in there now. Have you got a pathologist in that mob at the gate?'

Bell shook his head. 'Half that gang won't be needed now, and most of the people we need will take ages getting up here.' He sighed. 'I'll be glad when all this is done with. Bloody nightmare.'

'Good luck,' said the fire chief. 'I'll leave the appliance here for a while just in case there's a flare-up, but we'll keep out of your way. Cups of tea on offer in the kitchen. See you later.' He handed over the radio.

Bell looked across the yard at the farmhouse. 'Ah, the lovely Rose,' he said. 'OK, Pritchard,' he said into the radio. 'This is going to be interesting. Body in the barn.' The radio squawked back at him. 'Not confirmed, but who do you reckon? Anyway, this is now a crime scene. Everyone who comes up wears the full crime-scene rig. We'll need Wong straight away and he'll probably need help. And a pathologist. Can you sort all that out? Tell them to get a move on. Scene's pretty messed up already but I'm not moving the body until someone's examined it where it is.' More squawking. 'If Penrose can suit up and hobble up here, tell her to come. We could do with someone in the house just watching and listening. There's all sorts going on.'

The two men, evidently father and son, were still standing by the gate, staring across at him. Whatever they'd been saying to each other had fizzled out. The older man's face was blank with exhaustion and the younger one's eyes flitted around nervously as Bell approached them.

'Mr Heslop?' said Bell. 'This must be a blow for you.'

Eric Heslop shrugged and mumbled something inaudible.

Bell looked at the younger man. 'This is Aidan, is it? We've not met, son,' said Bell, 'but I know quite a lot about this farm already.'

Aidan stared. He looked as if he was about to burst.

Bell pointed towards the farmhouse. 'Need you both to go inside. This whole area's a crime scene. You know the firemen found someone in the barn?'

They both nodded. Aidan asked, 'Is he dead?'

'You'll be informed in due course,' said Bell, 'but for now we need everyone out of the way so our blokes can examine everything. OK?'

He stood back and ushered them both towards the door. From the other end of the yard a small group was approaching, looking like something from a science-fiction film, except that one of them was using a very low-tech walking aid.

Eric noticed. 'What's up with her?' he asked.

'Minor accident,' said Bell. 'DS Penrose is perfectly able to do her work. Just wait here a moment, will you?'

Bell kept his back to the two men and said quietly to Anna, 'When these two go in the house, get them tea, butties, anything they need, but keep them apart. They've already had an argument according to the fire chief and I don't want them cooking anything up between them before we get them down to the station.'

'Right,' said Anna. 'Is Rose inside? What about her?'

'Keep her busy too,' he said. 'And watch them all. Put Aidan in another room with Bob. The lad's agitated, Farmer Eric looks as if he couldn't care less. We'll get them away as soon as we can but I want to hear what the pathologist has to say first.'

'He reckons he'll be half an hour minimum.'

Eric held the door for Anna, who hobbled awkwardly into the porch and on into the kitchen. She stopped suddenly. The crutch clattered to the floor. Rose Heslop was standing by the Aga. Behind her, sitting in the big chair, was a girl. She was pale and looked exhausted but very familiar. It was Helen.

Chapter 23

Rose went to stand by her daughter, one arm around her shoulders. Brian stood by Helen's chair, holding a toy lamb in his arms. His eyes were wide, and he moved over to hide behind his mother.

Rose said quietly, 'She got here last night, late.' She stroked her daughter's damp hair. 'Walked all the way from the other side of Cockermouth, didn't you, pet?'

Anna was speechless, questions bouncing in her head. 'Why…' she began. 'Why didn't you get help, Helen?

The girl looked up at her mother, who nodded. Helen's voice was very weak. 'He said – he told me the soldiers would lock me up if they found me, for spreading the disease. I was afraid so I hid in a shed.' The girl began to cry. 'Then I was sick.'

Rose held her close. 'She needs a doctor.'

'Stay with her,' said Anna. She turned to Aidan, silent and watchful. 'Go out in the yard and ask DI Bell, the policeman who's out there, to come in here. Tell him it's urgent, and we need a doctor or a paramedic.' Aidan stood silent, rooted to the spot. 'Now, Aidan,' said Anna firmly, and the boy looked at her blankly before doing what she said.

Bell pushed open the kitchen door and he too stared at Helen. 'Bloody hell!' he said. Anna repeated what Rose had said.

Bell asked, 'When did she get back?'

'Late last night, early hours. I'm not sure,' Rose replied. 'She was in a bad way. She's had some food and a sleep, and she's much better now. But we still need a doctor.'

Bell stood quite still, working out what to do first. He turned to Anna. 'DS Penrose, you and DC Pritchard will be in here. DC Carruthers will stay with Aidan in the other room. We need statements from everyone, and I must ask you not to communicate with each other, any of you, until those are complete. Is that understood?' He looked round the crowded room. 'I'll be outside, in the barn.' He hesitated. 'There are things out there that need my attention. The fire is under control now, so there's no danger to the house or to the other buildings.'

'Cows need milking,' said Eric, who was standing on the far side of the room. 'We were out there to do it earlier on when we saw the fire, moved the beasts out of the way, but they still need milking.'

Bell understood nothing about milking cows, and cared less. Anna helped him out. 'Milking can wait, sir, until Mr Heslop has made his statement.' She needed to say more. 'After that, I think we should take everyone down to the station in Workington. Much easier to leave the scene and do the rest of the business down there.'

Bell thought about this. 'Agreed,' he said. 'Thanks.'

Eric persisted. 'What about the cows, later on?'

'Leave that with us, Mr Heslop,' Anna said. 'We'll work something out.'

Out in the yard the wind had dropped and a watery sun was appearing periodically between high clouds. It was less cold but the forensic team that was straggling up the lane looked anything but thrilled to be there. Tony Wong briefed his colleagues and the work was divided between them. Wong himself started examining the quad bike that stood just inside the gate on the eastern side of the yard, close to the barn from which wisps of smoke still issued, floating round the yard and catching in their nostrils. Bell walked down the lane to check on a doctor for Helen and the pathologist's arrival, update Tognarelli, and explain the change of circumstances to the firearms team, half of whom were already asleep in the relative warmth of their minibus. He watched as the bus manoeuvred a tight turn and set off back down the hill, and then he plodded back to the farmhouse.

'Just a word, DS Penrose. Can you step outside for a moment?' Anna leaned on the wall by the porch door and Bell leaned in close to speak to her without being overheard. 'How the hell did a kid with asthma get all the way back home from where we found the van, without help and without being noticed?' he asked. Anna shook her head. 'Sounds like Wetherall told her that she'd be locked up if anyone saw her. She's lucky to be alive. We could have two bodies on our hands now.' She paused. 'Topped himself, did he?'

'Looks like it. See what the doc says when he gets here. No one here seems that bothered. All standing around like zombies.'

'What do you make of Rose?' Bell whispered.

'Calm as the day is long,' said Anna. 'Look at her. Making tea like nothing's happened.'

'I reckon Pritchard had it wrong all along,' said Bell. 'Wetherall's a psycho, kidnapped her kid, topped himself when she didn't give in to him.'

Anna shrugged. 'Well, there's her, the husband, and the son who looks like he's seen a ghost. Between the three of them, we should be able to squeeze out what went on here last night.'

Bell looked up at the last wisps of smoke on the wind. 'I wouldn't put it past Farmer Heslop to have torched his own barn.'

'To cover up the body?'

'No, for the insurance money. If he's not getting any compo for the cows, the insurance on the barn might be handy.'

'What about my car?'

Bell waved his arm in the general direction. 'One of the forensics guys is checking the fields beyond the barn. There's a lane over there where Wetherall could have left it. Think of the prize at the end: his beloved Rose. And she's still looking like butter wouldn't melt.'

Around the farm buildings the forensic team was busy, but inside the farmhouse the atmosphere was subdued. With Alex dead, tension had drained away like the water from the firemen's hoses. The doctor from Cockermouth arrived, examined Helen and sent her back to bed. He had gone, and the silence in the farmhouse had resumed when the forensic pathologist finally arrived. 'Farmer suicide again, is it?' Dr Mukerjee said to Bell as they walked across to the barn together. 'Seen a few of those recently. Why don't they talk to someone instead of blowing their brains out?'

'Bit different this,' said Bell, stopping outside the closed barn door. 'The deceased has no connection with this farm, except for a suspected relationship with the wife. Before we found him here he held my sergeant captive for a while in her own home. She managed to wound him and escape, and made the ID this morning. Nothing on the body to identify him other than that, but we know who he is.'

'Quite a charmer by the sound of it,' said Dr Mukerjee. 'Have the forensics boys been in the barn yet?'

'Plenty more for them to do so they've left this for you. Take your time.' said Bell. He didn't know this doctor except by reputation, and had heard he was thorough and slow. Given the state of this investigation so far, thorough and slow sounded very welcome.

Back in the farmhouse Bell helped himself to tea and a piece of cake from the tin on the table. Anna had taken a preliminary statement from Eric but it didn't amount to much. He'd finished work around seven, come in, eaten supper, drunk too much and fallen asleep, first at the table and then on the couch in the other room. The power had gone off just after they'd eaten and hadn't come back on. The phone didn't work. That's why they hadn't called the fire brigade when they spotted smoke in the barn as they were about to start milking. No, he hadn't been out of the house all night. Aidan had been in the house all night too, after supper. Yes, he'd been tired and a bit tight but he would have heard the quad bike. And his wife and younger son were in the house too, he was sure of that. Lousy night, they weren't going anywhere, were they? No, he wasn't awake when Helen got home. His wife had looked after the girl and put her to bed, straight away. He'd only heard she was back first thing this morning.

Now Eric sat at the table with his arms folded and eyes closed. Anna pulled herself up and limped across to the porch to have a whispered conversation with her boss. 'Saw nothing, knows nothing, and lying through his teeth, is my guess,' she said. 'Claims he and Aidan were arguing earlier about the future of the herd.'

Bell rolled his eyes. 'He must think we're really stupid. What about the blessed Rose?'

'She and the doctor took Helen upstairs to be checked out, and she stayed up there with both the younger kids. Came down briefly to get some food for them, but nothing was said and she went back up again without a word.'

'How does she look?'

Anna thought for a moment before she answered. 'In a word, calm,' she said. 'Weird.'

'Do you want a break?' Bell asked. 'You probably shouldn't be here at all, with the ankle and all.'

'I'm just tired,' she said. 'Back of the car for a kip sounds good. Can I leave this with Pritchard for a while?'

'Go,' said Bell. 'I'll call Wong in to organise getting clothes off our three stooges. Might look like an open and shut suicide but I'm not taking any chances. We'll have all the clothing checked for trace and firearms residue. By the book.'

Bob and Maureen had finished the preliminary statements. As they waited for further instructions, Bob took Aidan off into the other room to calm him down and Maureen was making another pot of tea. Bell found Bob and the agitated boy playing cards, which were hastily swept off the small table when the boss appeared. Bob jumped to his feet. 'Statement all done, sir,' he said. 'Waiting for forensics now, are we?'

Bell nodded. 'SOCO will be collecting clothing, so can you ask Mrs Heslop about spare stuff for everyone?' Bob edged past him, glad to be back in action, and Bell turned to Aidan. The boy looked back at him, and then said quietly, 'He shot himself. That man, the one in the barn.'

'Did he?' mused Bell. 'And do you know who he is?'

Aidan looked down at his hands. 'He knows my mam.'

'Well, well, small world, isn't it? And how do you know that?'

The boy didn't look up. 'She told me about him. He's a friend of hers from way back.'

'And does your father know about this?'

'We all know he took Helen,' said Aidan, 'not my dad, the man in the barn.'

'So it's worked out rather neatly, hasn't it?' said Bell, winking at Bob. 'Tidy, as my old mam would have said. And you put all that in your statement to the constable, did you?'

Aidan shook his head. 'He never asked me about all that,' he said. 'I just told him what happened last night.'

'And what did happen last night? Tell me.'

Aidan began to talk, rather too quickly. 'I was in all night, after supper. The power went off. It was really windy, things were banging around. Dad got pissed, like he does. Then this morning before milking we saw smoke and Dad opened the door of the barn. He said some of the hay bales were on fire, and there was a man lying on the floor. We thought he was dead. We had to get the cows out of the shed in case the fire spread.'

'Any sign of a mobile phone in there, or some money lying around?'

Aidan shook his head. 'What money? Where?'

Bell carried on, still standing over the boy who strained his neck to look at him. 'And what about calling us or the fire brigade?'

'Couldn't, could we?' said Aidan, with growing confidence. 'No power, no phone.'

'No mobile?'

'Doesn't work, no signal here.'

'OK, that's your story, is it?'

Aidan's face flushed. 'That's the truth. Ask my dad.'

That's two out of three of them lying, Bell said to himself as he went back to the kitchen. He'd already noticed the fresh mud on the tyres of the quad bike that showed it had been used overnight since the rain had started. Why did people always think that they could lie and get away with it? Wong was in the porch taking off his boots, and several large brown paper bags sat waiting to be filled with clothes. 'Getting what you need?' Bell asked the SOCO, who looked the happiest man in the place.

'Fine, thank you, sir. We've got as much trace as we can, although the yard's a bit of a write-off and the barn's been affected by smoke and water obviously.'

Maybe that was the idea, Bell thought. Not much chance of the body being consumed by a slow-burning fire, but it would be bound to mess up the forensics. He crossed the yard and pushed open the door to the barn. Dr Mukerjee was standing looking down at the man Bell had spent the past several days chasing fruitlessly round the county. 'First impressions?' he asked.

Mukerjee rested his hands on his hips. 'Interesting,' he said. 'I'll know more when we get him on a slab, but there's something about this entry wound,' he pointed to the side of Alex's head, 'that doesn't look quite right, if this was the gun that was used.' He rubbed his gloved hands together. 'I'll let you know the details as soon as I can. Workington CID, yes?'

'What about personal possessions?' Bell asked. 'Any sign of a phone?'

Mukerjee shook his head. 'Nothing in the pockets. Empty bottle of whisky beside the body, and the gun still in his hand. The forensics boys have taken those and the man's bag. I'll get my report to you as soon as possible.'

'We'll be at the station. We're taking all the family members down there as soon as we're done here.' Another thought occurred to Bell. 'What about money?' he asked. 'A lot of it.'

Mukerjee shook his head. 'Just a few pounds in his wallet. Could be more in the bag. Apparently there was some whisky in there, and some pills. But no one mentioned a phone or a lot of money.'

Bell nodded. 'Any idea about time of death?'

'Well,' said Mukerjee, 'from the state of the body, I'd say several hours ago.' He checked his watch. 'Let's say between midnight and five this morning.'

'But the fire wasn't spotted until we got the helicopter here about nine,' said Bell.

'Good luck,' said Mukerjee. 'Not sure this one is as straightforward as it looks. You'll get the body out as soon as you can?'

Bell followed him into the yard. Nothing in this case had been as straightforward as it looked, right from the start. He called to Wong who was emerging from the farmhouse carrying several large bags.

'You picked up Wetherall's bag from the barn?'

Tony Wong nodded.

'Any sign of a phone, or a large amount of money?'

Tony shook his head. 'Not in the barn. Do you want us to search elsewhere?'

Bell looked around the yard and the buildings all around it, and his heart sank. If someone wanted to hide two small items they could be anywhere. Ten men could tear the place apart and still come up with nothing. He needed to think about it. 'Not now,' he said. 'Maybe later.'

Chapter 24

The first priority for Bell was to cover his back by checking with Tognarelli. This involved standing ignominiously behind the crime scene in the only place on the farm where the mobile signal actually worked.

'Strictly speaking, DI Bell,' said Sam Tognarelli, 'the search for Helen was my investigation, and interviews with her would be done by my team, but all these events are so bound up with each other that it makes more sense to leave it up to you. Have you got enough people?'

'Not really, sir,' said Bell, 'but I'd still prefer to keep all the information we gather in one place. DS Penrose is fit for duty and very keen to carry on. She says she's better off with us, doing her job, than staying on her own at home.'

'Pretty impressive, from what I hear,' said Tognarelli.

'Army training, sir… self-defence, all that stuff.'

'And it worked. Could have been far worse.'

'Well, if we can keep her working we should have enough bodies. We're taking all the parties involved down to Workington, now preliminary statements are sorted. They'll probably want solicitors, all that.'

'That's their right, of course,' said his boss. 'All this will need doing by the book.'

'Exactly, sir,' Bell said. 'and we need to think carefully about how to deal with the two younger children. Helen's statement will be critical in clearing up the case against Wetherall, but it's hard to know what we could get from the younger child.'

'How old is the little one?'

'Six, and very tied to his mother.'

There was a pause while Sam Tognarelli weighed the implications of various courses of action. In the end it was agreed that Mrs Haile in Carlisle was the best choice to support the children while the family's adults were being held for questioning.

'One last question, DI Bell,' said Tognarelli. 'This looks at the outset to be a suicide – motive, opportunity, means, all quite clear, aren't they?'

'I thought so too, sir,' Bell replied. 'But now I'm not so sure.'

'Keep an open mind,' said Tognarelli.

It took a while to arrange the logistics of getting everyone away from the farm. Once forensics had finished with Anna's car it was brought round to the main gate. Wong would drive it back, with Eric Heslop alongside Anna in the back. Rose and Aidan would be with Bell, and Maureen would be taking both the younger children to Carlisle. She would interview them there, in the presence of their grandmother, and then leave them both in Mrs Haile's care.

Maureen talked to Bell before she set off. 'I've got an idea. Why don't I take Rose with the children? They've been through a lot and it might be reassuring for them, to have Mum hand them over to Granny.'

'And?' said Bell. He knew what Maureen was after.

'Rose is in a funny frame of mind, don't you think, sort of dreamy?'

Bell nodded. 'Penrose said she looked calm.'

'Exactly,' said Maureen. 'With all this going on, is that normal? I reckon I could get her to talk, like people do sometimes, sitting side by side not across a table.'

'Inadmissible, all of it,' said Bell.

'Of course, but priceless even so, when the formal questioning starts. If we get the truth out of one of them, we can turn the others. Guilty pleas to whatever charges we end up using, no trial, public money saved… you know how the bosses love that.'

'They'll lawyer up, bound to.'

'OK, but we're not dealing with hardened crims here, are we? This family's a mess, at odds with itself, secrets smouldering away. Just a bit of air, that's all it needs to start it flaring up.'

Bell looked at her. 'They'd have thought you were a witch a few centuries ago, you know that?'

She grinned back at him. 'Better hair though, eh?'

As soon as they arrived in Workington, Aidan and Eric were cautioned and checked into separate interview rooms. Eric insisted on his phone call and pulled a scrap of paper out of his pocket with the number of a solicitor in Cockermouth. He's come prepared, Bell thought: there was more to Eric Heslop than met the eye. In this different environment he seemed to have grown taller, with a mind that was working properly, now that the alcoholic haze had lifted.

The statements that the two men had given were patently false: it was just a question of which would be the first to fall apart. Given Eric's freshly cleared head, it was Aidan that Bell and Carruthers began with, but before that another young man had arrived at the station and introduced himself as Ian Featherstone, the family solicitor.

'Just you, is it, sir?' Bob had asked as he met Featherstone at the desk.

'Why, do you think they're going to turn on each other?' Featherstone asked, with more energy than his slight frame hinted at.

'Well, you never know, do you?' said Bob, cheerily.

Bell turned on the tape recorder in the cheerless interview room and spoke the necessary introductions into it. He made a great show of reading Aidan's statement, with care and without comment.

'I'll call you Aidan, if that's OK?' he began mildly. 'Well, Aidan, according to the statement you gave to DC Carruthers up at the farm, you were at the house all last evening, is that right?'

Aidan nodded. 'After milking we had supper, and then we stayed in. It was a bad night.'

'So you didn't go out at all?'

'No, I said, didn't I?'

'There's a quad bike at the farm, isn't there?'

Aidan nodded.

Bell looked down at his notes. 'I need you to answer, Aidan, for the tape, see?'

'Yes.'

'So who took the quad bike out last night, I wonder?'

'No one did,' Aidan said.

'It was wet last night, wasn't it?' There was no response to this, but it didn't matter. Bell pressed on, 'And the tyres of the quad bike this morning were covered in fresh mud, still wet.'

Aidan shook his head and this time Bob pointed at the tape machine.

'Dunno,' said Aidan.

'Your father took it out, maybe?' Bell asked.

'No,' said the boy with conviction. 'He didn't go anywhere. He had a drink after supper and went to sleep.' He hesitated. 'He often does that.'

'So who could it have been, I wonder?' mused Bell. 'Your mother?'

Aidan laughed. 'Never,' he said. 'She wouldn't have a clue.'

'So it's a mystery, isn't it?' Bell shuffled his papers. 'Let's leave that open, shall we, and talk about mobile phones.'

Aidan looked up, from Bell to Carruthers and back again. 'Haven't got one. No signal at the farm.'

Bell leaned towards him. 'Oh, but there is a signal actually, just behind the barn that caught fire, something to do with the skyline and the transmitter, a little pocket of signal. You remember when we found your mum's earring, after Helen went missing? That's where your mum took off her earring to use the phone, the one she claims she doesn't have.'

'So?' said Aidan. 'None of us have one.'

'So why was Alex Wetherall, the man we found in the barn this morning, ringing your mother on a mobile number over the past few days? Actually, over the past few weeks, months, years?'

'That's a lie,' said Aidan. 'You made that up.'

'What if we found Alex Wetherall's phone?' said Bell, 'in the barn. Doesn't take long to check the calls.'

Aidan looked at the solicitor sitting beside him. Bell gestured him to go ahead and Aidan whispered to Featherstone, who then looked up and asked if he could have a moment to consult with his client. Bell nodded mildly, turned off the recorder and stood up. He and Bob picked up their papers and stepped out of the room.

Outside, they looked back through the window. Aidan was sitting looking at his hands. Bob pointed to the switch that would amplify what was being said in the room, but Bell shook his head.

'Let them talk,' he said. 'Aidan's falling apart already. Plan A is crumbling. Eric must have known that it would, so he'll have to come in with Plan B. But let's see how much Aidan will give us now that the dam has been breached.'

They waited, and shortly Mr Featherstone opened the door and called them back into the room.

'My client would like to add to his statement,' he said.

'Add to it, or change it?' Bob asked.

'Well,' said Featherstone, 'let's see what he has to say.'

Aidan looked up. Whatever confidence he'd shown had ebbed away. 'I did go out, on the quad bike,' he whispered. 'I came back after it started raining, in the mud.'

'Time?' asked Bob, without looking up from his notes.

Aidan shrugged. 'Must have been about eleven, maybe midnight.'

'And where had you been?'

'Meet up with mates, lads from other farms. We're all stuck on them now, see. It gets boring, so we meet up at night, have a drink, you know.'

He rubbed a hand over his eyes. 'We have a den, like, in the wood, just down the lane.'

'A den.' Bell's disparagement was clear in his tone. 'Like kids. Bottle of cider and a few ciggies, is it?'

'We're not kids,' said Aidan, irritated by the man's tone. 'We do men's work. Can't go to pubs or Young Farmers while the outbreak's on, can we? Anyway, we didn't stay long, it was too wet. So I came back.'

Bell pressed on. 'And when you got back to the farm after this excitement, what did you do? And don't tell me you parked the bike and went off to bed like a good boy.' He leaned forward.

'You went into the barn, didn't you? Did you see something in there, a light maybe?'

'I...' said Aidan, and then stopped himself. He looked again at Featherstone, who didn't respond. Aidan looked up at the ceiling and closed his eyes. He has no idea how to tell a lie, Bell realised. Whatever else his mother taught him, she forgot to teach him that.

'I heard something,' said the boy finally. 'In the barn. I opened the door and looked in. He was smoking, the man who was in there, I could see his cigarette end.'

'Smoking and talking to himself?'

'No, he was with someone. They had a lamp.'

Bob interrupted: a change of voice was sometimes enough to be disconcerting in an interview. 'Who was it?' he said loudly. 'Who else was in the barn?'

'Do I have to say?' Aidan asked Featherstone desperately.

'Yes,' said the solicitor. 'Tell them.'

'It was my mam.' Aidan's voice was just a whisper. 'I heard them talking and I went in. She was standing looking down at the man.'

'And what did you do then?' Bell asked. Bob Carruthers looked up.

'I went for the shotgun,' said Aidan. 'I pointed it at him and told him to get out.'

Bell pushed his chair back, then leaned forward to say into the tape, 'Interview suspended, 13.20 hours. DI Bell and DC Carruthers leaving the room.'

Back in the office, Bell slammed the file down on his desk. 'A shotgun! Why didn't we know there was a shotgun? I don't want any more surprises. Where's that bloody Chinky SOCO, and the forensics report, and the pathologist's? We have to sit on our thumbs waiting for people to tell us what's been going on, and I won't take surprises from a wimp like that Heslop kid!'

Bob retreated to the safety of his desk, tucked away at the far end of the office, on pretence of checking any messages. Bell was being his usual petulant self, but they could have guessed a working farm would have a shotgun somewhere around. The surprise was they hadn't already found it.

Bell was still fuming, pushing papers round his desk in a display of misplaced irritation. 'So it's back to the drawing board on this interview. Bob, get up here,' he roared. 'I want the pathologist's report before we go any further. He said there was something funny about the entry wound and I want to know what he meant. I can't be asking questions I don't already know the answers to.'

'Right, boss,' said Bob. He knew there was no point in arguing.

After some calls with furious whispering on Bob's side, the phone on Bell's desk rang and was quickly picked up. It was Mukerjee calling him.

'Inspector, I promised you my report as soon as I could provide it, and I simply haven't had time yet to investigate as thoroughly as you want.'

'OK, OK, Doctor,' said Bell, trying to control his response. He'd realised that there was little mileage in pissing off an expert he needed as much as he needed this one. 'One of our witnesses, and a possible suspect, has just mentioned the presence of a shotgun that we previously knew nothing about. The full report isn't ready yet, I accept that, but is there any evidence you can see regarding the involvement of a shotgun, anything at all?'

'Well,' said Mukerjee, 'since you ask, there is. You recall I suggested that something was a bit odd about the entry wound?'

'I do, that's one reason why I'm calling now.'

'Well, if this is a suicide, it's the first suicide I've seen where the victim has shot himself in the ear.'

'The ear?'

'Yes, I take it our deceased person was right-handed?'

Good question, thought Bell. Someone must have checked that, surely. 'As far as we know, yes.'

'And the gun would therefore be held in the right hand and aimed to do the job. Sometimes that means in the mouth, for some reason, more often to the side of the temple or under the chin.'

'Yes,' said Bell, impatient to get to the point. 'But this man shot himself in the ear, you say?'

'That's where the bullet entered, but the damage to the skin around the entry wound was a puzzle until I got a closer look. The ear had been shredded by shotgun pellets at some point before the fatal bullet was fired.'

'How long before?'

'At least an hour, I would say. There was a fair amount of blood loss, from that wound and from the earlier injury inflicted by your officer as I understand it?'

'Yes, DS Penrose caught him with a breadknife in her efforts to escape. He was threatening her with the same gun, the SIG Sauer.'

'Aha,' said Mukerjee. 'Well, the combination of blood loss, shock and too much whisky must have left our victim pretty vulnerable, I would say. Very weak.'

'Too weak to shoot himself.'

'Oh, I couldn't say that, but too weak to get away.'

I couldn't say. What a mealy-mouthed expression that is, Bell thought to himself.

'Well, thank you, very helpful,' he said, politely. 'Is there anything else at this stage?'

There was a lengthy pause. 'I would say that's probably all I can give you definitively for now, Inspector. The full report should be with you by, say, six this evening.'

Bell sat for a few minutes at his desk, digesting this information. It would be very difficult to shoot yourself in the ear with a shotgun, and why would you when there was a handy little gun so close at hand? So he could assume the shotgun did not belong to Wetherall, and was not fired by him. In that case, who fired a shotgun, why at the man's ear, and where was the weapon now? He picked up the phone and rang forensics.

Chapter 25

'Gun shot residue results?' said Wong. 'Hang on a minute... Yep, those are in. Some trace, not much, on the right sleeve of the boy, Aidan, from a shotgun. Nothing on Rose's clothes. No residue on the father, but some indication on his fingers of oil from a shotgun. Can't hang much on that, though, because of the time lapse. They could all have changed their clothes before we turned up and hidden or destroyed the ones they'd been wearing at the critical time. There are some other bits and pieces that we're trying to figure out at the moment and I'll keep you posted. Fingerprint results are in too, do you want those?'

Bell listened hard and scribbled furiously as those results came through. 'Just the one set of Wetherall's prints on the pistol, that's all? Smudged round the trigger, you said? Aidan's prints on the quad bike, yes. Don't worry about the car for now, we know who that belongs to. Listen, there's something else. Did any of you find traces of shotgun use in the barn?... No, we didn't know either until just now. Cartridge could have been picked up, but looks like most of the pellets went wide, past our victim and presumably into the hay bales behind him. Can you get up there again? And have another look for a mobile phone, just in case it got missed.'

He was about to ring off in sheer frustration when he remembered the question of the money. 'That £50 note we found at Wetherall's hide-out near the Solway, did you have a look at it?' There was a slight pause. 'Traces of cocaine, well no surprise there. No other notes like that found anywhere, in the bag or near the body?… OK, thanks. I'll be creative with what I've got so far and see if I can frighten the lad into a confession… Yes, the lad… OK. Let me know, as fast as you can, right? PACE clock's ticking.'

Bell looked up. He wanted food and a cup of tea, but it would have to wait. 'Bob?' he bellowed. 'Come on, we'll have another go at the lad. Let his dad stew a bit longer.'

Rose had been upstairs almost all the time since giving her initial and very brief statement to Bob Carruthers. She must have realised that the evidence so painstakingly gathered by the forensics team would make it impossible for her to deny that she'd been in the barn with Alex the night before. Yes, she'd found him there. No, she hadn't expected to see him. He was injured and unable to move and they couldn't call the police because of the power cut. Yes, she did have a mobile phone at one time but it was lost. No, she hadn't seen Alex's phone and knew nothing about any money. Yes, she tried to dress the man's wound, and had given him some food. She was shocked that he shot himself but he was a strange sad man and was obviously at the end of his tether and knew that he would be charged with taking Helen. It was a terrible situation and she was so relieved to have her daughter home safe. That was all she had to say, she needed to be with her children.

When it was time to take the children to Carlisle, Rose had changed her clothes and Maureen could finally see why the men seemed to fall for her. She was wearing what she would probably put on for work, with her hair pinned up, just one dark curl escaping by the side of her face. Earrings, smart shoes, a skirt.

'Work clothes.' She smiled when Maureen looked admiringly at the outfit. 'Haven't had the chance to get dressed up for weeks, ever since the outbreak started. It feels good.'

Maureen had to remind herself that this woman had just experienced someone she knew well being found shot dead a few metres from this house, unless they'd got the story completely wrong. They still hadn't found the damn' phone that could have told them so much. It could be anywhere.

Helen looked more like herself too. There was a spare puffer in the house and she'd been able to use just enough to open up the clogged airways and bring some colour back into her face. A bath and food and sleep had worked wonders, although she was clearly suffering from the whole experience. She clung very close to her mother and Brian too, Maureen noticed. Hardly surprising. She wondered what the long-term impact on the girl might be.

'We need to talk to Mum and Dad and Aidan too, Helen,' Maureen said to her, as they put some clothes into a bag in Helen's bedroom. 'You understand?'

Helen nodded.

'And you can tell me all about what happened since you left school on Friday. Granny Jo will sit with us while we talk. Will that be OK?'

Helen nodded again. Maureen hoped she'd be more relaxed at the interview or the conversation would be fruitless.

Downstairs Brian was waiting with Rose, clutching his toy lamb. 'Shall I take Lamby for you?' said his mother. She held up the toy to her face. 'I lost my sheep,' she said to Maureen, 'and they weren't even sick.'

'So you told me,' said Maureen. 'Let's go, shall we?'

The day was much brighter now and milder too, the wind less strong and from the south-west rather than the easterly gale that had hit them overnight. The road to Carlisle was quiet and familiar. Brian and Helen went to sleep in the back of the car almost immediately, lolling against their seat straps, their heads almost touching.

Maureen peered into the rear-view mirror before she spoke. 'There'll be some tough questions, Rose, you know that, don't you?'

Rose looked steadily straight ahead. 'I know,' she said. 'I've been expecting them.'

'You'll need to be straight about your previous relationship with Alex. It's going to come out, if not from you then from Christine, or your mother even, or Alex's. It could be painful.'

Silence.

Maureen asked, 'Does Eric know?'

Rose looked down at her hands. 'He knows that Alex and I were close, before I was married. He may have heard rumours about us, while he was working away. But we don't talk about it.'

'Working away where?' Maureen asked. 'When?'

'When we were first married Eric was working for contractors at Sellafield, and they sent him south sometimes. That was before Eric's dad got ill and we took over the farm.'

Maureen nodded. What Christine Strong had told her was making sense now. 'What about Aidan, does he know about Alex?'

Rose shook her head. 'He was just a bairn.'

Maureen drove a little further, deciding what line to take. She only had the hour or so that the journey would last, and half of it was already behind them. It was early afternoon, not much chance of traffic hold-ups. She needed to get Rose to reveal more.

'You know that Alex attacked my colleague Anna in her own home, don't you?'

Rose said sharply, 'Attacked her? I thought he just stole her car.'

'He held her at gunpoint. She was lucky to get away. He's a violent man, Rose. How could you get involved with someone like that?'

If there was ever a time for her to tell me to piss off and mind my own business, this is it, Maureen thought. But Rose didn't react. If anything she seemed flattered, smiling at the idea that someone was curious about her.

Rose openly scrutinised the police officer. 'How long have you been married?' she asked.

'Nearly thirty years,' said Maureen.

'And it's still, you know, fresh?' She paused for a moment, choosing her next word with care. 'Passionate?'

Maureen chuckled. 'We have our moments.' She took her eyes off the road momentarily to glance at Rose. 'Is that why you wanted a lover? For the excitement?'

Silence fell again, so Maureen continued, as if she were talking to herself. 'I wouldn't know where to start. Making arrangements… furtive meetings. I'd be too worried about things going wrong.'

It was enough. Rose began to talk. 'I was worried to start with, but then… I got careless. I was flattered. It was, you know, exciting. You don't think things through sometimes, do you?'

'What kind of things?

'Oh, these modern gadgets. The kids know how to use them properly, but I never learned.' Her voice tailed away. In the back seat, Brian and Helen slumbered on. They were nearing the outskirts of the city.

Maureen tried again. 'Are you talking about the phone?'

‘That damn’ phone,’ said Rose. ‘He gave it me. Wish he’d never bothered.’

‘Where is it now?’ Maureen asked, without looking at her or changing her tone.

‘I don’t know, do I? I told them already, I lost it.’

When Maureen glanced sideways, Rose was smiling at her.

‘I need to ask you again,’ Maureen began, but Rose cut her off.

‘Did I know he had Helen? I thought he might have wanted to see her, but… no, of course not. I didn’t know what he’d done.’ Rose turned back to stare out of the window at the road ahead. ’I’m not saying any more.’

And that was it. No more was said as they drove into the city. Maureen wondered if they would ever discover enough to crack Rose’s composure and find the truth inside, hiding like a sea creature in its impregnable shell.

Chapter 26

Helen dissolved in tears when she saw her grandmother, and the two of them stood holding each other in the dark hall of the guesthouse. Rose held on to Brian's hand and Maureen saw that both of them were crying too. Fortunately there were few guests around at that hour of the day and Jo Haile could give her full attention to what needed to be done. She'd asked a friend to come in after school with her little boy, and Brian was able to relax for a short while with a child of his own age and just play, away from the tensions of home. Rose sat with them, but didn't say or do anything. She looked exhausted.

In Jo's small untidy office Helen perched on the best chair and Maureen and Jo sat side by side on a bench carried in from the hall.

Most of the details about Helen's movements immediately after school on the previous Friday were already known, pieced together from other witnesses, but there were still a few things that Maureen needed to know, even though the case against Alex Wetherall was now moot.

'Where did you first meet him?' Maureen asked.

Helen looked at Jo, who smiled. 'Go on, pet,' she said. 'You can tell Maureen, it's OK.'

Gradually the story emerged. Helen remembered how surprised and annoyed she'd been when Alex had referred to her mum as 'my Rose'.

'I thought that was silly,' said the girl. Jo Haile looked down at her hands.

Helen showed Maureen the raw scars on her wrist where Alex had tied it. 'But I told him it hurt and he took the cord off,' she said.

'Why did he have to tie you up? Were you trying to get away?'

Helen looked puzzled. 'He said I needed to get to know him… something like that. And then he said he had to protect us from the police and the army, that they would lock us both up for spreading the disease.' She shook her head. 'Was that true?'

Maureen smiled. 'No, pet. We were all out looking for you, the police and the army too. We were very worried about you.'

'When the van crashed, I thought he might be dead, and he wouldn't be able to protect me any more, so I had to get away.'

'Is that why you didn't want people to find you, because you thought they might lock you up?' said Maureen.

Helen nodded. 'I heard dogs early on, but then they stopped. And another dog frightened me when I was in the shed behind the garage.' She began to cry. Jo glared at Maureen, then reached out to hold her grand-daughter's hand.

Maureen made a note to herself to give the garage a piece of her mind about how a young girl in obvious need of help went unnoticed by their staff, despite all the publicity about a missing child.

'And what about last night, before you got back to the farm? You walked a long way,' said Maureen.

Helen used the hankie Jo had given her to wipe her eyes. 'I felt funny, like I was sleep-walking. My feet hurt but I knew which road to take and I just kept walking. If the wind was too strong or I got tired I sat down by the wall for a while. But I wanted to see my mum and Brian, so I kept walking.'

Maureen knew the next question would be critical.

'When you got to the farm, pet, what did you do?'

Helen hesitated. 'I found my mum.'

'And where was she?'

'In the kitchen.'

'In the house, not outside?'

'In the kitchen,' said Helen again, raising her voice slightly. 'She cried when she saw me.'

'You didn't go into the barn yourself, where Alex was?'

'No. Mum said not to.'

'Did she tell you that Alex was there?'

'Yes, but I didn't see him. I had some food, and cake, and Mum said I had to have a bath. And then I went to bed.'

'Did you hear anything else during the night? Did anything wake you?'

Helen shook her head.

'What about this morning?'

'I heard Dad and Aidan getting the cows out of the shed.'

'Where was your mum then?'

Helen shrugged. 'Don't know.'

'Did you go out into the yard yourself?'

Helen shook her head again. 'We heard the helicopter, and I could smell the smoke, and then the fire engine came.'

'And then we arrived, didn't we?' said Maureen smiling. 'We were very surprised to see you, and very pleased too.' She took Helen's hand, but the girl pulled it away. 'Don't,' she said, and stood up. 'Is that all?'

Jo stood up and held Helen close to her. 'She's had enough now Maureen, you can see that.'

Maureen smiled and closed her notebook. Clearly Helen didn't want to talk any more, but Maureen felt there was something she was holding back. Whatever it was would have to wait.

'Thanks for talking to me, Helen,' she said. 'You've been a great help, and so strong, to come through all of this. Maybe we'll talk again, but no more for now, eh?' She turned to Jo. 'I'll get back. Are you sure you'll be OK?'

'We'll be fine, won't we, Helen?' said her grandmother. 'You and me and Brian, having a wee holiday together.' She looked at Maureen again. 'Just overnight?'

'We'll see. I'll ring you, OK?'

Rose looked up when Maureen walked into the residents' lounge where the two boys were playing.

'All done,' Maureen said. 'Your daughter's very brave, she's been through a lot. What did the doctor say this morning?'

Rose lowered her voice. 'He said she was obviously suffering from exhaustion, and that the puffer had been too strong for her, but she would be fine in a few days.' She paused. 'I need to be with her.'

Maureen didn't respond to this request. 'We must do our jobs, Rose,' she said quietly. The boys were busy playing, taking no notice. 'A man has died,' she went on. 'We have to find out exactly what happened.'

'Isn't it obvious?' Rose said with sudden annoyance, turning towards the door. 'He was ill, and in terrible trouble for what he did to Helen.'

'And now we need to go and find out exactly how he died,' was Maureen's only response. 'I'll wait in the car while you say goodbye to the children.'

Rose put her hand to her mouth, holding back a sob.

As soon as she reached the CID room Maureen could tell that the interview with Aidan had not gone well. Bob was hiding, and Bell was grumpy and mumbling about ticking PACE clocks and questions being asked.

'Any luck with Rose?' he asked, but Maureen shook her head. 'Admitted to a past relationship with Wetherall, hinting that it was just a fling while Eric was working away, before they moved to the farm. Admitted having had a mobile phone, but claimed it was lost.' She remembered Rose's smile. 'I think she knows that we can't prove anything without that phone. That was it really. She was very upset about leaving the kids.'

'And what about Helen?' Bell asked.

Maureen thought for a while. 'She says she walked home somehow, Rose was in the house when she got there, and Helen slept the rest of the night. I still think she's holding something back.'

Bell swore under his breath. 'I reckon they're all lying through their teeth. We've got the rest of today and overnight before we have to charge someone, or all of them, or see them all walk. That Featherstone bloke looks about twelve but he knows enough to call us if we can't make anything stick.'

'And if we can, there's still the CPS to deal with,' Maureen added. Her years of experience warned her that the Crown Prosecution Service were unwilling to take anything to court unless there was a pretty good chance of a guilty verdict.

Now that Bell had calmed down a little, Bob Carruthers came across. Bell was telling Maureen about the shotgun and asked Bob what Aidan had said about it. Bob checked his notes. 'He said, "I went for the shotgun. I pointed it at him and told him to get out".'

Maureen frowned. 'And Rose was there at the time?'

'Yes,' said Bell. 'He heard them talking when he was crossing the yard towards the house, presumably.'

'He didn't hear what was being said?'

'Not that he told us,' said Bob.

Maureen sat back in her chair. 'If I were interviewing Aidan, I'd want to know where he got the gun from, and what happened next – what did Rose do or say? Alex got that ear wound somehow, and it could be connected to the fatal wound that came later. Too much of a coincidence otherwise, isn't it?'

Bell seemed to be cheering up. 'So what did Rose tell you, exactly?'

Maureen made a face. 'She said she thought Alex might have been curious to meet Helen but she didn't expect him to pick her up like that. She's a convincing liar, sir. That's what bothers me about getting it to court.'

Bob nodded. 'She's the smart one in the family, I reckon. If she really wanted Wetherall out of her hair, she's got that now, hasn't she? Job done.'

The door opened and Anna hobbled in. She'd been for an X-ray to check that the ankle wasn't broken.

'Just a sprain,' she said. 'I could have told them that myself. What have I missed?'

They looked at one another. 'Watching us going round in circles,' said Bob. But Maureen shook her head. 'I think we're making progress.'

'Not fast enough,' grumbled Bell. 'Still more to come from forensics and the full post mortem report. Getting details out of Mukerjee is, you know…' He struggled for a metaphor.

'Blood out of a stone?' Anna suggested. 'Look, why don't I have a go at Aidan? He's obviously rattled. His story about being at home all night fell apart straight away, and Eric's been caught in that lie too. Who's going to deal with him on that?'

Bell nodded. 'OK, you go back to Aidan. Ask him about the shotgun, and the alibi deal he must have made with Eric. We'll leave Rose for now.' He looked around. 'And there's another loose end we need to track down. So far there's no sign of Wetherall's phone. We know he had one. I made Aidan think we'd found it, but SOCOs didn't find it. If someone's deliberately tried to hide it, it could be anywhere on that farm. They had long enough to stash it or destroy it before we turned up.'

'What about the money?' Anna asked. 'That must be why he headed for that place near the Solway. Why take such a risk unless it was something he needed. Where's that money now?'

Bell nodded. 'I've been wondering about that. There were traces of cocaine on the note we found up there, by the way.'

Anna went on. 'He must have had money. You don't turn up to take your lover and her children away without cash, and lots of it. Nothing was found in the search of the barn, but the family could have found it when he died, split it up, hidden it.'

'Burned it?' Bob asked. 'The Aga was on in the kitchen.'

'Unlikely, I reckon,' said Bell. 'Heslops needed money. Can't see them just throwing it away, or handing it over to us. But it's the same problem, they had so much time to stash it somewhere we'd never find it.'

'Rose wouldn't throw money away,' said Maureen. 'That I'm sure of. She loves what money can buy. Good clothes, all that. I still can't fathom why she agreed to move to the farm.'

'Maybe she didn't have a choice,' said Bell. 'Eric's no women's libber, is he? If he wanted to take on the farm, for whatever daft reason, she'd be expected to go along with it.'

Anna shook her head.

Maureen pressed on. 'I checked with Rose's GP about her medication, but he wouldn't say much. Patient confidentiality blah blah. But from what I saw of her in Carlisle, she's much brighter now. We need to have another go at her.'

Bell hesitated. 'Not yet. Make her wait. The others could cough up more yet, box her in. We'll leave her a while. I might take the interview myself.'

Maureen frowned and glanced across at Anna, who looked away.

Anna turned on the tape in the interview room and spoke the necessary introductions before she sat back and looked steadily at Aidan Heslop. Outside, beyond the mirrored window of the room, Bell was watching and listening, checking his new sergeant's interview skills.

Anna began, 'You told my colleague earlier that you "went for the shotgun" when you found Mr Wetherall in the hay barn with your mother. Is that right?'

Aidan nodded. 'Yes, but I didn't use it.'

'Let's come back to that. Just for now, I want to know where you went to find the gun. Into the house?'

Aidan shook his head.

'But a shotgun wouldn't normally be lying around in a barn, would it? It should be locked up, kept secure.'

Aidan shrugged. 'We have to use a gun when the foxes come after the sheep.'

'But there are no sheep now, are there?'

'The foxes are still around. I saw one last week, across the field.'

'And you shot it?'

He shrugged again. 'Missed.'

'So, I'll ask you again. Where is the shotgun normally kept?'

This time the boy said nothing. He looked back at Anna and she saw that his eyes were damp. For a few moments he was silent, then he lowered his gaze. 'I had to move it,' he said quietly, 'out of the house. I hid it in the barn, behind a bale, beside the door.'

Suddenly she understood. 'Your dad's been very depressed, hasn't he?'

Aidan nodded, without looking up. 'One of his mates, last week…' He paused.

'Did one of his farmer friends kill himself, Aidan?'

He nodded again. A tear fell off the end of his nose. 'I was afraid. Dad never says much, you know, but he was drinking bad.' He looked up. 'So I hid the shotgun in the barn. That's why I could point it at that man.'

Anna sat still for a moment. 'Did you fire the gun, Aidan?'

'Don't answer that,' Featherstone interrupted. Anna tried again. 'Your dad told us you'd not been out, and that you were all in the house together, all evening. He's lying, isn't he?'

Aidan was suddenly angry. 'Of course he said that. He's me dad. He wants to keep me out of trouble. He knows I go out at night, and I shouldn't, in case I bring the infection back to the farm. And anyway, he's usually drunk, so he doesn't care.'

'Are you saying he knows that you were out last night?'

'I told him, when I came in.'

'Did you tell him about the man in the barn?'

'Yes.'

'And did you tell him that you'd shot at the man and missed, and just winged the side of his head?'

Featherstone leaned towards his client, but Aidan pushed him away and put his hands over his face. 'I just told him the shotgun went off.'

'And what did your dad do?'

'He told me to keep quiet about it, and stay in the house with Brian.' The boy hesitated. 'And then he went out.'

Featherstone raised his hand. 'I know,' said Anna. 'I won't ask Aidan to speculate about what happened then.' Another tack. 'OK, Aidan, let me ask you about the man you found in the barn with your mother. Did you know him?'

'He's called John.'

That was a surprise, and Anna tried not to show it. She looked again at her notes. 'You said earlier that this was the man who took your sister.'

'I recognised him,' said Aidan.

'From what? Had you seen him before?'

He froze, eyes flickering sideways. 'No, but I'd heard about him.'

'From whom? From Helen?'

He shook his head. He'd painted himself into a corner, and they both knew it.

Suddenly Anna guessed what had happened. 'You found your mum's phone, didn't you?'

Aidan stared at her, his mouth open, and shifted uncomfortably in his chair. 'I found a phone, in our house. Actually, Brian found it, and gave it to me. When I looked at the messages…'

'Who did the phone belong to?'

Aidan took a while to respond, remembering the shame of seeing his mates reading the words. His face burned. 'My mam.'

'Did you ask her about it?'

Aidan looked down, moving slightly in his chair. 'No comment,' he said at last.

'One final question, Aidan, for a while at least. Where's that phone now?'

'I chucked it away.'

'Where?'

'In the slurry pit.'

Anna groaned inside her head. If that were true, the search would be a nightmare, and she dreaded to think what the corrosion would do to the evidence. Her ankle began to throb.

'Interview suspended, 17.43, DS Penrose leaving the room,' she said for the tape, pushing back her chair.

'What about the cows?' the boy asked.

'What about them?' she said.

'They have to be milked. We'll have to go and do it.'

Anna nodded and walked out of the room.

As she stepped into the corridor on her way back to the office, Tony Wong was right in front of her.

'I brought the forensics report in,' he said. 'Are you OK?'

She could feel herself blushing, remembering the touch of his fingers on her face. 'Just a sprain. The doc said someone had done a good job cleaning me up. Thanks for that.'

'You're worth cleaning up,' he said.

She had to move and brushed past him, walking as confidently as she could towards the office. He followed behind. In the office Bell was standing in front of the big whiteboard. 'Good guess about the phone,' he said. 'No wonder the kid was upset.'

Maureen added, 'That accounts for Rose's frustration about "modern gadgets".'

'And Aidan must have had a shock, thinking that the man who'd been pawing his mam was sitting in the hay barn. I'd not be surprised if he shot him on the spot,' said Bob.

'He wouldn't cough to that,' said Anna, 'but I reckon he would if we pushed him. I thought there'd be more from the pathologist.'

'Still nothing more from Mukerjee,' Bell said. 'I told him I wanted the full report by six, and it's almost that now.'

They all sat for a few minutes, thinking.

‘Oh, God,’ said Anna, ‘I forgot about the cows. They’ve got to be milked.’

Bell looked as if he were going to burst. ‘Milking the cows? For fuck’s sake.’ They were sharing their collective ignorance about dairy farming when Featherstone put his head round the door.

‘I checked with the neighbours about the cows,’ he said. ‘It’s all sorted. They saw the cars, realised the milking problem and someone’s already been.’

‘Bloody hell,’ said Bell. ‘I take back all I’ve ever said about farmers.’

‘They look out for each other,’ said Featherstone reproachfully.

‘While you’re here,’ said Bell, ‘do we take it you’re representing Mr Heslop and his wife, as well as the lad?’

‘I’ve called in one of my colleagues,’ said Featherstone. ‘Miss Daly will be here shortly.’

‘Ah, the fragrant Miss Daly,’ said Bell. ‘We’ll be so delighted to see her again.’

‘Thought you would be,’ said Featherstone, as he left the room.

‘We need to sort these bloody cows out,’ said Bell. ‘What was the name of that bloke Rose used to work for, the one who went to the farm when the sheep were being culled?’

‘Barry Blake,’ said Maureen. ‘He and Rose looked pretty pally.’

‘See if you can track him down,’ said Dinger. ‘Tell him we could have a problem with the Heslops’ cows, see if he can sort something out for tomorrow, or longer.’

Maureen got up to check the information she’d gathered on Blake. She wondered how he might react to the news of the Heslops’ whereabouts, although he probably knew already on the farmers’ grapevine.

Anna said, 'Eric's been stewing for a few hours, away from his friend the bottle. I could have a go at him.'

Bell looked at her. 'Let me think about that,' he said. Maureen glanced across at Anna from her desk, and caught her eye. Both of them guessed Bell would want to keep the juiciest interviews for himself, and that could include Rose.

'Do you want the rest of the forensics, while I'm here?' said Tony. 'Virtually impossible to prove who was in the barn or when. The gun shot residue evidence is weak too. Some evidence on Aidan's clothes, and Eric's. Nothing at all on Rose. Whatever prints might have been on the pistol were wiped before Wetherall held it for the last time.'

'Or someone who handled the gun was wearing gloves,' said Anna.

The phone rang. Bell picked it up. 'Dr Mukerjee, just in time.' He listened for a while. 'We know there was a fair amount of whisky involved. The deceased brought almost a full bottle with him and there was very little left when we found it.' The team fell quiet, straining to hear what was being said. Bell looked around, his eyes wide, the phone very close to his ear. 'How long will that take? Yes, of course we want it done. If the man topped himself, we need to know when and how. Yes, as soon as possible.'

Bell hung up and told his team, 'Mukerjee reckons there was more than just whisky in Wetherall's system. He's sending for further blood analysis. Could be a while.'

Maureen asked, 'Is he saying that Alex could have died from a cause other than the bullet – from a mix of alcohol and something else, for instance?'

Bell raised his hands in exasperation. 'The bloody man insists he can't say. He has to check exactly what else was involved, and what effect it would have. We'll just have to wait.'

Chapter 27

'Miss Daly, how delightful,' said Bell with exaggerated politeness as he greeted the solicitor at the main entrance to the police station in Workington.

'Yes, right,' said Joyce Daly. Like most of the women in Dinger Bell's life, apart from his wife, she was taller than him, and high heels enabled her to look down at his beery face from a height that pleased her and infuriated him. She was also, as ever, immaculately dressed, this time in a pale grey suit and a green shirt that was unmistakeably silk. Bell was suddenly and uncomfortably aware that his own clothes were creased and badly in need of refreshment.

The other thing that Bell disliked intensely about Diva Daly was her voice. Wherever she'd been educated, it was long way from Workington. 'My colleague tells me,' she said, 'that you have three members of the same family here, and that your time with them is running out. Charge or discharge, Inspector, you know the rules as well as I do.'

'Thank you, I'm aware of the time,' said Bell. 'We are waiting to interview Mr Heslop, but I expect you'd like a few words with him first.'

'Of course. Lead on, DI Bell.' Joyce Daly managed to make even this suggestion sound like an insult. Bell was pleased he'd handed this interview over to Penrose, but he'd be watching and listening, just in case he wasn't happy with proceedings.

Both he and Anna watched as Joyce Daly questioned her client and listened to his halting responses. Eric Heslop seemed to have deflated like an old balloon during the course of the day, cheered only by the news that his neighbours had taken over the milking. But even that was quickly followed by embarrassment that they all clearly knew something serious was going on. At one point there was quite an animated exchange, and Miss Daly looked less than happy when Anna entered the room with Bob behind her and formally began the interview.

The solicitor immediately held up her hand. 'Before we start any interview, DS Penrose, my client wishes to make a statement. Against my advice, I might add. He believes this whole business can be cleared up and wants that to be as fast as possible.'

'I understand he's worried about his cows,' said Anna.

'Really, Sergeant,' said Joyce. 'That was extraordinarily callous, if I may say so. My client's first concern is for his family.'

'Of course,' said Anna. 'My apologies. Do continue, Mr Heslop. And please speak up, for the tape,' she added, pointing towards the microphone.

Eric cleared his throat. 'I admit I lied about us all being in the house last night.'

Anna interrupted, realising that the story would be far from smooth. 'Can you explain what you mean by "us all", please, for the record?'

'Me, the wife, and Aidan our older son. The young 'un, Brian, was upstairs asleep right through.'

'OK, do go on.'

'Well, we had supper after milking like always and then I fell asleep. When I woke up there was no one else in the house, apart from Brian. I was wondering what were up when I heard the noise.'

Anna raised her eyebrows, and he took the hint and back-tracked. 'The noise of the shotgun going off. Thought it was our Aidan after a fox again, but it were too close. So I went outside. Aidan was coming out of the barn, right upset. He had the shot-gun in his hand. I've told him a million times not to carry it like that…'

'That's fine, Mr Heslop. So what then?'

'Well, he said summat like, "It went off". I went into the barn and Rose were there. She was kneeling beside a man who was sort of lying up against a bale on't floor. She were holding his head.' Eric stopped talking. His mouth was moving but nothing audible was coming out.

'Take your time, Mr Heslop,' said Anna.

'Looked like the feller's ear was bleeding but he were OK. Just lay there. Didn't say owt. I thought he might be drunk.'

'Did your wife say anything?'

'She said that Aidan had waved the gun around and it went off, like, but there was no real harm done.'

Anna waited. Beside her Bob Carruthers was scribbling furi-ously. Wetherall's passivity, if this account were to be believed, was at odds with the violence and agitation he'd shown when he was with her.

'So you contend that the man who had been hurt just lay there while his ear was bleeding and your wife was mopping it up?'

'Aye,' said Eric. 'I said I'd go and call the police, but Rose said no. She said she knew the man, that he was drunk and needed to sleep it off, and then he would go away. She said the police would arrest Aidan if they came, and we didn't want that. She was right. The lad meant no harm.'

'So you went back to the house?'

'Aye, and Rose came too. Aidan were in the kitchen with the gun. He were right upset. I took the gun off him and threw it in the slurry.'

'Was that your idea?'

'Rose said she'd do it, but it were a wild night, so I did it meself.'

'No harm done, Sergeant,' said Joyce Daly. 'The boy was in a panic, I'm sure you understand that.'

'Miss Daly,' said Anna. 'If and when we decide to charge Aidan Heslop, he will be represented by your colleague, not by you. So please limit your interest to your own client.' She turned back to Eric.

'So your contention is that, having thrown the shotgun into the slurry pit, you went back to the house along with your wife and son and you all stayed there until you got up in the morning to do the milking?'

'Aye, that's right.'

'And how can you be sure of that?'

He hesitated. 'Well...' he began.

'Your son says that you fell asleep again, having had more to drink, as is your habit.'

'Well, it was night-time.'

'Did you go up to the bedroom you share with your wife?'

Eric looked very uncomfortable. 'No. Well, she was with the kiddie, you know, in our bed, so I went on the couch in the other room downstairs.'

'And Aidan went to bed.'

'Aye. He was very upset. I told him not to worry, that we'd take care of it.'

Anna looked down at her notes. 'Mr Heslop,' she said. 'Did you know the man you saw in the hay barn?'

Eric looked at Joyce Daly, who looked glacially back at him with an expression that said: I told you this was a mistake.

He thought for a while before he said, 'I think it was someone my wife used to know. His name's Wetherall.'

'And when did your wife know this person?'

Eric squirmed on his chair. 'When I was working away a lot. We went through a bad patch, you know. He were always sniffing around, before we moved out here.'

'And since then?'

He shrugged. 'I haven't seen him, not since then.'

'But has she, I wonder?'

Eric shrugged again. 'She could have, you know, bumped into him or summat.'

'Mr Heslop, are you aware that this was the man who abducted your daughter last Friday?'

'I am now. You lot never told us owt. When Helen came back, she told her mam.'

'And when did Helen come back?'

'Last night, late. Rose didn't wake us, she didn't want Helen upset by all the fuss.'

'So why was Wetherall in your barn?'

Another shrug. 'Dunno. If he was drunk, like. People do daft things when they're drunk.'

Joyce Daly's face was a picture. 'May I have another word with my client?' she asked. 'We seem to be straying off track somewhat.'

'Certainly,' said Anna. She and Bob picked up their folders, she stopped the tape and they both left the room.

As they walked out into the corridor they heard raised voices, followed the sound. Beside the main reception desk stood a man with the build of a rugby forward. His face was flushed under his thick brown hair, and he was pointing an accusatory finger at DI Bell.

'You have no right to keep her here,' he was saying. 'I know her, she's doing her best to hold her family together in impossible circumstances and this is how she's treated.' His voice grew louder. 'It's disgraceful! They've been through enough, God knows, without this... this harassment.'

Dinger had wisely decided to wait until the man's anger blew itself out. Anna went to stand alongside him in a show of professional loyalty and Bell turned to her. 'DS Penrose, this is Mr Blake, Mrs Heslop's employer, very concerned for her welfare.'

'It's not just Rose,' Barry Blake persisted, 'it's the whole family. I've known the Heslops for years.'

'I've explained to Mr Blake,' Bell went on, 'that we are investigating a death, as yet unexplained, and that we have to conduct our investigation as we see fit, in keeping with all the required procedures, and that these allow us to talk to anyone who may be involved, for twenty-four hours.'

This long-winded speech was having the desired effect. Blake simmered down. 'What about the dairy herd?' he asked.

'All taken care of by the neighbours for this evening,' said Anna. 'We may need your help with that if the Heslops' absence continues.'

'You mean if they're arrested and charged?' he said. 'But that can't involve Rose... Mrs Heslop... surely?'

Anna knew what Maureen would do, and took her chance. 'If you'd like to see Mrs Heslop, Mr Blake, and reassure yourself that she's being properly looked after, we could arrange that, just a brief look-in.' She was keen to see this, given what Maureen had suggested about the relationship between Rose and her boss.

Blake seemed mollified by this. He lowered his voice and his face returned to its normal healthy outdoor tan. 'That would be... yes,' he said. 'It's been a tough time recently, for all of us.'

'Of course,' said Anna. She looked at Bell, who nodded.

Anna led Barry Blake through the double doors and down the corridor to the room where Rose had been sitting alone for hours. 'I'll leave the door open,' she said. 'Procedure. Just five minutes.'

Rose stepped forward to greet Barry, who took her in his arms and gave her a hug. 'What a dreadful business,' he said. Anna wondered how Rose would explain what had happened, but she made no attempt to do so, lingering in the man's embrace longer than was necessary. 'Oh, Barry,' Anna heard her whisper. 'It's been awful. I'm so glad you're here.'

'Can't stay, pet,' he said, pulling away. 'You won't be here much longer, I'm sure. I heard that Helen was back. Is she OK? Where is she?'

'She's fine, considering. My mother's looking after her and Brian. It was awful,' Rose said again. 'I haven't had the chance to tell the police anything. It's been hours. Can you get me out?'

One of them must have realised that they were being overheard: the voices dropped to whispers and they moved out of Anna's line of sight. A few moments later Barry Blake emerged, his face quite pink. Behind him, Rose stood plaintively at the door to the interview room. He turned to give her a parting hug. As he pulled away, Rose looked over his shoulder at Anna, who was watching this encounter with mounting irritation. Rose caught her eye and smiled, a knowing, confident smile that said, 'Look how they love me.'

Blake appeared to be on the offensive again, spurred on by Rose. 'I'm sure you'll quickly discover,' he told Anna, 'that Mrs Heslop has nothing to reproach herself for, and that you'll send her back to her children. I'll be here tomorrow morning if I can rearrange some things first. Mrs Heslop should be released around mid-morning, I understand.'

'Unless we decide to charge her, sir, yes.'

He rolled his eyes. 'I'm sure that won't be necessary, Sergeant. Mrs Heslop has worked for me for several years, and I can vouch for her unreservedly.'

I'm sure you can, Anna said to herself, watching Barry Blake stride away.

'We have to rethink our approach,' she said to Bell back in the office, with a conviction that surprised even her. 'All three of them are lying, or telling us half-stories. Two of them have solicitors butting in all the time, and we haven't even got to Rose yet. From what I see of her and our friend Mr Blake, he'll be finding some fancy brief to look after her. They'll just play off each other, and tie us up in knots.'

'So what are you suggesting we do differently?' said Bell.

'Something that puts them at a disadvantage. It's all too cosy in here. Why don't we take them all up to the farm, have them walk through it, show us what happened, who did what when, throughout that night?'

Dinger said, 'What about the briefs?'

'Them too.' She leaned forward across the table. 'This whole case is wrapped up in that family and how they live in that isolated place. Having them down here, we're missing something.'

Dinger pulled out a chair and sat down. 'OK, it might work.' He paused. 'But what a carry on, and for what? That Wetherall was a pain in the arse, a nutter who attacked his mam and one of ours, and then topped himself. Half of me says, "Good riddance, next case".'

'Too easy,' said Maureen.

Bob laughed. 'Easy's good, isn't it?'

'No.' Maureen raised her voice. 'Not if it gives a manipulative bitch like Rose Heslop the chance to bend things the way she wants them and get away with it.'

'Ooh, get 'er,' said Bob. 'Someone getting too involved maybe?'

'Shup up, Bob,' said Dinger. 'You said yourself that Rose is the smart one.'

Maureen persisted. 'Have we heard back from Mukerjee about the extra tests they were doing?'

Dinger shuffled through the accumulation of messages on his desk. 'Not that I know of.'

'OK,' said Anna. 'Sir, you'll need to ask for an extension. Tell them we need till midday tomorrow – it's only a few extra hours. We'll take everybody back to the farm, boots and all.'

'And there's that slurry pit,' said Bob. 'Some poor bastard's going to have to fish around in there for the shotgun.'

'And the phone,' said Anna. 'Maybe Alex's phone is in there too.'

Dinger pushed back his chair and got up. 'OK. The Heslops all stay here overnight, and we can get some kip. Everything kicks off again at first light, right?'

The prospect of a night in their own beds was a bonus for all of them, with the single exception of Anna. The power was back on, but she realised that her isolated little house didn't feel as inviting as before. She wanted company.

Chapter 28

The alarm was set for six, and when the radio clicked into life Anna stretched out a hand to switch it off. She lay back, aware of the strapping round her ankle, and felt the unaccustomed warmth in the bed, a warmth that stirred and moved closer to her, kissing the back of her ear.

'Morning,' he said. 'Cup of tea?'

She turned to face him. 'Just what I've always wanted.'

'Really? Hope it didn't disappoint.'

She laughed. 'Not that – the cup of tea, in bed.'

'Stay here,' he said. 'I'll find everything. That's my job, right?'

She heard the stairs creak under his bare feet. This development was probably a mistake, but right now it felt like a really good idea.

When Tony had responded to Anna's phone call the previous evening they'd lit the stove and found food in the freezer and wine in the fridge and spent the best evening that she could remember for a long time. Yes, he was a bit younger, and he was a colleague, but what the hell? She needed comfort and company and he provided both, and more. He was funny and easy-going and not frightened of her or intimidated by her rank. They would have to explain both arriving in his car the following morning, but it made sense that he would pick her up, as she couldn't drive herself to Brinfell Farm where the next stage in the Heslop drama would be played out.

Anna had wanted the weather to be difficult for the re-enactment at the farm, and the day promised exactly that. The tall trees around her house were creaking in the wind as they'd done the night that Alex had attacked her. It would be a while before she felt secure here again. When she and Tony left for the farm a heavy shower was blowing through. As they dropped down the hill the air cleared again, but they could see the next shower approaching, blotting out the fell tops to the north and west.

'You OK?' he asked, turning towards her.

'More than OK,' she said. 'You?'

He was smiling broadly. 'Never better.'

'We'll talk, right?' she said. 'But not now.'

He nodded. 'Yes, boss.' She reached across and pinched his knee.

Tony parked the car at the farm gate and walked down ahead of Anna so they didn't arrive together and draw attention to themselves. He wore his full crime-scene kit and Anna decided to do the same. Trace evidence would be either collected or compromised by now, but at least the overalls and boots protected their clothing.

As she turned the corner into the farmyard she could see that everyone else had made the same decision, prompted by the stringent rules about FMD contamination. It made for a strange sight as they crowded into the big kitchen, out of the wind and the rain that bounced off the flagstones and concrete in the yard.

Anna noticed that both Featherstone and Daly had turned up, but they looked satisfyingly misplaced and uncomfortable. Many townies, even in Cumbria, had no idea about the subsistence lives that hill farmers lived. There was poverty here, just as grinding as anything in the cities.

Dinger was clearly in charge, behaving as if the whole idea had been his from the start. He and the Heslops were seated at the table in the kitchen. Bob, Anna, Maureen, Tony and the two solicitors stood in an outer circle. Anna glanced at Rose. She was still looking calm but the corners of her mouth twitched slightly.

'We need to be clear exactly what happened the night that Mr Wetherall died,' Dinger began. 'At one time or another, each of you' – he gestured to the Heslops – 'was in the house or in the barn across the yard. Helen arrived back at the farm very late. After midnight, we understand.' Rose nodded. 'And Brian was in the house all night.'

'He was,' Rose interrupted. 'Leave him out of this.'

Anna raised an eyebrow and caught Maureen's eye. Touchy, she thought, and clearly Maureen felt the same. It might be worth pushing that button again.

Dinger pointed at Bob. 'Now DC Carruthers here has agreed to be Mr Wetherall.' Bob looked startled, having not been asked any such thing. 'We'll start with him already in the barn, having parked DS Penrose's car and walked across the field.'

Daly interrupted. 'I understand that the deceased was already injured, by one of your own officers?'

Anna spoke up before Bell could respond. 'Mr Wetherall attacked me in my own home,' she said. 'When he threatened to kill me, I defended myself with a knife in order to escape. He had a knife wound to the knee, but it wasn't serious enough to hinder his walk across the field to the farmyard. My only aim was to slow him down.'

Daly sniffed, but didn't say any more.

'So,' Dinger continued. 'Mr Wetherall is in the farmyard. What happened then?'

Rose spoke up. Her voice was clear but quiet. 'I was here in the kitchen when I saw him at the window. He must have been watching and knocked on the glass to attract my attention.'

'And then?'

'I gestured to him to go away, and he must have gone into the barn, out of the rain. It wasn't locked.'

'Do you have legal representation?' said Featherstone, out of the gloom at the far side of the room.

'No, not yet,' she said, 'but that's OK. I've nothing to hide. And Mr Blake has said that he will find someone to advise me if necessary.'

'Mr Blake is Mrs Heslop's employer,' Anna added. She hoped Blake would turn up at some point. Eric Heslop needed to see his wife in full 'Damsel in Distress' mode.

'Why didn't you call the police?' Bell asked. 'A strange man is outside your house in the middle of the night, in a very isolated spot. Weren't you afraid?'

'Firstly, the phone was down because of the power cut. And anyway Alex isn't... wasn't a stranger,' she said. 'I'd known him for many years, since we were at school in Carlisle. It took me a minute to recognise him, but I wasn't afraid of him. I felt sorry for him.'

'You are aware that it was he who kidnapped your daughter Helen?'

'I am now, but I wasn't then.'

Lies, lies, Anna thought to herself. She and Maureen exchanged the usual blank expression that revealed nothing and meant everything.

'So, you left the house and followed Mr Wetherall into the barn.'

'Yes,' said Rose. 'As I said, I felt sorry for him.'

'OK, so let's go over there, shall we?' said Dinger. They all looked around. He was really going to do it. Daly spoke up again. 'Is this necessary, Inspector?'

'Believe me, Miss Daly,' said Dinger with matching pomposity, 'we wouldn't be here unless my superiors agreed with me that the complications of this case require extraordinary measures to be taken.' He stood up, walked to the door and led the way across the yard to the hay barn. Fortunately it had stopped raining for a few minutes.

Inside the barn the smell of smoke was still strong.

'DC Carruthers, can you sit down on that bale, which we believe is roughly where Mr Wetherall was sitting. Is that right, Mrs Heslop?'

She nodded as Bob reluctantly perched on the bale.

'We were talking,' said Rose, 'when my son Aidan came in.'

Anna would have loved to ask what was being talked about, but there was no point. Rose would only continue to lie as she was already doing.

Bell said, 'Right, Aidan, if you could come and stand here now?' Aidan looked warily at Featherstone, who nodded, and the boy stood awkwardly by the door. They all had to shuffle into the barn to make the space he needed, and stood around the seated Bob Carruthers, like a surreal Nativity tableau.

Bell said, 'In your statement, you said that you "went for the shotgun"?'

Aidan nodded. 'I wanted to get him out. I'd moved the shotgun out here...' He hesitated.

'Tell us why,' said Bell.

'My dad,' explained Aidan. 'I hid it from him, in case...' His voice tailed away.

Anna stepped in. 'Were you afraid that he might be tempted to harm himself, is that why you hid the gun from him?'

Aidan glanced across at his father who was leaning against the scorched wall of the barn, his head bowed. 'He were in a bad way. First the sheep went, and we had a scare with the cows. One of his mates, Keswick way, he… did it, and…' Again he couldn't finish the sentence.

'Where was the gun?' Bell asked.

Aidan shuffled to his right and pointed to a spot where bales had spilled onto the floor. 'Behind the bales that were stacked here. It was out of sight, but I knew where it was and I picked it up.'

'You shot at Mr Wetherall, didn't you?'

'No!' Aidan shouted. 'I just waved it around, to scare him, and it went off. The man cried out and put his hand to his ear, and I saw blood on his hand. Mam was upset. I kept the gun in my hand and went out. My dad came out of the house and saw me.'

Bell peered around the barn until he spotted Eric, who still hadn't raised his head. 'Mr Heslop, we need you to step out into the yard with Aidan for a moment.'

Eric walked through his actions like a zombie. He'd found Aidan in the yard, offered to call the police but Rose had said no. Then he'd left her in the barn and gone back to the house, taken the gun from Aidan and thrown it into the slurry pit. Yes, it was his wife's idea, but he did it.

This is going to break him, thought Anna. She asked, 'What did you think was going to happen about the man in your barn, Mr Heslop?'

All Eric did was shrug. He didn't want to go back into the barn, but Bell insisted that they all return there. Whatever Rose had to say needed to be heard by everyone.

For a while, she presented herself as the concerned old friend, helping out a poor chap who was in a mess. Suddenly Maureen stepped forward. Anna was taken aback: this must have been agreed in advance with Bell, who seemed content to stand back and let his DC take charge.

'Mrs Heslop,' Maureen began, 'you and Mr Wetherall go back a long way, as you've said yourself.' Rose smiled wistfully. 'But you'd seen him recently, hadn't you, and you'd been in touch with him by phone.'

Rose opened her mouth to respond, but Maureen carried on. 'He gave you the phone, didn't he, when you met him in Cockermouth, so that you could talk about your plans?'

Suddenly Rose looked less sure of herself. She didn't know what Aidan had told them. 'I bumped into Alex… Mr Wetherall in Cockermouth one day, after work.' She hesitated. 'And he gave me a phone when I said I would find one useful for work, even though there was no signal here at the farm.'

Maureen let that go but pressed on. 'When Aidan came into the barn, Mrs Heslop, did he know who the man in there was?'

'I don't know.'

'He guessed, didn't he, because he'd seen the messages on your phone? On his own admission Aidan threw the phone in the slurry. But what if we have found it there, along with the shotgun?'

Rose stared. No words came.

Surely she won't fall for that old trick, thought Anna. But there was doubt, enough to undermine Rose's boast that she had nothing to hide. Go on, Maureen, Anna urged silently. Push her, now.

And then they heard it: the hiss of tyres on wet concrete and the banging of car doors, two, three. All eyes turned towards the door of the barn as it opened. Barry Blake stood in the doorway, silhouetted against the pale March daylight. Behind him another man appeared, and then a policeman in uniform.

'Rose,' Barry called. 'Hugh Chetwynd's here. He's a lawyer. Are you OK?'

The tears came, just for a moment, before Rose wiped them away and smiled up at him, her saviour. Anna looked across at Eric, who was standing, open-mouthed, his humiliation complete.

'DI Bell?' called the tall well-suited man who'd come in with Blake. 'I need a word, now, if you please.' He looked disdainfully around the barn. 'Not in here, in the house.' He turned and left. Bell had a choice to make. Hugh Chetwynd was big league, with friends in high places and in the Lodge. Bell said nothing, but followed Blake, Rose and Chetwynd out of the barn and across the yard to the house.

Anna looked up at the smoke-blackened ceiling of the barn. They'd been so close. Just at the point when Rose's composure had started to crumble she'd been rescued. Now she wouldn't say another word without her lawyer's advice. Maureen's bluff about items recovered from the slurry would be called.

The police constable was still standing by the door, looking confused. 'Ma'am,' he said, spotting Anna. 'I've got some information for DI Bell, but…'

'The pathologist's report. I'll take it,' Anna said, holding out her hand. She tore open the envelope and read for a few minutes. 'DC Pritchard, a word, please.' She took Maureen's arm and propelled her outside. 'Did Rose's doctor say what drugs she was on?' Anna asked, keeping her voice low.

'Tranquillisers of some kind, he said.' Maureen stopped and stared. 'Is that what's been found?'

Anna nodded, reading from the paper in her hand. '"Clear traces of Paracetamol and Valium together with alcohol in the deceased's system, likely to have rendered him incapable, with possibly fatal consequences." She drugged him! She took her pills and fed them to him with the whisky during the night.'

'If he was dead before the final bullet, there wouldn't have been so much blood,' Maureen added. The rain was getting heavier. The two women looked for shelter and found it in the doorway of the cowshed.

'Alternatively,' said Anna, 'the bullet may have killed him, but he must have been comatose with these levels in his blood. Eric said he thought Alex looked out of it. So how did he manage to shoot himself?'

Across the yard the farmhouse door opened and Bell appeared. 'Get the others and come in here,' he called across. When they all crowded into the kitchen, Hugh Chetwynd took centre-stage. 'I've advised my client to say nothing more at this time,' he said, then paused for effect. 'And I must add that it beggars belief this unfair treatment should be inflicted on a woman who did nothing more, as she told me herself, than to hold the hand of a very troubled man.'

Maureen made a strangled noise. 'That's it!' she whispered to Anna. 'That's how she did it. She held his hand.'

Chapter 29

The lawyer from the Crown Prosecution Service looked up from the file and took off her glasses. 'It's not enough,' she said. 'Even with the remaining pills that you found in Mrs Heslop's possession, it's still not enough. No one saw Rose give Wetherall the pills. Her story is that she left them with him because he was agitated, and he must have taken too many, but still been able to hold the gun and finish himself off. Everything else, well, it's circumstantial or inadequate.'

Maureen rolled her eyes. 'The phone?'

'Badly corrupted by the acidity of the slurry. Some messages, but they were careful. She calls him "John", not even his real name. It wouldn't stand up in court.' She checked her notes. 'Alex's phone wasn't found?'

Bell shook his head. 'SOCO's had another look in the barn. Nothing. Beyond that immediate location, the phone could be anywhere. Too many possibilities. Same with the money he must have had with him. All in high-value notes I'd guess, wouldn't take up much space. Could be buried in a plastic bag, somewhere we'd never find it.'

'The gun shot residue?' said Wong. 'Prints?'

'Shaky,' said the lawyer. 'Gathered hours after the event, after various washings of hands and changes of clothes. Some traces on husband and son, but nothing that would carry a case against either of them. Nothing on Rose. She looked again at items in the folder. 'Only Wetherall's prints on the gun, but some smudging round the trigger. The entry point of the bullet, by the ear, is unusual, but we can't hang a case round that either.' She shut the folder. 'Sorry, it just won't hold up.'

She looked around, smiling. 'Not all bad news though. There's enough to charge the boy Aidan with unauthorised discharge of a weapon, and Mr Heslop admitted starting the fire himself, didn't he, back at the station after that unnecessary drama at the farm? Something about wanting to claim the insurance, as I recall. He can't seriously have expected that a slow-burning fire like that would hide a dead body.'

Bell said, 'Wrong people, wrong charges. Is that all we've got?'

'I'm afraid so, yes,' said the young woman brightly. 'Right-ho, got to run. Let me know how you want to proceed.'

They sat disconsolately round the big table. On the wall above their heads the whiteboard was covered with detailed information that mocked their impotence.

'That's it then,' said Bell finally. 'I'm damned if we're going to throw an arson charge at that poor bugger, and the son doesn't warrant any more than a caution.'

He closed the file on the table in front of him and pushed back his chair. 'That's what comes of playing by the rules. In the good old days we'd have slammed someone up against a wall or intimidated Rose until she squawked. Now it's all ticking clocks and warrants and bloody lawyers telling us what we can take to court and what we can't.'

'Wait a minute,' begged Maureen. 'We can't let this go, not yet. Rose is lying, I'm sure of that. Maybe we can still trip her up.'

'How?' said Tony Wong.

'Helen?' Anna suggested. 'You said you thought she was hiding something.'

Maureen nodded. 'I was sure of it when I talked to her in Carlisle. But she'd had such a bad time, I couldn't pressure her, not with her granny clucking around.' She hesitated. 'And there's someone else we haven't talked to at all.'

They looked at her. 'Brian,' she said. 'Sweet little Brian who watches everything and says nowt.'

'But he was asleep upstairs all night,' Bell objected.

Maureen leaned forward. 'That's what everyone said, but how do we know for sure? Eric said Brian and Rose were in the parents' bed, that's why Eric stayed downstairs. But Rose wasn't there with him, was she, not all the time? Brian could have got up, gone to the loo or back to his own bed. Or he could have woken up and gone downstairs.'

Bell sat down again. 'Someone would have seen him and mentioned it, surely,' he said. 'Helen was upstairs too, wasn't she, after Rose had sorted her out?'

Maureen went to the whiteboard and scrubbed the redundant scribbles off it with her sleeve. 'Look,' she said, picking up a pen. 'Here's the plan of that big kitchen at the farm. The porch is here, the Aga here, the table, the door to the other room, and the stairs. If someone was standing at the top of the stairs, here,' Maureen marked a large cross on one corner of the plan, 'what could they see?'

'Right across the room to the door into the porch,' said Anna.

'Right,' said Maureen. 'How do we know that Brian didn't see who was coming and going that night? We've never asked him.'

'How old is he,' Bell queried.

'Six,' said Maureen. 'He's clingy and doesn't say much, but he's not daft.'

'It wouldn't stand up.'

'OK,' said Anna, 'but it might help to undermine Rose's story. Look how quickly she froze when Maureen spun that tale about the phone.'

'Before the cavalry arrived,' sighed Bell.

They sat for a moment, thinking through the implications. 'If we crowd him, he'll only clam up,' Maureen said. 'There'd have to be just one person for him to focus on.'

'And you couldn't take notes, you'd have to keep looking at him, paying attention to him,' Anna put in.

'Video,' said Wong. 'We could set up a video that he might not even notice.'

'He'd have to have an adult with him,' said Anna.

Maureen nodded. 'Good old Granny Jo. She could sit right next to him, but we could still ask him a few questions and see what happens. No pressure.'

'Better still,' said Anna, 'why not have Helen there as well, the two kids together with Granny Jo. Why not? What have we got to lose?'

On Friday afternoon, just a week since Helen had driven happily away in Alex Wetherall's van, there was more activity in Jo Haile's private sitting room at the Carlisle guesthouse. Rose had very reluctantly agreed that her mother should be with the children for their chat with DC Pritchard. The case was still open and there could be no valid objection if all the protocols involving interviews with children were observed.

Tony Wong set up a video camera on one side of the room and a microphone under the table by the settee where the children would be sitting with their grandmother. Maureen would be at the side, visible in the video image but not blocking the camera's view. In a neighbouring room Tony sat watching and listening. Anna was back at the office with Bell, trying to decide if there was any way to challenge the CPS decision.

'How are you doing, Helen?' Maureen began.

'I'm fine,' said the girl. 'But why do you want to talk to me again?'

'We realised that no one had talked to Brian,' said Maureen, 'even though he was in the house all that night, wasn't he? And Brian would feel better if he had his big sister with him.'

'But he was asleep,' Helen insisted. Brian was kneeling on the floor by the low table, drawing on a piece of paper. He'd been working on it for a while as Tony and Maureen were arranging the room. The toy lamb that he often carried in his arms was perched on the table top beside him.

'Look, he doesn't want to talk to you,' said Helen. 'He just draws all the time.'

'Let's see if he'll talk to me if I ask him nicely,' said Maureen. 'You're here to look after him, aren't you, like you always do?'

Helen smiled. 'He's my little brother,' she said. 'I've missed him, while I've been away.'

'I'm sure you have,' said Maureen.

Brian looked up, still kneeling on the floor. 'Do you remember me, Brian?' Maureen asked him. 'I brought you and Helen here in my car, with your mummy, the other day.'

He nodded. 'I played with Tom,' he said.

'You did, that's right, while I talked to Helen.'

Brian nodded again.

'Do you remember the day when the fire engine came?'

Brian blinked, but said nothing.

'He remembers that,' said Helen. 'He thought it was great.'

'And what about the night before?' said Maureen. 'Do you remember that too?'

'I was asleep,' said Brian.

'Was Mummy there with you?'

'Yes,' he said. He looked gravely at Maureen. 'And no.'

'She wasn't there all the time?'

He shook his head.

Maureen kept her voice quiet and level. 'Did you see her somewhere else?'

Brian nodded. 'In the kitchen,' he said slowly. 'With Helen.'

The girl fidgeted. 'He doesn't remember properly,' she said. 'He's just a baby.'

Brian looked at his sister and poked her leg with his finger.

'You're not a baby, are you, Brian?' said Maureen. 'You're a big boy now, going to school when you can.'

He nodded and got to his feet. 'Mum was with Helen, they were talking.'

Maureen turned to his sister. 'Was this when you got home? What did you and Mum talk about?'

Helen shrugged. 'Just about how I walked there, you know.'

'You were whispering,' said Brian.

'Of course we were,' said Helen impatiently. 'We didn't want to wake everyone up.'

'And you showed Mum your arm. I could see.'

Helen was flustered. She wanted her brother to stop talking, but didn't know how to make him do so with the camera staring at them both.

'Brian,' she said, 'you couldn't see everything from the top of the stairs, could you?'

'I could, I could,' he insisted. 'I saw Mum look at your wrist, and then she went out.'

Maureen had to ask. 'What was your mum looking at, Helen?'

She pulled up her sleeve. The welt on her wrist was still angry and red.

'Did Alex do that?' Maureen asked. Jo Haile frowned and shook her head. Helen nodded, pulling the sleeve down. 'Mum…' she began, then stopped. 'She asked me about it, and then she told me to go to bed.'

'And she went out again,' Brian shouted, jumping up and down where he stood. 'I said that.' Jo reached out to hold him still.

'And you went to bed, Helen?' Maureen asked.

The girl nodded. 'I was very tired.'

Brian put up his hand. 'I heard it,' he said.

'Heard what, pet?' said Jo Haile.

'The bang,' he exclaimed. 'I heard it, after Helen went to bed.'

Brian looked triumphantly at his grandmother and then at Maureen. At last he had their attention. 'Mum came back,' he said, bending down to pick up the piece of paper he'd been drawing on.

'Can I see that?' said Maureen.

The picture was of a stick figure with brown hair, a blue top and black trousers. The arms of the figure stuck out to either side. At the end of each arm was a large hand with fingers, and they were purple. To one side was a red box with little doors in its front. Helen, Jo and Maureen all stared at the picture.

Maureen was the first to speak. 'That's very good, Brian,' she said. She pointed to the red box. 'Is that the Aga in the kitchen?' He nodded. Then he pointed at the purple hands. He held up his own hands, peeled off some imaginary gloves, opened an imaginary door and pushed the gloves inside. Then he pulled an imaginary garment over his head and did the same, before folding his arms and standing still.

For a moment there was silence. Helen looked anxiously at her grandmother. 'He's mixed up, Granny,' said the girl. 'Mum uses purple gloves for the sheep.'

'Of course she does, dear,' said Jo Haile.

Brian shook his head. 'But the sheep are all dead. And they killed my lamb.'

No one spoke. The boy turned and faced his grandmother. 'I was at the top of the stairs, Granny,' he said, pointing at the picture again. 'Mum came in and took off her gloves and her jumper.' 'Don't be silly, Brian,' Helen shouted at him. 'You're being silly!'

Brian started to cry. Jo put her arms round the boy and looked up at Maureen. 'That's enough now. He's upset.'

Helen turned on Maureen, her face twisted with anger. 'Leave us alone!' she shouted. 'Go away!'

The moment had passed. Brian and Helen cuddled up to their grandmother. 'OK,' said Maureen, getting to her feet. 'Thank you, Mrs Haile. I'm sure the children are ready for some fresh air or their tea.'

Helen sat back on the settee. 'Are you going now?'

Maureen smiled. 'Yes, pet. All finished. Mr Wong and I will leave you with Granny and go home.'

'Good,' said Helen. 'My mum's coming for us and she won't want to see you.'

And I don't really want to see your mother either, Maureen thought to herself, unless she's standing in the dock facing a murder charge.

Three hours later Tony and Anna were sitting side by side on the sofa in the little house in the forest. He'd driven from Carlisle, arriving after Bob Carruthers had dropped Anna off at home. Whatever suspicions the rest of the team might have about Anna's private life, she was determined to keep it private.

Anna had her bandaged foot up on a low table in front of them, next to a bottle of wine. 'Will it be enough for the CPS?' she asked. 'Sounds as if Brian was really clear about what happened, and it explains why we found nothing on Rose's clothes.'

Tony shook his head. 'Maureen went back to the office with the video, and Bell had a look at it. I rang Maureen later, to see what they said. Bell didn't think the CPS lawyer would change her mind.'

They sat in silence for a few minutes, watching the flickering glow of the log burner.

'I think Maureen was probably right all along,' Anna said. 'She reckoned Rose had lied to Alex about Helen being his child, but then she'd hesitated about leaving Eric, so Alex took the girl to force her hand.'

She took a sip of wine, thinking about how the case had unfolded. 'Maureen's old school, actually, like Bell. She had a gut feeling about what was going on, but he wouldn't have it. Not enough evidence, he said, too much instinct.'

'Plus she's female,' said Tony. 'Blokes like Bell have a hard time accepting that women can deal with difficult cases.'

'Do you think he feels the same way about me?'

'Yes, probably. But he knows that Tognarelli supports you, so he'll put up with it.'

He poured himself more wine and offered Anna more too, but she put her hand over the glass. She was still thinking about what had happened. 'Rose must have realised that the bloke was crazy, and when he turned up at the farm it wasn't difficult to get him under control with booze and pills. She took the phone and the money and hid them somewhere. When all this is over she can wait as long as she needs to, and the money will come in very handy.'

'That's it,' said Tony. 'When he was out cold, just to make sure, she got a pair of the latex gloves she used with the sheep, put the gun into Alex's hand and pulled the trigger. There was smudging round the trigger, remember, but nothing to prove that anyone but Alex pulled it. Enough of the evidence pointed to suicide to make the CPS reluctant to take a murder charge to court.'

'But why the ear?' Anna asked. 'She must have known that would look odd.'

'I wondered about that,' said Tony. 'I think she was trying to cover up the shotgun wound Aidan had caused. Trying to keep her son out of it if she could. Didn't work. She should have shot Wetherall from the other side, blasted the side of his head off. Much harder to see the shotgun wound then, but it would have been on the wrong side for a right-handed man.'

Anna grimaced, trying to envisage the final seconds of Alex Wetherall's life. 'Could he have been dead already, before that final shot?'

'Possibly, but it would have been close. Rose needed to be sure, and wanted it to look like a deliberate action. That would fit what she wanted us to believe: that Alex was a crazy violent man who'd stalked her and tried to coerce her into leaving her husband by kidnapping her child. Then he'd proved his madness conclusively by shooting himself. An accidental overdose wouldn't have been dramatic enough – he might have survived, and she didn't want that.'

'And good old Barry Blake is standing by, all too willing to help her out of the jam she's got herself in,' Anna added. 'Very clever. Bob Carruthers may be pretty thick, but even he realised Rose was the smart one in all this. And now she's got away with it.' Anna shook her head. 'It doesn't seem right.'

Tony stroked her hair. 'I know. Basically, the CPS thinks Brian is too young to be credible and there are too many loopholes for a good defence barrister to exploit. Rose would get the sympathy vote from enough of the jurors. "Plucky farmer's wife from the heart of a disaster zone." Press would be all over it.' He put his arm round her shoulders. 'There's nothing we can do it about it. Have you told Maureen that you think she was right all along?'

'No.'

'Are you going to?'

Anna took another sip of her wine. 'Not sure. Maybe. A few days ago, I wouldn't have bothered. But things have been much better between us since my fight with Alex. Maybe she's decided I'm OK after all.' She put down her glass and turned to look at him. 'Actually, all sorts of things have been better since then.'

Later, curled up next to Tony in her bed upstairs, Anna said,

'Women like Rose must spend their whole lives wheedling and conniving to get what they want. They don't have the guts to make their own way, so they use men to do it for them. My mother was like that.'

'But that's not your way, is it?' said Tony. 'You know what you want, and you go and get it.' He smiled at her. 'So do I. Come here.'